# JAG IN THE TURN

*To*
*Dear David,                    May 2020*

*I hope you enjoy Chris's book*

## JAG IN THE TURN

*With very best wishes,*

*Mark*

Chris Davy

Copyright © 2019 Chris Davy
All rights reserved
ISBN: 9781074050924

In Memory of Maria Allison

Strength and Compassion Personified

'everything happens for a reason'

- unattributed

## Chapter 1

Mary Abbot-Glover checked the date on the calendar. *June 29.* No matter how hard she might wish otherwise, this was *the day.* She closed her eyes and gripped the edge of the countertop, fighting off a wave of panic. There was nothing she could do. Goodness knows she had tried. She had pleaded with the Fade, reminding them Jonathan was only fifteen, and a *young* fifteen, at that. They had listened to her politely, but the course was already set. To interfere in any way could have serious, if not catastrophic, consequences.

Her son entered the kitchen. His school uniform was immaculate, set off by regulation black shoes which were polished to perfection. The mop of curly hair which adorned his head had been carefully groomed. But a quick glance at his watch made his head rock back as though he'd been punched. "Oh, no!" he said.

He opened his eyes wide and dug his fingertips into his temples, he looked at her briefly. "Mum, I'm running late!"

She glanced up at the clock that hung above the sideboard. How ironic that she had turned to *that* clock, with its three painted characters. "Jonathan, you are just a minute or two behind your schedule. Relax, your eggs are ready; so is the toast—and your tea is brewing. You'll be fine."

Jonathan did not appear to share her confidence. She watched as he downed his breakfast. Her eyes were stinging. He must not see her crying.

"Allergies," she said, pulling a handkerchief from her apron. Why did she say that? She had never suffered from any kind of allergy and Jonathan knew it. Luckily, he was too busy playing catch up to take in her words.

"Right! I'm off!" he said, picking up his lunch bag and carefully placing it in its allotted space in his backpack.

"Wait, Jonathan, your phone."

He snatched it from her.

"Jonathan?"

3

This time her voice broke, and Jonathan looked at her briefly.

"Sorry, mum," he whispered, as he carefully placed the phone into his pack.

She wanted to say something, but her throat was too dry.

A surge of emotion welled up inside her, and she knew she was about to lose control.

"Go, go, go," she whispered and followed him to the front door.

"I love you!" she said.

She stood in the doorway as he hurried away down the pavement. Curls bouncing, he turned without slowing his jog. "Yes, I know that, mum." He turned right at the end of their street and was gone.

*****

Jonathan checked his watch as he passed the ironmongers. Even allowing for the extra stop he would be making this morning he would be on time. His mum had been right. Why had he rushed her? What if she had forgotten his secret message?

He had to fight an impulse to stop and check for it. She had never forgotten before, he rationalized. Why would she today? Besides, his sixteenth birthday was just a few weeks away. He was getting a little old for this game.

The ritual had been going on for as far back as he could remember. She packed his lunch bag for him every morning and slipped a message inside with his sandwich. A simple gesture, just a folded piece of white cardboard, which, when opened, would reveal a handwritten message. She never wrote the exact same thing twice. Sometimes, she'd give him a short piece of advice—or "wisdom," as he thought of it. Perhaps she'd write only one or two words, like "breathe" or "be strong." On another day, she might share a joke—he liked her jokes—or a piece of news she thought would interest him. But no matter what she put on that little piece of white cardboard; he could count on feeling better after reading it.

He reached the newsagent. As he entered, the customer door monitor spluttered out its flat pitched alert. Jonathan covered his ears till it had finished.

"Well good morning Jonathan," said a lady in a blue print dress sitting behind the counter. She lifted a plump arm and gave Jonathan a friendly wave.

"Hi Audrey-Vanessa, was it delivered?" he asked breathlessly.

Audrey-Vanessa smiled as she turned around and picked up a magazine from a table behind her. "First delivery this morning."

"Complimentary, as promised on TV?" asked Jonathan as he poked a hole in the protective wrap.

"Nothing to pay for the first issue. Just remember to go on-line and cancel your subscription now, or you will end up with a large bill in no time."

Jonathan discarded the wrap. A well-oiled muscle man wearing nothing, but a dazzling smile and a pair of leopard skin briefs dominated the front cover. He was posing like 'The Thinker' statue Jonathan had once seen at a museum in London. Above him in large print was the banner headline; *MAX MUSCLE*. Below in a smaller font: *Say hello to the new you! Measurable improvements guaranteed within two weeks!* Jonathan opened the magazine to its centre pages. Stapled to them were four sachets of off-white powder.

"Wait, what are those?" said Audrey-Vanessa standing up. "You didn't tell me anything about samples."

"It's fine," said Jonathan. "They are completely safe – it said so on TV. You'll be saying hello to the 'new me' within two weeks. I have to run – I'll be late for school."

Audrey-Vanessa sighed. "You know Jonathan, I kind of like the old you. Promise me you'll talk to your mother before you touch those samples?" Jonathan was already half way to the door but he stopped and turned to answer her.

"Why do you think I asked you to hold them for me? Mum worries about everything!"

Audrey-Vanessa exhaled loudly, "Jonathan, wait." She grabbed a plastic bag ."At least put the magazine in a bag. Not all the kids at school will understand why you ordered it." Jonathan came back and slipped it into the bag, and then the bag, into his backpack.

"Please Jonathan, you have no idea what's in that powder. Talk to your mother – you don't want to end up looking like me."

Jonathan looked her up and down, "Why not? You're not a bad looking woman – especially considering how overweight you are."

"Thanks, Jonathan – I think."

Jonathan nodded an acknowledgement and sped out of the shop. He was pleased with how that had gone. It wasn't that he wanted to look like Max Muscles on the cover page. That would be gross. He just wanted to look a little more athletic so that he wouldn't be the butt of the jokes flying round the boy's locker room before and after gym. His mother wouldn't understand…

"Yo! Jonathan!" came a call from behind.

Jonathan turned around and continued walking backward. "Hey, Freddie, you're not late today."

"Yes, that happens occasionally," replied Freddie as he playfully slapped Jonathan on the back.

Jonathan worked hard to keep pace with his long-striding friend. They were soon discussing cricket, the sport that had brought them together. Freddie Patel was the star of the Pendleton Secondary Under 16 cricket team, and Jonathan—who didn't *do* sports—was the team scorer. He liked the challenge of recording the game's complex activity and better yet, designing and running custom analytical reports for the coach.

"You hit the ball square of the wicket, it was his call, and I have to say he was right, Freddie; even you weren't quick enough to make it in time," Jonathan said. "Maybe you can make up for it this afternoon."

"If the weather holds," said Freddie, pointing towards the Cudleigh Hills.

Jonathan's stomach sank. There was a bank of very ominous-looking storm clouds forming on the horizon. "That wasn't in the forecast. Do you think maybe it will miss us?"

Freddie didn't answer right away, and Jonathan looked over at his friend. "Freddie?"

"Check that out." Freddie said, breaking into a run.

They were passing the last building on the high street. The abandoned shop. At least, they had always assumed it had once been a shop. They couldn't be sure because it had been empty and boarded up for as long as Jonathan could remember. The front facade had become a favourite graffiti target for the local taggers. A heavy link chain and lock secured a makeshift front door that hadn't been opened in a long time.

Jonathan followed Freddie until he came to a stop near the shop's front door. A large wooden panel that bordered the area to the right of the door, along with the area above it, had been forcibly removed. The remnants of the splintered wood lay scattered on the pavement.

"Looks like someone tried to break in!" said Freddie, kicking a piece of the fractured board over to one side.

"Pinhorn and his bozo pals probably." Jonathan stepped closer to peer through the large gap left by the broken hoarding.

Freddie nudged him to one side.

"Well, whoever it was, they didn't get very far." Freddie pulled hard on the adjoining panel.

The vandals had provided them with their first glimpse inside the hoarding. In the past, they had tried to look through the diminutive gaps between the wooden slats, but it was too dark, and the cracks were too narrow to allow any view. Its inaccessibility only added to the mystery and made the place that much more intriguing. Today they could see the old red brick wall that formed the front of the building. Thick green moss covered most of the bricks. There was a gap of about eighteen inches between the wall and the board. Freddie turned around and, arching his back, leaned into the space, flicking on the light function on his phone.

Jonathan looked up and down the pavement nervously, but there were no people in the immediate area. He twisted around and leaned back, craning his neck so he peered upward. Jonathan's gaze followed the beam of light produced by Freddie's phone.

"Oi, what are you two doing?" The question, asked in a loud voice, came from the other side of the street.

Jonathan and Freddie instinctively tried to stand up straight and banged their heads on the boarding.

"Damn!" Jonathan yelled as he negotiated his way out of the space.

"Pinhorn, you moron!" Freddie shouted.

The bully sat watching them from his motor scooter.

"Private property. I should call the cops," said Pinhorn.

Jonathan studied Pinhorn's ride. The scooter looked several sizes too small for him.

"Go ahead," Freddie scoffed. "They're probably looking for you anyway."

"Losers." Pinhorn revved up the small engine to a high pitch and slowly pulled away down the street.

"Is it weird to feel sorry for a scooter?" asked Freddie. "Oh, no. Not the journal."

Jonathan had already opened the book and was noting the event.

Boarding protecting old shop was broken—unable to investigate further due to interference of Kevin Pinhorn, formerly of Pendleton Secondary.

Freddie read the entry over Jonathan's shoulder. "You might add: *all of which caused us to be late for school.*"

These words woke Jonathan from his thoughts with a jolt. "Oh no, what's the time?"

"Don't worry," said Freddie, "we can still make it on time if we run."

With that he turned and ran towards the cinder path, his long, easy stride taking him out of sight in no time. Jonathan trudged after his friend, resigned to being late. He didn't *do* running. Something else was bugging him, too. He'd noticed something odd behind the hoarding on the old building. What was it? Pinhorn's interruption had been untimely.

By the time he turned the corner at the cinder path, Freddie had already entered the school gates. Jonathan looked up—the heavy black clouds were closing in behind the school. His shoulders slumped forward, and he walked the remaining yards to the school gate.

Mrs. Brownlow didn't appear to be upset with Jonathan for being three minutes late for class, but his mood got worse when she handed out copies of Tolkien's *The Hobbit* and told the students this would be their new reading assignment. Jonathan's mother had tried to read the book to him when he turned ten but had given up when Jonathan showed no interest. He didn't see the point of listening once his mother had confirmed there were in fact no real hobbits in the world. Why should he care about a small, fictional character that was foolish enough to leave the comfort of his home and the security of his daily routine to go on a treasure hunt with a bunch of short men?

Worse still, there were not enough books to go around, and he would have to share with Gillian Andrews. Gillian had the ability to make him feel very uncomfortable, just by looking at him, which she seemed to do regularly. She missed out on a book, and her friends suggested she share with Jonathan. Gillian glanced at him briefly as she joined him on his bench. Freddie was no help. He looked around from his desk and grinned from ear to ear while he gave Jonathan a thumbs up. Jonathan edged farther away from Gillian—any further and he would be off the side of the bench. His cheeks burned.

The storm broke during maths. Jonathan looked through the classroom window, for once paying no attention to 'four-eyes' Ray who was scribbling algebraic formulas on the white board. The rain was teeming down. A few minutes into the deluge monstrous thunderclaps rocked the building, and wild lightning strikes illuminated faces around the classroom.

Ten minutes into art, Mr. Simmons, the team coach, knocked on the door and made the announcement Jonathan was dreading. The inter-school cricket matches were all cancelled due to water-logged pitches. Jonathan sighed and stared at the blank canvas in front of him. Late for school, forced to share a book with Gillian Andrews, cricket cancelled. How much worse could it get?

He detested art. What was the point?

He started sketching randomly, and to his surprise, the scribbles developed into the likeness of a woman's face. By his standards, the picture wasn't half-bad and bore a striking resemblance to his mother. He must have been thinking of her on a subconscious level. Why?

"Not bad. She looks like your mum!" Freddie came over and took a seat on the table.

The class had reached the point in the lesson where students were encouraged to look at one another's drawings and give feedback.

"Well, we've got the afternoon off. What's the plan?" said Freddie.

"I should get home; my mother will be worried about me."

"Well, that's the thing," said Freddie, "she won't worry about you because she'll think you're at the cricket. Plus, doesn't she work on Friday afternoons?"

"Yes, but—"

"Dude, she gave you that phone for a reason. She's expecting you do teenager type things. We're fifteen. People are going to think there's something wrong with us if we don't do the odd senseless thing from time to time. It's an important part of our development."

Jonathan arranged his pencils on the table to prepare for packing. The addition of the magazine earlier that morning had upset the order of items in his pack. He needed to address that now. He emptied the contents onto his table and set the magazine to one side whilst he considered his options. He glanced quickly out of the window. The clouds were clearing.

"It's no good, Jonathan; they've called off the match. They won't change their minds now, no matter what the weather does. Let's make the most of it. My vote is that we go explore the Cudleigh Hills train tunnel. Maybe we could even 'do the two'."

8

A shiver ran from Jonathan's neck down into his spine. He had never been to the old railway tunnel that snaked under the Cudleigh Hills to the west of Pendleton. But its status was legendary among the children of the town. The single-track railway had been closed in the late 1940s, though the tunnel remained accessible by foot. Over the decades, many tales had evolved about the decaying tunnel. Jonathan had heard plenty of them. He knew they were just random ghost stories and should be ignored, but the thought of being underground in a damp, pitch-black tunnel was not his idea of a good time.

To "do the two," a person had to walk the entire two-mile length of the tunnel without the aid of a light. Pinhorn boasted he had done it twice. Others made similar claims, but Freddie's older brother Min said they had to be lying. According to Min, at some point since the forties, they'd blocked off the tunnel roughly fifty yards in from the entrance.

A group of girls clustered round a table at the back of the classroom clamoured with excitement, laughing and giggling like a bunch of, well, *girls*. Several of their classmates joined them to see what the fuss was about. One of the guys, Gerald Hopkins, roared with laughter and reached in among the girls to pick up the object of the group's amusement— Gerald held up a Max Muscle magazine. Jonathan looked at the adjacent table where he had left his copy. Nothing – they had his copy.

"Hey, everyone, check out Mr. Abbot-Glover's magazine of choice! Max Muscle!"

Jonathan briefly considered trying to deny it was his, but he was almost incapable of telling a lie. Then he remembered his details were printed onto the address label anyway.

"So, tell us Jonathan; do you want to look like Max, or are you hoping Max will like you?" The burning sensation returned.

Jonathan poked and prodded at the remains of his lunch. Freddie sat opposite him. They were in a large cafeteria, known by students as 'the grub room." Students sat at tables scattered around the large, open dining hall.

"I think it was one of Gillian's friends who picked it up," said Freddie. "You should be happy - they like you."

"They don't like me. They want to humiliate me," Jonathan bit hard into an apple.

"Gillian has a crush on you dude. Anyway, you know how girls work; they embarrass you to show how much they like you." Having finished his food several minutes ago, Freddie was flicking crumbs off the table with his straw.

Jonathan punched his fist into his hand. "Well, that's just stupid! Girls! What's the point?"

As he spoke, he pulled his notebook out of his pack. He scribbled a quick entry, which he kept out of Freddie's view.

"We're missing an opportunity here. Why don't we invite them to come to the tunnel with us? They'll be scared stupid. We might get a snog!"

Jonathan blushed, and Freddie laughed.

"All right! Not such a bad idea, huh? I think we should give you an image makeover. Time to launch the new Jonathan. Let's start with your name—Jonathan Abbot-Glover. Not exactly cool, is it?"

Jonathan slammed his journal onto the table. "Who cares about being cool? I want to be me. Jonathan is a good name. I don't care what those idiot girls think!" Preoccupied with his rant, he pulled the card containing his secret message from his pack.

"Nothing wrong with your name…we just need to spruce it up. Everyone calls me 'Fast Freddie', and I take that as a compliment. Let's think of a cool nickname for you. You don't get to choose it yourself. It has to come from someone else. It has to…" Freddie stopped mid-sentence, his gaze going to Jonathan's journal. "You know what? I guess you did choose it yourself." Freddie laughed, pointing at the cover of the notebook. In the top right corner, Jonathan had printed his initials. "Jonathan Abbott-Glover—Jag! I like it!" Freddie held up the book to Jonathan.

"No!" Jonathan snapped, what did Freddie not get? Jonathan hated being the centre of attention.

"Oh, come on! It's cool. Tell you what, let's break into the old shop."

"No." Jonathan shook his head. "I'm heading home." He began to open the folded piece of cardboard.

"Okay, I tried," Freddie said. "One day we'll get to do something different together. You know what? I think I'll go check out the tunnel by myself."

Freddie threw his belongings together, including his cricket bat, which his coach had told Freddie to take home and oil. Without glancing back, he started towards the grub room exit.

Jonathan watched him go and then held his head in his hands. Why couldn't he be more like Freddie—gung-ho and carefree? But Jonathan didn't have it in him. He unfolded the message from his mum. Six words, all in caps and printed in large, block letters, stared back at him. He gazed at them in disbelief, and his hands started shaking. How could she have known? For a moment, he sat there, staring off into space, his thoughts racing. He couldn't have read it right. He glanced down at the slip of paper and read it again:

TAKE A CHANCE. GO WITH HIM.

The piece of cardboard fell from his hands and fluttered to the floor. An image of the hobbit Bilbo Baggins running down the garden path came into his head. He jumped up, grabbed his pack, and hurried towards the exit.

"Freddie, wait!" he called out as he chased after his friend.

Freddie turned around as Jonathan caught up, "Whoa! You look like you've seen a ghost, Jonathan!"

"I've changed my mind; I'm coming with you."

"Great!" Freddie clapped Jonathan on the back.

Jonathan fell into stride beside his friend, and they headed off towards the school gates.

"Oh, and one more thing..." Jonathan added as they started up the cinder path.

"Call me Jag."

## Chapter 2

Jag gazed up at the light blue sky. The weather had turned full circle. The stifling humidity that had preceded the storm had gone. The leaves on the oak trees bordering the road rustled in the warm breeze. Cabbage white butterflies fluttered across their route. Pollen filled the air, causing Jag's eyes and nose to water. Songbirds were in full voice, and a tractor engine hummed as a farmer worked an adjacent field.

But Jag was unmoved by the perfect summer afternoon. The initial bravado he'd felt after reading the secret message was fast disappearing. Every step forward was a step closer to the tunnel. Yes, he knew all the ghost stuff was a load of rubbish, but he couldn't stop those thoughts from bouncing around his head.

"Freddie, slow down. There's no rush, you know. I think I should stop and call my mother. Just to let her know where I am."

"Nonsense," Freddie replied. "Why would she worry? She's at work, remember?" Freddie looked at him. "This will be fun. If at any point it isn't fun, we'll stop and turn around; I promise. The spooky tunnel thing is stupid. Trust me, we'd know if there was anything to it."

Jag stopped for a moment to update a note regarding bridges. Freddie paused, a hint of frustration showing in his tightened jaw as he looked back at Jag.

"Jag!" Freddie widened his stance and put his hands on his hips. "Let's go!"

After another mile of uphill walking, the old railway bridge finally came into view. Loose pebbles and dirt covered a worn path that wound its way up the embankment to where it intersected with the top of the bridge.

Jag frowned. "We have to get up that?"

Freddie didn't answer. Apparently, something on the other side of the lane had distracted him. He crossed the road and leaned out over a guardrail, looking down. Jag followed him, but Freddie thrust his arm back, palm raised in a gesture that told Jag to stop. He froze. A shiver ran down his back. What the heck was Freddie looking at? After a few tense seconds, he motioned for Jag to join him.

Jag raised his head above the safety fence. Instantly, a wave of vertigo made him sway on his feet. He hadn't realized until that moment how high they had climbed. It was at least a hundred feet down to the river below. Gripping the fence, he steadied himself and then looked in the direction Freddie was pointing. About sixty yards upstream three people stood by the edge of the water. Two were holding what appeared to be long sticks, while the third stood with his hands clasped together behind his neck and his foot propped on top of something laying in the grass. Even from this distance, Jag recognized the third person.

"Is that—?" Freddie began.

"Pinhorn... Yeah." Jag nodded.

Which meant the two guys holding the sticks had to be Pinhorn's constant sidekicks. The lanky one was Gerald Hopkins, who had shown off Jag's Max Muscle magazine during art class, and the other was the much shorter and considerably wider Hamish Blunt.

Hopkins and Blunt were in Jag's year at Pendleton. Pinhorn was two years older and had left school the previous summer...although, Jag had seen him on the school grounds several times that term.

What were they up to? The object under Pinhorn's foot shifted, and Jag caught sight of a boy with a shock of blond hair.

"Jeez, it's that new kid. Year seven. What's his name?" Freddie asked.

"Farley," Jag said in a hushed tone.

He knew Farley but not well. The boy had only started at the school a few weeks before, but he seemed nice enough, always smiling. He was a bit on the short side for his age. There wasn't a chance he deserved what Pinhorn and his cronies were meting out.

"Poor kid... We've to do something!" Freddie backed away from the fence.

"Us? *We* can't do anything. There's three of them and only two of us. We need help!" Jag said.

"There isn't time. You know how these guys operate. We have to free the kid."

Jag shuddered. He'd rather face the tunnel than Pinhorn and his friends. "Freddie, they'll beat the crap out of me. I'm not a fighter."

"I have an idea." Freddie turned his back to Jag. "Open the lowest zipper on my pack."

Jag frowned. What was Freddie up to? Reaching into the backpack, Jag grasped a pair of well-worn cricket balls. He pulled them out.

"Good, now give them to me."

Jag handed the balls to Freddie then followed him back to the fence. Pinhorn said something, and although Jag couldn't hear the words, the tone of Pinhorn's voice was menacing.

The other two idiots were poking Farley with the sticks, and he writhed on the ground at their feet. The ends of the sticks were covered in a distinctive green—the colour of stinging nettles. Those bullies were pressing the stinging plants onto the exposed skin on Farley's arms and legs.

Pinhorn aimed a kick at the younger kid's gut, and Farley rolled over to the edge of the bank. Any further movement would put him into the water.

"Are they mad? He could drown..." Jag said.

"Time for a little distraction." Freddie chucked the first of the balls as hard as he could at the three bullies, but it landed a good thirty yards short of his target, disappearing into a large thicket bush. "Damn it!" Freddie mumbled.

"It's too far," Jag pointed out. "You can't throw that far."

"Yup, I know that now. Thanks, Jag." Sarcasm and frustration filled Freddie's voice. "Wait...lob the ball up."

"What?"

Freddie thrust the second ball into Jag's hand. "Toss it up into the air about a foot in front of me."

As Freddie gripped his cricket bat and raised it behind him, Jag understood his friend's plan. But they were too far away, weren't they?

"Quick!" Freddie whispered.

As he under armed the ball up in front of Freddie, Jag heard a splash. Farley had tumbled into the river! At the same instant, Freddie swung the bat in a long arc. He connected perfectly, and a loud, satisfying crack echoed from the bridge as the ball flew away towards its target. Jag turned to watch the flight of the ball, mesmerized by the power with which Freddie had struck it. A split second later, it caught Pinhorn square in his forehead. Despite the distance, Jag heard the impact. Pinhorn, who had been laughing at Farley as the poor guy tried to stand up in the river, staggered backward. He flapped his arms like a chicken having a seizure; his legs folded, and he went into a slow-motion spin before hitting the ground. Freddie and Jag dropped behind the fence as Hopkins and Blunt looked up in their direction.

"Blimey, Freddie, what if you've killed him?"

"Then I'll win some kind of community award." Freddie shrugged.

Jag assessed the scene below through a gap in the fence. It looked like Hopkins and Blunt were dividing their time between tending to their stricken leader, who was flat out on the grass, and looking back towards the bridge. No doubt, they were trying to locate the source of the projectile. Meanwhile, Farley had scrambled out of the water twenty yards downstream from his attackers and was making his escape, running towards a point that would intersect with the lane Jag and Freddie had come up.

"Right. Jag, you stay here. I'll fetch him."

Before Jag had a chance to protest, Freddie was gone, racing back down the lane. Jag sighed and reached for the phone in his pocket. They needed help. He held up the cell to check the signal and sighed. No reception—not even one bar. Mobile phones...what's the point? He returned the device to his pocket and looked back through the hole in the fence.

Pinhorn was up. *No accessory to murder charge then.* Jag puffed his cheeks, but the sense of relief didn't last long. Hopkins was pointing straight at Jag's position. The little band of thugs started making their way along the riverbank towards the bridge. Jag looked back down the lane, but there was no sign of Freddie or Farley...and then voices sounded from directly below him.

"Never mind the runt. We'll sort him out later. I want to get my hands on the S.O.B. who threw a frigging cricket ball at me. Where are the stairs, Hamish?"

Stairs? Panic rose in Jag's stomach. If there were stairs by the river leading up to the bridge, he was in trouble. He looked back down the lane. Still no sign of Freddie. What was taking him so long?

"I'm sure I saw someone running back down the lane."

The sound of Hamish Blunt's gravelly voice came from just below Jag. They'd found the staircase, and they were close.

"Okay, let's get to the top, and if we don't see him, we'll sniff them out in town."

Pinhorn spoke slowly, as if he were having trouble putting his thoughts into words. Maybe that knock on the head had given him a him concussion.

Jag had to move fast. He weighed his options; he could run down the lane the way Freddie had and hope Pinhorn and his buddies didn't spot him, or he could continue up the lane. The second option frightened him a bit; he had no idea where the trail led. Actually, he didn't like either choice.

"Darn it, Freddie, why did you disappear on me?" Jag scanned the lane again. Freddie would know what to do.

Don't think about it. Do it, and then think about it.

Freddie's advice sounded in Jag's mind.

The gang of three moved closer. *Don't think, Jag, don't think!* He ran back across the road and clambered up the small wall that allowed access to the path that angled up to the railway line. Against all his better judgement, something was telling him he had to head for the tunnel.

The scramble up the path would have been challenging, but fear proved to be a powerful motivator. Jag reached the top of the embankment in seconds. He took cover behind a blackberry bush. If he kept still, he wouldn't be visible from below. Pinhorn and his gang appeared on the bridge, walking back and forth, looking in every direction. They were so close Jag could make out the black bull tattoo on

Pinhorn's biceps. Rumour had it he'd been just twelve years old when he'd got the tattoo, and all the kids said it made him look even more frightening. Jag fought to keep still. Instinct told him to run away, to bolt down the railway embankment, but any movement would give away his position, and Jag was no runner. He tried to control his breathing, forcing himself to take slow gulps of air. The three searchers scoured the area for what seemed an eternity. At one point, Blunt looked straight up at Jag's hiding spot. Jag held his breath, fearing the game was up. But although the chunky kid squinted and stared for several seconds, he finally shrugged and turned away.

Pinhorn barked his next orders. "Okay, he must have gone back down the hill. There's no rush; I bet the little blond brat knows who hit me with that damn ball. Getting the information out of him will give us another good reason to kick his scrawny butt."

Hopkins and Blunt both laughed as they fell into line behind their leader who was already heading back down the lane.

Jag rolled over and breathed a sigh of relief. He was worried about Freddie but took some comfort from knowing he could outrun just about anybody. Of course, he might have Farley with him, which would slow Freddie down. Jag shook his head. Nothing he could do for them now. He looked at his watch. *Four-fifteen*. The gut feeling telling him he should go to the tunnel entrance had grown even stronger. Jag set off, tracing the route of the old line. The sleepers, rails, and ballast stones that would have once marked the way were long gone, but the route of the old track wasn't hard to follow, even though nature had reclaimed much of it. Long, lush grass, huge ferns, and even small trees now grew on the path.

What a day. Jag found an open spot with a grassy bank over to the side and sat to update his journal. He recorded more random thoughts about the old shop. He logged his exact arrival time at school, though it pained him to do so. Then he added a brief description of the secret message incident along with a few theories about how it could have happened, although none were very plausible. He recorded detailed information about the walk they had taken into the Cudleigh Hills, charting statistics about intersecting roads and paths, as well as the river's course. He also wrote in as much detail as he could about the Pinhorn encounter. When he had finished, he felt much better. He set off towards the tunnel again. Why was he going there? What had Freddie said that had made Jag take this course? What was he going to do when he got there?

A shout came from behind him. Jag froze.

# Chapter 3

Jag turned. Gillian was just a few yards behind him. She scanned the ground as if she were looking for something. Dust covered her skirt and tunic, one sleeve had a big rip, and both buckles on her shoes were broken.

"Why are you following me?" he asked, trying to regain his composure. "Are you helping Pinhorn?"

"Pinhorn? What are you talking about?" she replied, still scanning the ground.

"Have you lost something?"

"Yes, a charm from my bracelet. I heard it...oh, found it." She picked up a small figurine caked in dust and brushed it down as best she could before tucking it away in her skirt pocket. "I'll fix it later."

"Have you seen Pinhorn?" Jag asked.

"Yes, at the bottom of the lane. He was with his two numbskull friends. They were cutting across a field back towards town. Why? Is he after you or something? I know he's a bully..."

Jag found a grassy area over to one side of the pathway and sat down. He didn't look back at Gillian, but she joined him, pressing her skirt to her sides as she tucked her feet under her legs.

"You're a bit of a mess," said Jag.

Gillian laughed and ran her hand through her shoulder-length hair, creating a small cloud of dust. "Yes, I underestimated how tricky the access path to the bridge was. Did you lose Freddie?"

"Well, I was with him, but Pinhorn is on the war path, and Freddie left me to go help one of Pinhorn's victims. That new boy, Farley."

"Oh no, Farley? That sweet little guy? Someone needs to teach that ignoramus Pinhorn a lesson. What happened?"

Jag linked his hands together behind his neck and gave Gillian a detailed account of his walk with Freddie and the encounter with Pinhorn. Gillian listened attentively. When he finished, she looked at him.

"I didn't see Freddie or Farley. Sorry. Are you still heading for the tunnel?"

"Yes, I am. I don't know why." Jag reached back into his pack for his journal. "You still haven't told me why you're following me."

Before Gillian could respond, Jag heard a familiar voice from behind them.

"Where you headed, Jagmeister?"

Jag looked over his shoulder. Freddie strolled towards them, a big grin on his face.

"Freddie. What happened to you?"

"Well, young Farley here runs a lot faster than you would expect."

Jag raised his arms as Farley stepped out from behind the much broader Freddie. Farley nodded a greeting, a sheepish grin on his face. His clothes were still wet from his dunking in the river, his messed-up blond hair was plastered against his forehead, and the skin on his arms and neck were covered in red stinging nettle rashes.

Gillian's expression softened, and she walked over to him and put a maternal arm round his shoulders. "Oh, what did they do to you? You poor thing," she said as she examined the rash on one of his arms.

"I ran as quickly as I could, but this speedster beat me to the junction, and I had to chase him all the way back to town. Once I reeled him in, I told him our story and suggested it might be a good idea for him to stick with us until we got this thing sorted out."

Jag filled them in on what had happened after Freddie left.

"And then Gillian got here," Jag said, concluding his story.

Freddie gave Gillian a look of indifference.

"I'm impressed with you taking on the Pinhorn monster. I suppose cricket isn't a completely useless game then?" she said, smiling at Freddie.

"We've come this far; we might as well go look at the tunnel," Freddie said, ignoring Gillian.

"Hey, what's your problem, Freddie Patel?" Gillian jumped to her feet and stood hands on hips, glaring at Freddie.

Freddie said nothing and started walking in the direction of the tunnel. Jag got to his feet and followed. He glanced back. Gillian was following him, and Farley brought up the rear, walking several steps behind, looking around, his expression dreamy.

"Sorry, Jag, you should have come with me. How was Pinhorn? Did the cricket ball improve his looks at all?"

"I didn't get to see. Most of the time I was hiding. How did you miss them when you were coming back up the lane?"

"They sounded like a herd of elephants coming down the hill. We heard them long before they had any chance of seeing us. We got off the road and hid behind a wall. Once they passed, we got back on the road and continued up to where I left you. Of course, when we reached the bridge, we had to guess which way you'd gone. At first, I thought you'd headed up the lane, but I wasn't sure. I was thinking it through when I turned around and saw Farley halfway up the embankment. Decision made... Hey, keep up, Farley; we don't want to lose you again!"

Farley had fallen even farther behind and didn't seem in any rush to catch up. They waited for him.

"Ah, that's what we need, Farley!" Freddie put down his bat. He stepped off the trail, bent down, and picked some reddish-green leaves from a large plant. "Doc leaves! Nature's answer to stinging nettles." He broke off a handful of the leaves and rubbed them vigorously together, so they emitted a sap. "Rub that wherever your skin still burns. It'll help."

Smiling, Farley looked up at Freddie and took the crushed leaves.

"Farley, you can talk, right?" Freddie asked.

The blond boy nodded.

"Do you want to tell us why Pinhorn and the *ugly sisters* were torturing you?"

The smile left Farley's face. He remained silent.

"Okay, feel free to talk your head off any time the mood grabs you."

Farley's smile returned, broader than ever, as he turned his attention to applying the doc leaf residue to his rashes.

Freddie shook his head. "Oh, boy, you're going to fit right in with us!"

Five minutes later, they reached their destination. They came upon the entrance so suddenly, Jag froze, a bit shocked. The wild plants thinned out, the ground on either side of them rose, and then there it was! A large, red brick edifice that framed the opening of a dark tunnel. A line of lighter bricks bordered the brickwork, meeting at the apex of the tunnel. A roughly hewn keystone held everything in place. Above the keystone was a concrete slab with a barely discernible inscription on it. Years of weathering had taken its toll on what must have been the name of the tunnel or a date—or maybe both. Above the slab the damp had discoloured the red bricks, creating a curious pattern. On either side of the tunnel entrance, long trails of ivy cascaded down the face of the brickwork, their dark leaves shimmering in the breeze. The ivy's tendrils gripped the stone and, wherever there was decay, burrowed their way into the wall.

Jag could not bring himself to look at the tunnel. Pure darkness—the type in which you couldn't see your hand when held up directly in front of your face—filled the large hole. The tunnel gave off a forbidding aura, and yet, Jag found himself being pulled into it. He stopped, as though waking from a stupor, and reversed course several yards, all the while keeping his eyes on the entrance. He squatted on his haunches and looked towards his friend. For once, Freddie was still, leaning forward on his bat, as if he was taking it all in. His unhappiness showed in his expression.

"You know what, Jag?" he whispered. "This place is genuinely disturbing. I don't like it at all."

Gillian looked worried, too.

Of the four of them, only Farley appeared unaffected. He had taken a seat in the grass and was applying more doc leaves to his sore limbs.

"Well, we can tick it off the list. I'm ready to head home. It's sealed off a few yards into the tunnel. We need to sort out the Farley situation. I'm thinking we should report the attack to the principal or maybe even the police. We need to make sure he gets protection from those cavemen…"

Jag stopped listening, returning his attention to the spot where the water damage had created the curious pattern above the archway. Now he was a few steps farther back, the angle of the sunlight gave him a different perspective. That wasn't water damage at all. *It's a brick mosaic…* Difficult to make out after years of weathering but he knew what he was looking at.

He stared at it in disbelief. "Freddie! Freddie…look!"

As Freddie turned, something hit Jag on the shoulder…a glancing blow, but it hurt.

Jag looked from the stone lying at his feet towards the hill above the tunnel. "What the…?"

Hopkins and Blunt stood above them. How had they managed that? Hopkins threw another stone, while Blunt sat next to his buddy like a chubby pit bull waiting for his orders. Jag glanced around. Where was Pinhorn?

"Hey, Max Muscle!" Hopkins launched another rock in their direction. "And your boyfriend, Freddie, too! Looks like you brought along a girl to protect you. Did you think you would lose us? Kevin's seriously pissed off—you gave him a headache!"

Laughing, Hopkins sped up the stone throwing. A piece of flint caught Jag on the leg. Gillian cried out as one hit her elbow.

"Where is that oversized jelly? I'll cure his headache once and for all," Freddie yelled, swinging his bat.

"Well, as a matter of fact…" Hopkins said, lowering his voice.

Pinhorn came barrelling down the trail that had taken them to this point. He blasted into Freddie, hitting him at a dead run.

"Bingo!" Hopkins shouted.

"Run, Farley, run!" Jag yelled to their young companion.

Farley sped off, straight into the tunnel, the darkness swallowing him in a fraction of a second.

"Not that way! Farley! Back to the road! Back to the road!" Jag called out.

But Farley did not reappear.

Freddie and Pinhorn were grappling on the ground, Freddie getting the worst of it.

"Go after him; help him! Help him!" Freddie said from beneath Pinhorn.

Tears streamed down Jag's face. What should he do? Freddie had told him to help Farley… *But how can I leave my best friend at the mercy of this thug?*

Noise from above drew his attention. Hopkins and Blunt were scrambling down the embankment. They were seconds away, and Jag had no good options.

Freddie threw Pinhorn off him for a moment—a small victory in a war he was losing. "Go!" he yelled in a strained voice.

Pinhorn leaped on Freddie again, pushing his face into the dirt.

Jag ran towards the fight, but Gillian beat him to it. In a blur of motion, she charged in and landed an almighty kick on Pinhorn's back. Pinhorn emitted a loud groan and grabbed her ankle, trapping her. Jag aimed a kick at Pinhorn's wrist. The bully let go of her for a second. She took full advantage, turning and sprinting for the tunnel entrance, yelling out Farley's name.

"Go! Jag, leg it!!" Freddie had escaped the fight and scrambled to his feet.

Jag turned towards the tunnel entrance…took one last look behind; Hopkins swung a clenched fist towards Jag's head. He ducked the punch and ran for the tunnel.

Just as he reached the opening, Jag glanced up at the mosaic above the arch. *No way!* The image depicted a man intently studying a sun dial…an exact copy of the timekeeper featured on the kitchen clock at home!

The adrenalin coursing through his veins fuelled Jag's sprint into the tunnel. Within a few seconds he was running blindly because the tunnel veered to the right just twenty yards in, and the bend cut off the natural light. He slowed. The chill in the air bit into his exposed skin; a strong smell of sulphur burned his nostrils. He continued at a walking pace; his hands held out ahead of him. A strange silence surrounded him. Even the sounds of his footsteps on the ballast seemed muted. He wanted to call out but was afraid. What was happening? Where were his friends? And where was Pinhorn?

He edged forward and bumped into the tunnel wall. The first touch of his hand against the clammy, wet stones did nothing to ease his fears. He recoiled and stood motionless for a moment. Nothing—no light, no sound of any kind. How could this be? He had seen Farley, Gillian, and Freddie all run in ahead of him, and he had sensed Pinhorn chasing from behind. Jag had a healthy fear of Pinhorn, but it was nothing compared to the terror of being alone in the pitch-black, silent tunnel. He needed to think.

*Slow your breathing, Jonathan,* his mother always said when he used to have panic attacks. He put his hands on his knees and leaned forward, gaining more control by increasing his intake of cold air. Okay, had he somehow passed the others? Yes, that was the only logical explanation. But wasn't Freddie behind him? How far in had he run? It couldn't have been that far. As Freddie had said, the tunnel was blocked off fifty yards in. They would all have to come out the way they had come in. Pinhorn knew that, too, and he was probably waiting for them at the entrance. The situation was hopeless. Jag had to find his friends.

"Freddie?" he said, breaking the silence for the first time. No answer.

"Freddie?" he called out a little louder. But each time he spoke, the sound of his voice was flat and toneless, as if the dark itself devoured his words. Panic rose inside him again.

"Freddie, Farley, Gillian! Where are you guys?"

He shouted as loud as he could, but it was as if his words just tumbled out in front of him and disappeared. Silence was the only response. If only he had a flashlight...

The thought brought back the memory of what Freddie had done so they could see inside the abandoned shop. Jag fumbled in his pocket for the phone his mother had reminded him to take that morning. He pulled it out and flicked it open; the device came to life with a musical sound, barely audible in the tunnel. But to Jag's relief, the screen emitted a shard of light. Only enough to see a few yards around him but he felt a lot better. He could make out the wall of the tunnel now. Rivulets of moisture meandered down its damp surface. He pointed the phone in the direction he had come from, but the light wasn't strong enough to make out any details. Then he turned half circle and shone the light deeper into the tunnel. Again, there was not enough light to penetrate the pitch darkness. But as he lowered the phone to check his immediate surroundings, he caught sight of a tiny pinprick of light some distance farther down the tunnel. At first, he thought it was the reflection of his phone on the wet wall. But when he snapped the phone shut, extinguishing his light, the glow was still there, and it was moving from side to side. Someone was signalling him!

How stupid he had been. He hadn't passed the other three; they were still ahead of him, probably close to the blocked area of the tunnel. He strode towards the light; whatever lay ahead, it would be a lot easier to handle with Freddie beside him. Jag flicked his phone open again, and now he could see the ground in front of him, he broke into a trot, heading deeper into the darkness. He smiled as he said to himself, "Just follow the light!"

After a few minutes of jogging, Jag's anxiety started to build up once more. The light was still ahead of him, but it no longer moved, and despite his progress, he didn't seem to be getting any closer to its source.

"Freddie is that you?" he called out again, but his words fell flat, the sound of them going nowhere.

The smell of sulphur was becoming overwhelming. He had slowed his pace to a walk, his eyes fixed on the pinprick of light ahead. The other end of the tunnel? How far had he come? He was now certain that nothing blocked the way fifty yards into the tunnel. No point in turning around now...might as well go for it. He ran towards the light, moving faster and faster. No matter how bad this experience might be, it wouldn't get any better until he got out of the tunnel. He ran, and he ran. *Follow the light, follow the light.*

"Freddie!" he yelled. "Gillian! Farley!"

Follow the light.

The reek of sulphur and the cold air were affecting his mind. He imagined something evil was chasing him. He ran even faster to get away. Several times, he stumbled and fell flat on his face. But he jumped to his feet each time. Nothing was going to stop him now. Minutes ticked by... *Follow the light.* His lungs ached... *Follow the light.* And his heart thudded against his ribcage from his exertions.

How far had he run? Half a mile? A mile? He didn't know, but he wanted out of this tunnel. The light from his phone disappeared. Without stopping, he lifted the phone to see what had made it go.

"Oomph!" He collided with the wall at a dead run. The sound of the impact—a very alarming, crunching noise—met his ears before pain exploded through his body.

His torso hit the wall first, and all the air left his lungs. His head took a vicious blow, which sent him spiralling unconscious for a moment. He twisted around and collapsed in a heap, his back ending up against the wall. As he tried to catch his breath, he felt warm blood trickling down his face. In the darkness he caught sight of the gentle glow of the light from his phone, which had fallen a few feet from him. He stretched to pick it up, making the pain in his chest worse as he did so. A wave of nausea swept through his head as he tried to lift the phone. At the same time, the phone sounded a musical chime and then powered off, leaving him in total darkness.

"Battery..." Jag uttered.

So, Min had been wrong. They hadn't blocked off the entrance; they'd walled off the exit on the other side... Jag was sinking fast, but he thought he sensed a vibrating sensation coming through his back, accompanied by a loud grinding noise. Was the wall pushing him? *I wonder if they'll ever find me.*

Although his eyes were shut, he could see the tiny light right in front of him again, and it was growing. If only he could open his eyes...

But he didn't want to open his eyes; he wanted to rest.

The last thing he remembered was the girl's voice.

"Jonathan, is that you? Jonathan!"

He thought about trying to answer, but he felt too far away. He let himself drift off into a quiet place that didn't require thought.

# Chapter 4

The salty flavour on the breeze stirred him. The gentle wind caressed his face, dissipating the remnants of the sulphurous odour. The unnatural cold he had been exposed to earlier was gone. Earlier? Where had he been? Where was he now? His head spun, and he kept his eyes closed, knowing instinctively they would hurt if he opened them.

Follow the light.

That's what he had been doing, but that had been a long time ago. An hour? Several hours? Darkness, cold, fear, pain. He drifted away again.

A loud shriek pierced his ears, waking him with a jolt. The sound was familiar but not one he would normally associate with the farmlands of the Cudleigh Hills. Where the heck was he? He'd been in a tunnel, hadn't he? He arrested the swirling in his head and avoided the nausea. He was winning the fight.

Follow the light.

He was *in* the light! A bright glow blazed through his closed eyelids.

A second louder shriek filled the air, close by this time. Jag blinked in alarm. Bright sunlight burned his retinas, and he clenched his eyes shut again, covering them with his forearm for extra protection. A seagull… His mind registered the source of the noise, and he relaxed a bit. Just a harmless bird…

"Hey, shoo, shoo!" A girl shouted from nearby.

The seagull shrieked again, this time angrily as it took flight. The bird must have been close to him because he felt the turbulence created by its wings as it flew off.

"I've been watching you for a while. I think you're going to live. But try to open your eyes."

The girl's accent sounded foreign, but Jag couldn't place it. He angled his head away from the sun and tried to open his eyes again. He sighed. Much better…only a small amount of pain, and he could make out images. He turned his head to look at the girl.

"What is your name?" she asked.

Jag squinted, and her face came into focus. She was young, about his age, and had dark-brown eyes.

"Urgh." Jag reached for his voice—it was there, croaky and dry, but he could talk. "Jonathan...err...Jag..." Still finding it difficult to breathe, he coughed.

"Pleased to meet you, Jonathan Ur-Jag. I am Ulma of Three Widows. Which town are you of, and where is your allegiance?"

Jonathan lowered his head, trying to make sense of the words.

"Which town am I of?"

"Yes, and where is your allegiance?"

Jag looked up at her again. She was quite pretty.

"I've never cut anyone before, but I am not afraid to do so." She raised her hand.

To his horror, Jag realized she was holding a short dagger.

"Cut me? What the heck is going on? Why would you cut me?"

Ulma looked at him silently, dagger still held aloft.

"To be honest with you, I think I'm in the middle of a crazy nightmare, and you are part of it. I'm not sure when the nightmare started or where." His throat was so dry he coughed again. "This is terrible for my routine."

Ulma looked at him coolly. "Are you of the lost?" she asked.

"Yes, yes. I think we can safely say I'm lost." Jag coughed out the words.

"Okay, Jonathan Ur-jag," said Ulma, lowering her dagger, "Nikolas says the lost are usually without malice. Here, drink of this." She sheathed her dagger and from the other side of her belt unclipped a leather flask, which she opened and pressed against his lips.

The fluid tasted like water but sweeter and with a little fizz. It was delicious. Jag realized how de-hydrated he was. He swallowed thirstily.

"Not too much." Ulma laughed and pulled the flask away. "A little Anika water will restore you, but too much will make you crazy!"

Jag let the effect of the draft work its way around his body. Much of his pain had dulled, and his head was clearing. His voice became stronger, too. "Wow, that stuff is good. I should make a note of it for future reference!" He reached behind him to pull his notebook from his backpack, but the pack was gone. When had he lost it? He tried to remember the last time he had opened it. Most likely before he entered the tunnel. He rarely went this long without making a note about something.

"What have you lost, Jonathan Ur-jag?"

"I had a backpack. I was wearing it before I ran into the wall."

"What wall is this?"

"The one at the end of the tunnel." Jag pushed himself into a sitting position and then onto his feet. His balance wasn't great, but for the first time, he could look around. "Where is Cudleigh from here?" he asked, shielding his eyes from the sun to take in his surroundings.

"No tunnels near here. What is Cudleigh?"

"The tunnel entrance should be right here. It's blocked, but I came through it somehow...right after I banged my head." He turned around slowly. He had been propped up against a small granite cliff, perhaps thirty feet high. He looked left and right; the cliffside stretched both ways. There were a lot of loose rocks lying at its base but no sign of a tunnel entrance or exit. He turned a semi-circle. The ground sloped gently upward. The soil was sandy and covered in clusters of long wild grass. Jag shook his head. The ground didn't rise enough to accommodate a tunnel. What the heck? Further proof he was in the middle of an ultra-vivid dream?

"Cudleigh must be close. We're near the tunnel exit. Okay...it disappeared, but it can't be far away." He took in the position of the sun, which had sunk low on the horizon. "So that is west. Cudleigh lies to the west of Pendleton. My guess is that it's located just over the rise ahead of us."

"That is unlikely, Jonathan Ur-Jag."

"Well, let's look." He walked up the slope, surprised how well his legs worked. That Anika stuff was good.

Ulma stepped alongside him. He looked over at her as they went up the hill. He wasn't one for fashion, but her dress looked like a sack, given shape only by the belt she wore round her waist. Her bare arms and legs were deeply tanned, and on her feet, she wore laced up moccasins.

He turned his attention back to locating Cudleigh. "It has to be here," he said.

They crested the slope, and Ulma glanced across at him.

"Do the residents of this town breathe underwater?" she asked with a hint of a smile.

Jag stumbled to a halt and took a sharp breath. The other side of the hill dropped away steeply. After thirty yards or so, the clumps of grass disappeared. In their place were rolling sand dunes, and beyond those, an ocean. A vast ocean that stretched across the horizon as far as he could see. There were no people. No buildings. No signs of civilization. Jag slumped to his knees. A seagull—maybe the one that had been stalking him earlier—flew over his head towards the ocean. The bird gave out an elongated shriek as it caught an updraft that sent it soaring into the heights. Ulma was right; they were an awfully long way from Cudleigh.

Jonathan sank down to sit on the grassy hilltop and looked all around, hoping to find something familiar. But the landscape was alien to him. Waves crashed on the beach ahead, a sound he was familiar with, as his mother had taken him to the seaside for a week every summer. But the nearest resort area was a hundred miles from Pendleton. On a good day, the drive took two hours. The sun was setting fast. What on earth should he do?

Ulma stood next to him. Hands on hips, she looked down at him. "Which direction is your home, Jonathan Ur-Jag?"

Jag buried his head in his hands. What was happening to him? "I don't know," he replied. "I really don't. Please tell me where I am."

"You are on the edge of the Western Wastes. My home is a few hours to the east; let me take you there. Nikolas may be able to help you. You cannot stay out here. It is dangerous, especially at night. The RagaRaga patrol these shores."

"The who?" replied Jag.

"You do not know of the RagaRaga?" Ulma asked. "Come, Jonathan Ur-Jag, you need counsel. We head east. But before that, let us return to where I first saw you."

"I think we should just go," said Jag quickly. He had had enough excitement for one day, and he didn't like the sound of the RagaRaga.

"We need to see if your woman has returned. She may be looking for you."

"What?" exclaimed Jag. "I don't have a woman! I'm fifteen years old!"

"The one dressed in grey. She cries a lot."

Jag couldn't think straight. Then it came to him—the voice he'd heard after he'd run into the wall. A girl calling him. *Gillian*... Was it possible she was here, too? His pulse racing, he started walking back to the granite cliff where he had first woken from his trauma.

*****

Gillian Andrews sat with her head in her hands. What had happened to her? Where was she? Was this real? Was it a dream? Now she'd lost Jonathan, too. When she'd first found him after exiting the tunnel, she'd been sure he was dead. He lay on the ground in a tangled heap by the granite cliff. She'd stayed with him for a while, crying. Finally, she'd come to her senses and had gone to look for help, but she couldn't find anyone. She saw no evidence of people. No roads, no buildings, no utility pylons, no farm fences. Nothing. When she returned to the spot where she had left Jonathan, he had disappeared. How was that possible? She'd flopped down onto the ground and wept.

How had she gotten into this mess? Gillian had felt guilty about Tessa and Hopkins humiliating Jonathan in art. Gillian could and should have stopped her friend from sharing the magazine with anyone, not least Gerald Hopkins. But she'd stood and watched silently. She'd seen the pained expression on Jonathan's face as they mocked him. Once they had finished, she'd quietly picked up the magazine and placed it in her pack. Her friend had overheard Jonathan and Freddie talking about going to the old railway tunnel. After school was finished, Gillian turned down an invitation from her friends to go hang out at the mall. Instead, she set off on foot towards the railway bridge. She wanted to return the magazine and apologize.

Her thoughts were interrupted by a familiar voice.

"Gillian?"

Jag looked at the pitiful girl sitting on the ground sobbing into her hands.

"Gillian?" repeated Jag, his voice still raspy. "Gillian, are you okay?"

"Jonathan!" She dropped her hands, jumped up, and ran the short distance between them. She threw her arms around his neck. "Jonathan! Thank goodness! I thought you were dead." She held him tighter still, pressing her tear-streaked cheek to his neck. "What happened to us, Jonathan? Where are we? Where are the others?"

Gillian released him and stepped back, looking at him with wide, wet eyes. Jag wasn't big on physical displays of affection or comfort, but he had felt strangely reassured by the embrace. Gillian didn't look anything like her normal self. Her uniform was now a write-off. Dirty, torn, and blood stained. Her normally smooth and shiny hair was tangled

"I don't know. I don't have any answers. I believe I'm having some sort of nightmare…"

"Me, too. But this feels so real!" Gillian spread her arms. She looked at Ulma. "And who is this?"

Ulma scowled back at her. "I am Ulma of Three Widows. Which town are you of, and where is your allegiance?"

"What?" said Gillian.

Ulma moved her hand towards her dagger.

"No, no! Her name is Gillian," he said. "We go to school together at Pendleton Secondary. We're in the same year."

Ulma looked at him, her expression blank. "School? Penderton?"

"Pendleton, yes."

Ulma frowned, but her hand moved away from the dagger. She looked Gillian up and down. "Is she of the lost too?"

"Yes," he replied quickly, "we're both, um, of the lost… Well, we're both lost anyway. We ran down the same tunnel. We were trying to help someone. We were with—" Jag stopped.

Ulma was looking at him wide eyed, and he didn't think giving her more information would help.

"Then we hit a wall and ended up here." He finished his tale with a shrug.

"You hit a wall?" Gillian asked. "Is that how you got all those cuts and bruises?"

"Well, yes. The wall blocking the exit to the tunnel. Didn't you come up against it?"

"I didn't see a wall. I just walked out and found myself here."

Jag looked around. She just walked out? From where? His gaze fell on his backpack, which sat leaning against the cliff edge next to Gillian's. She must have picked it up earlier. He breathed out a sigh of relief.

"So, where is the exit?" he asked, as he walked over to his backpack, frantic to get his hands on his journal. He pulled the pack up by one of its straps and reached inside for the book.

"That's a good question. After I exited the tunnel, there was a loud bang behind me. I turned around, and the tunnel had disappeared," said Gillian. "It sounds crazy, I know, but it's gone."

"I have to go now; I'm already late," said Ulma. "If you come with me, you have to do as I say—no questions. I don't want to end up with a RagaRaga spear in my heart."

"Can you give us five minutes?" Gillian asked.

Ulma squinted at Gillian. "What are minutes? Whatever they are, I doubt I have any. I travel light."

Jag and Gillian exchanged looks. Jag opened his mouth to respond but Gillian jumped in.

"Jonathan, let's compare notes and make a decision based on that."

For the next several minutes, Jag and Gillian discussed their situation, and then Jag scribbled the options in his journal:

Search the area for the tunnel entrance/exit.
Do nothing. Remain by the cliff and wait to be found/rescued.
Go with Ulma and seek help from her people.

Gillian looked over his shoulder. "One is the most logical," she said, "but we have both done that already and found nothing. Two is also logical. But I'm not sure logic has much value here—tunnels disappearing and a new coastline appearing a few miles from home. So, I vote for number three. Let's see where this dream takes us."

Jag closed his eyes. He agreed with Gillian but wasn't really happy with any option. When had he last eaten? Was it normal to get hungry in dreams? He always had tea at exactly six o'clock—what was the time now? He didn't know. His wristwatch had disappeared—it must have broken and fallen somewhere in the tunnel. His phone was also missing. How was he going to explain this to his mother? Would Ulma's town have a shop where he could buy things they might need, like food? And if it did, how would he pay for it?

"There is water on the route and food in my town." Ulma said.

That sealed it for Jag. "Okay, Ulma. We're coming with you."

*****

Jag stumbled again as he and Gillian tried to keep up with their guide. They had been walking for half an hour with no sign of civilization.

"Are we the only ones who made it through the tunnel?" Jag whispered to Gillian.

"I don't know," she replied. "It was pitch black in there and totally chaotic."

Jag took stock of their surroundings. The scenery was a depressing panorama of barren rocks and featureless landscapes. Ulma seemed obsessed with the threat of a surprise attack by the RagaRaga.

"Hush!" Ulma came to a sudden halt, her arm raised. "To the rocks!"

The three hurried off the pathway and took cover among the ubiquitous granite boulders. This was at least the fourth time Ulma had made them hide since they'd left the granite cliff. As they lowered themselves behind one of the larger rocks, Ulma made sure they weren't visible from the pathway, signalling them to crouch lower still.

For Jag, with each successive false alarm the tension was easing. If these RagaRaga were truly a threat, wouldn't they have attacked by now? He was starting to think Ulma was being a bit overly cautious, and he was sure Gillian felt the same.

"Okay, clear," Ulma whispered, as she deftly retraced her steps back up to the trail. "We continue, but no more talking. You both speak too loudly; our foe can hear sounds many leagues from where they stand. You will bring trouble down upon us."

They followed Ulma but moved with nowhere near the same ease and lightness of foot she displayed. Gillian had been complaining about being thirsty, and now Jag desperately needed water, too, but Ulma did not offer her flask to either of them. He could use more of that nice potion. Gillian dislodged loose rocks with a misplaced step, which started a mini-rockslide and a series of loud clunking noises. Ulma turned and gave Gillian a daggerlike stare.

"So, just who are these RagaRaga?" Gillian asked, making no attempt to keep her voice down. "And why should we fear them?"

In a flash, Ulma stepped around Jag. She caught Gillian by her waist with one hand and put the palm of her other hand over Gillian's mouth before she had a chance to react.

"Lost girl, I am trying to help you." Ulma's mouth was right up against Gillian's ear, and she spoke softly but deliberately. "If the RagaRaga take you, you will never see your home again." She maintained the grip a moment longer and then slowly released it.

Jag looked on, mouth wide open, as Gillian's face turned white, and tears welled in her eyes, but he said nothing. Ulma stepped back, and Gillian dropped her head submissively as they picked up the trail again.

As the sun set quickly behind them and their three shadows stretched out ahead of them, Jag felt sure they must be getting close to the town. The unmistakable sound of running water came from up ahead. Seconds later, he picked up his pace, elated to see a small but fast-flowing stream crossing their path. *Water!*

"Yes, drink of this," said Ulma. "It is good water." For the first time since leaving the cliff, she spoke in a normal tone and not in a whisper. "It also marks the end of the Western Wastes. We are safe now."

Jag paid her little attention. Gillian had thrown herself face down into the shallow stream and was gulping mouthfuls of water. Jag debated the situation silently. His cautious nature told him it would be smart to test the water before drinking it, but his thirst drove him forward. He flopped down alongside Gillian and scooped water up to his mouth with cupped hands. It was cool and delicious. They could test it on the way back, he thought to himself, reaching down for another mouthful. Ulma joined them, laughing loudly and splashing the others playfully.

They drank their fill and then settled down for a rest on the far side of the stream. Jag had retrieved his journal from his backpack, worried it might have become wet from Ulma's splashing. But he had packed it securely, and it was dry as a bone.

As Ulma talked, explaining details of this strange world, Jag took notes.

"The stream runs down from the Maria Mountains. It is one of many that flow from the mountains located to the north of my homeland. They are small rivers, but they are reliable and allow my people to farm this region."

Jag put down his pencil and scratched his head. Why was he recording this? The geography she was describing bore no resemblance to the land he grew up in. Yes, maybe the stream could be part of the river that Pinhorn had dunked Farley in, but mountains to the north? There were no mountains to speak of in their part of the country. Nor was there an ocean just a few miles from the exit of the train tunnel! They'd quenched their thirst, but now he realized how hungry he was. And if the grumbling coming from Gillian's stomach was any indication, she was famished, too. Apparently, Ulma didn't have any food with her. How could she not be hungry? It must be well past six now. On Fridays—strange to think of this as a day of the week—his mother made pasta with a creamy mushroom sauce and garlic bread on the side. His poor mother… She had to be so worried about him. He had a mental picture of her sitting at the table with a steaming bowl of pasta in front of her, an empty place setting opposite her. Was she crying? He had to get back quickly.

"Jonathan, you're daydreaming!" Gillian shook his shoulder.

He looked around and blinked in surprise. The light had faded, the sun having eased its way down beyond the Wastes and the sea beyond them. Fortunately, it remained warm, because their clothing was still damp from the stream.

"How will we find our way in this darkness?" Jag asked, staring into the shadows that lay ahead.

"This is my country. I know every inch, Jonathan Ur-Jag. I do not need light. Follow me closely."

She started off into the darkness, Jag quickly following and Gillian right behind him.

"There will be food for us in your town?" Gillian asked, her tone somewhat curt.

"There will be food," Ulma replied without looking back.

Jag hesitated for a moment. "You wouldn't, by any chance, have creamy mushroom sauce on pasta with garlic bread on the side?" he asked.

Ulma did not respond, and Jag's shoulders drooped.

Despite Ulma's reassurance, something made him uneasy. More than once, he thought he heard someone following them. Each time, he looked back over Gillian's shoulder, but it was too dark to see anything.

"Are you sure we're safe now?" asked Gillian.

"Quite safe." Ulma sounded confident. "This is Mensa, the country of my ancestors and my family home for many generations. Another bell and we will be within sight of Three Widows. If I am with you, there is nothing to fear."

Without warning, she froze. Jag stumbled into her back, and Gillian walked straight into Jag.

"No!" cried Ulma.

A taught net swung into Jag, moving so rapidly it knocked him off his feet. "What the—?"

A great weight landed on him, punching all the air from his lungs.

*Not again...* The net swung around him on his other side and then rapidly tightened, cocooning him in a bundle of meshed rope.

"Let me go!" Gillian screamed.

She kicked out violently, her foot catching him square in his temple. Stars filled his vision. From nearby, Ulma shouted words Jag didn't understand, but he had no fight in him. He didn't resist as a knee pressed hard into his back and rough hands bound his wrists together. The sounds of others involved in their own confrontations became unimportant to him. For the second time that day, he sank into a dark pit of nothingness.

# Chapter 5

Something warm and wet sloshed against Jag's face, causing an unpleasant sensation—slippery and yet rough at the same time, like a large tongue. He woke with a start. It was a tongue! He stared up at the face of a donkey.

The donkey appeared to be amused to have woken him and was looking down on him, baring long, crooked teeth as if in a mock grin.

"Oh, yuck! Oh, no!" Warm, slimy saliva coated his face. He moved to wipe it off, but his hands were tied behind his back.

Gillian was beside him, lying on her side, her eyes closed.

"Gillian!" Jag nudged her with his knee. "Please help."

She awoke with a jolt. Her hands were bound, but she managed to get quickly onto her knees. "Move, David! Move!"

Surprisingly, the donkey backed away at her command. She looked down at Jag and grinned.

"Don't laugh at me. Help me wipe this off!" Jag was starting to feel sick. "And who is David?"

"He is." She nodded in the direction of Jag's new friend.

Jag looked again at the donkey. A rope hung from its neck, holding a wooden sign with the message, *Hello, my name is David*, painted in white letters. Jag blinked. The entire situation seemed crazy and unreal. He needed his journal fast, but his backpack was missing again. He closed his eyes against a wave of desperation. What had he done to deserve this? His routine had been obliterated, and he was hungry and thirsty and still suffering aches and pains from the attack. But being deprived of his journal? By far, the hardest thing for him to endure.

Dry straw covered the floor they had slept on, providing him a measure of comfort against the hard dirt. They were in what appeared to be a small stable made of four crudely constructed walls. Grimy-looking water filled a trough screwed onto the far wall, and a second trough adjacent to it contained what looked and smelled like old vegetables.

Some kind of tightly bound, reed-like material made up the roof. It wouldn't keep the rain out, thought Jag, as he looked up at a myriad of small holes through which tiny shafts of sunlight illuminated David's home.

At the front was a classic stable door made up of two sections, upper and lower, each fastened with rusty iron hinges

"Jonathan, we need to talk fast; I imagine our captors will be coming to see us soon. We need to get our stories straight. But first, get up on your knees like I am."

He pulled his legs under his torso, and then following Gillian's directions, he shifted his weight to one side. From that position he was able to pull himself upright into a standing position. Gillian was already standing facing him. She turned, showing him her back.

"Okay, now rub your face on my jacket." She moved a little closer.

"Oh, no, I can't do that! It's your school uniform, and we don't have a change of clothing."

"Jonathan, it doesn't matter. These clothes are so dirty and disgusting, the minute I can get them off, I'm going to burn them! Now, go ahead. You can't walk around with donkey spit all over you!"

As if on cue, David emitted a loud, braying call. Gillian giggled. Jag scowled in the donkey's direction.

"Be quiet, David!" he said firmly.

David made a muffled snorting noise and turned his attention to the vegetable trough.

Jag rubbed his face against Gillian's back as best he could, ridding himself of much of the slime.

Gillian was giggling again. "If they could see us at school now, what would they think we were up to?"

Jag jerked back, his cheeks burning.

"It's okay, Jonathan; no one is around to see us, and anyway, we are just being practical."

Jag ignored her attempt to reassure him and took another step back. "Let's compare notes."

They squatted on their haunches, and each related their recollection of the attack, but neither of them remembered much. Gillian had been only partially caught in the net. She had a vague memory of two people grabbing her and trying to pin her down. She had fought back as hard as she could, flailing her arms and legs.

"I'm pretty sure I managed to get one of them in the head," she said with a grim look of satisfaction.

She'd caught someone, all right... Without thinking, Jag reached towards the still-prominent gash on his head.

"Oh, no. Oh, Jonathan, I'm so sorry! I had no idea!"

Jag shrugged and dropped his hand. He didn't need her feeling sorry for him.

It turned out that her ill-aimed kick had been her last act of resistance. Their attackers had pinned her face down on the ground and had tied her arms and legs with strong rope.

"Then one of them put a sack over my head." Gillian shivered. "I've never been so terrified... I could still hear Ulma shouting, but I think they must have caught her, too, because I didn't hear any more fighting."

"I think we were outnumbered. We never had a chance," Jag said. "What happened next?"

"One of them picked me up. He was very strong and very tall, and he put me over his shoulder and carried me like a sack of potatoes! I don't know how far he carried me, but I'm guessing we walked for at least half an hour. The entire time, I kept wondering where you and Ulma were because I couldn't see, and I didn't hear anything except a bit of conversation from our captors."

"Could you make out anything they said?" Jag asked her. Maybe they'd given some clue about who they were or where they were headed.

Gillian shook her head. "I'm afraid not. It was a little difficult to concentrate while hanging upside down with my head in a bag." She shrugged. "The guy who was carrying me had a nice voice, though. He hummed sad melodies that calmed me and made me drowsy. Finally, we arrived here, and he lowered me onto the straw, and they pulled off my hood. It took a while for my eyes to adjust after being in darkness for so long. You were already lying here. I didn't panic like I did at the cliff, but I couldn't do much for you." She paused and looked around. "I wonder where they put Ulma. I would have thought she'd be here with us."

"Maybe they separated us to make it harder for us to escape?" Jag suggested. "If we can get out of here, we'll have to find her. We can't just leave her here..."

Gillian nodded. "True. Anyway, shortly after they put us in here, another man came in. He had the sharpest grey eyes I've ever seen, and he offered me some of that drink...that Anika stuff Ulma gave you. Normally, I would have refused, but I was and still am very thirsty and hungry. Jonathan, it was the best drink I've ever had! Instant pain and suffering relief! I vaguely remember feeling wonderfully sleepy, and I started to drift off." She hesitated and looked at Jag with a hint of confusion in her eyes. "There was one other thing...as I began to fall asleep, I heard Grey Eyes say something to me in a foreign language. It almost sounded like a prayer—or a chant."

"So, you think he's some kind of priest?" said Jag.

"Could be. But here's the really odd thing. I replied to him. I responded to him in what I'm sure was the same language!"

Jag furrowed his brow "What languages do you speak?"

"None. Well, a little schoolgirl French, but, Jonathan, this wasn't French—I'm sure I spoke a language I've never heard before. I know that sounds impossible, but I swear, I'm telling the truth."

"That can't be right."

Shaking his head, Jag looked across to the other side of the barn where David stood watching them. The donkey did his teeth smiling thing again. Jag quickly looked away.

"Maybe it was a side effect of the Anika water. No one simply starts speaking a new language." He looked around for his backpack again. "I wish I had my notebook. There's so much I need to record and review."

Gillian huffed and got to her feet. "Well, I can summarize for you," she said, her tone conveying her annoyance. She walked towards the barn door. "We're trapped in some sort of other world; we've been captured by a bunch of people, possibly the RagaRaga? Whoever they are, they've locked us up in a filthy barn with no food or drink, even though we haven't done anything wrong. We haven't eaten since I don't know when, and the only drink we've been offered is a questionable potion that's probably illegal. We have no idea how long they're going to keep us in this stupid stable, which we're sharing with a ragged, old donkey called David."

She kicked her foot against the door, and Jag and David jumped.

"Hey, Grey Eyes! Let us out of here!" She kicked again, harder. "We've done nothing wrong! We're starving and dying of thirst!" She let the door have it, kicking out several times. "We just want to go home. Please! We just want to go home!"

All the fight seemed to go out of her, and she leaned forward, balancing herself by propping her head against the door, breathing heavily.

But her outburst hadn't gone unheard. There was a commotion outside the door.

"Now, what is it, Tiny? Yes, of course, they were always going to stir at some point. No, just keep watching the door for now. No, I'll go and tell him. You've done a fine job, good lad. Just a little longer now. Oh, look, never mind, here he is now!"

Gillian backed away from the door, while Jag got to his feet and joined her. They exchanged a silent look. Gillian shook her head, indicating she didn't recognize the speaker's voice.

"Good morning, Anthony," said a deep voice.

"That's Grey Eyes," whispered Gillian.

"Well, good morning, Master, I was just commending Tiny on the fine job he did making sure our guests didn't go for a night-time walk."

"Were you, indeed? Well, that's praise well earned, providing, of course, that our guests are still in there!"

"Let's see," said Grey Eyes after a moment. "Now, Tiny, when I open the door, I want you to make sure our prisoners don't run off. You don't need to be rough; control that strength of yours! Just make sure they don't get away."

Jag could hear what sounded like the grinding of a large wooden block.

"Master, is the plan still to have a Circle at the tenth bell? I have prepared my notes accordingly."

"Indeed, Anthony. But there are a few matters to attend to before then. More happened last night than you might have realized. I'm also optimistic that Marcus and his troop may meet with success in their hunt and be back here in time. It's important to include everyone. Further, it seems the whole village knows about last night, and I don't need them all following us around like a litter of lost puppies. They will get their chance at the Circle. Now then, Tiny, help me with this block if you wouldn't mind. There we go."

The large doors swung open, the rusty hinges groaning under the strain as a stream of daylight lit the room. Jag and Gillian looked out at three figures silhouetted against the morning sun. Jag found it easy to work out who was who. Grey Eyes was standing a little to the right; he was tall and had a definite air of authority about him. His eyes were sparkling in the daylight. To his left stood the man who must be Anthony. He looked like Grey Eyes but not as tall and perhaps a little younger. He wore long, flowing robes, again, similar to those of Grey Eyes. They were both imposing-looking men, but the man standing to the right of Anthony drew Jag's gaze. He was a colossal figure—a giant—and had to be well over eight feet tall. He was broad, too, with tree trunk-like legs and massive, muscular arms. He wore sack cloth, like Ulma had, and a dark leather belt fastened around his midriff by a large brass buckle. Tucked into his belt was a wooden sword. His long, dark, unkempt hair framed a face that belied the rest of his physical appearance. His features were almost babyish, with a small nose and thin lips and green eyes that gave him a slightly vulnerable look. The giant stared at Jag and Gillian for a moment, then he took a long step forward and rested a hand on each of their shoulders.

"Now, you two," Grey Eyes said, looking down at them, "you already know of Tiny's strength. He effortlessly carried both of you back from the Western border. My point being, he is a strong fellow. So, just cooperate with our requests, and everything will be fine. The laws of our land forbid me to say much or respond to any questions you might have at this time. We have a forum for this, and we have scheduled an emergency hearing for you this morning, at which time you will have the chance to explain your agenda. It will be well attended. We have suffered recently at the hands of those who would do us harm. We trusted the people who have instigated these evil acts, and they were better known to us than you are. So, you see, we cannot afford to take any chances with you."

Jonathan opened his mouth to say something, but Grey Eyes held up a finger.

"I'm sorry, I fear I may have already said more than is permitted. Unfortunately, I have pressing matters to attend to this morning. I'm going to leave you in Anthony's capable hands." He turned to his colleague. "Anthony, I think a walk around the village would be most illuminating for our young friends here…"

"Please, sir." Apparently, Gillian could no longer contain herself. "We have many questions. You see, we are not from here—"

"No, no." Grey Eyes waved away her request. "No questions. Not yet. No questions, either of you, or from you, until the Circle. It is the custom and one that must be respected.

"I expect you are hungry?" he went on quickly. "Luckily for you, this region of Mensa is famed for its food. First stop, Madam Nan's Food Garden. Anthony, tell her the town will cover her for the expense, but see that these two are nourished to their complete satisfaction."

Tiny bent down and looked Grey Eyes in the face.

"Ha! Yes, Tiny, I'm sure the town has no objection to granting you a few morsels in recognition of your travails, too." Grey Eyes gave them another searching look before turning on his heel and striding away in the direction of what looked like rows of rustic, one-story dwellings. "So many questions," he called back at them, even though he was nearly out of hearing distance, "but that's for the Circle." He finally disappeared behind one of the closer structures.

Anthony led the quartet in the opposite direction. Jag and Gillian walked single file behind him, with Tiny bringing up the rear. It was a bright, sunny morning with just a few clouds, and Jag started to take in their new surroundings. They were in some sort of town, but he had never seen houses or streets like these. They followed a track that meandered past odd structures made of wood and plaster. Most of the buildings had glassless windows protected by shutters and small timber doors, many of which were open, though he couldn't see inside the buildings. Occasionally, they would pass villagers either walking up the track in ones or twos or, sometimes, leading a donkey or small pony, which were used for hauling carts laden with root vegetables, bundles of wheat, barley, or some other produce. Some of the wagons contained farm animals, like pigs, chickens, or other poultry. Animal pens or mini-barns stood in amongst the houses. Villagers were busying themselves with the maintenance of their holdings—feeding and washing animals or stacking crops. They appeared to be a hardworking lot, but the minute Jag and Gillian came into view, the workers stopped what they were doing to stare. Some of them ran over to get a better look. Mostly they just watched, but occasionally, they would call out or try to ask questions, most commonly, "Where is your allegiance?"

"No, no. You know the rules! The Circle at tenth bell," Anthony told the villagers, ending their barrage of shouts. "All are welcomed to speak or question then."

As the villagers went back to their homes, Jag frowned. Why were they so interested in a couple of strangers? Didn't these people ever get visitors from out of town?

Finally, they came upon Madame Nan's, located in a clearing that stretched out for some distance and was bordered by tall trees. The kitchen appeared to be a converted dwelling located in the centre of the clearing. Tables and chairs were positioned randomly around the grounds, and there didn't appear to be any other customers. They stopped at a table close by the kitchen. Anthony gestured for Jag and Gillian to sit on one of the long benches that served as seating for wooden tables. A large lady—both in stature and personality—came out to serve them.

"Good morning, Madame Nan," said Anthony.

"Hello, Anthony! Lovely Tiny, how are you? And greetings to your young charges...whose names are?"

"Hi, I'm Gillian, and this is Jonathan or Jag."

"Well, he's a handsome young man, regardless of which name he goes by, and you are as pretty as a rose. "Where's that brother of yours, Tiny? Not like Freckles to miss a meal!"

Before she served their food, Madame Nan scolded Anthony. "Are you going to untie these two poor creatures, or do you expect them to eat like pigs at the trough? Goodness, me, what are you worried about? They're barely older than children!" She playfully pinched Jag's cheek. "They won't be going anywhere once they get a look at what Nan is going to rustle up for them!"

Anthony appeared to think about it for a minute and then nodded at Tiny. The big man removed the ropes with no more than a couple of tugs on each of them. Jag and Gillian rubbed their sore wrists.

Madam Nan disappeared into her kitchen and spent the next twenty minutes ferrying an armada of wonderful food to their table. There was sizzling bacon, poached eggs, sausages, sweet grilled onions, a hot, spicy tomato dish, apple pies dipped in almond sauce, and a delicious yogurt sprinkled with flaked chocolate. To quench their thirst, she served piping-hot, full-flavored tea, iced water, and large flagons of apple cider.

Jag and Gillian left nothing unsampled.

"I think I may have, ever so slightly, overeaten," said Gillian, clasping her stomach.

"Me, too," said Jag.

He had half an eye on Tiny who was putting on a remarkable eating performance. The giant was putting away food as if he hadn't eaten in weeks.

Madam placed a very large plate in front of him, which she'd piled high with slow-roasted demi-chickens. He put away half a chicken at each mouthful, slowing only to add the occasional bowl of mixed vegetables, which he poured straight from the platters into his gaping mouth. Jag watched, amazed, as the giant then picked up several of the wooden kegs and pulled the cork stopper so he could swallow the entire contents of each in just a few seconds. Every now and then, he paused to let out a rip-roaring burp. Madam Nan clapped in appreciation.

"Oh, I love a man with a big appetite!" she exclaimed.

Tiny smiled broadly and let another one go for good measure. Gillian joined in with Nan's laughter, but Jag couldn't see what was so funny, and Anthony did not appear amused. He stood up from the table.

"Time to go. The tenth bell is not too many moments away. Besides, I don't want to be anywhere near Tiny when his digestive system starts finding other ways of expressing its appreciation of Nan's cooking."

Whether Anthony forgot, or he simply didn't deem it necessary any longer, he didn't order Jag's and Gillian's hands be re-tied after they had eaten. They said their goodbyes to Madam Nan, and she chuckled as she gave each of the four a warm embrace before they left.

They set off again. This time they took a much broader street. Anthony directed them to walk in the same formation as before, in a single line with Anthony at the front and Tiny keeping an eye on things at the rear. As they approached what looked like the centre of the town, the buildings became larger and grander, and the road grew crowded, filled with dozens of men, women, and children. They all seemed to be heading in the same direction as the four of them. Most of the villagers wore sack cloths, but a few wore robes like those of Grey Eyes and Anthony. Nearly all the men and some of the older boys carried weapons of some kind, including axes, short swords, dirks, and clubs.

All the people Jag, and Gillian passed stared at them curiously, and after a bit, a few people crossed in front of them or walked alongside them, as if trying to get a better look. Soon, a small, moving crowd surrounded the four of them. Jag's anxiety grew, and his breathing became laboured, as the onlookers pressed in against them, some only inches away and getting closer by the second.

Anthony tried to take command of the situation. "Clear now, clear now! Heed what is written!" He spoke in a voice full of confidence.

But the crowd pushed in harder.

Anthony shrugged. "Okay. You leave me no option; Tiny, if you please…"

The mountain-sized man came up from behind the group and with a simple flick of his wrist sent the closest four or five onlookers careening backward into those behind them, which initiated a domino effect as large numbers of viewers were knocked over by those in front of them. Within seconds, Tiny had cleared a path for the four of them. Nobody looked like they were ready to take on the giant. In fact, the whole thing took place with good humour, as many of those close by laughed at the shambolic sight. And though they continued to follow, they did so from a respectful distance. Jag breathed a sigh of relief.

At last they turned a corner, and there in front of them stood a very large, circular stadium. Painted a brilliant white, the building gleamed in the mid-morning sun. Jag estimated it to be about three stories tall—

considerably taller than any other building they had seen in the town—and flag staffs stood proudly from the highest point, giving the whole place a majestic appearance. Anthony looked 'round at Jag and Gillian.

"Behold, the Three Widow's Cirque." He waved his arm in the direction of the building as though they might somehow have missed it. "Here, you will have the chance to ask and be asked of."

Anthony had inadvertently answered one of the key questions. *The Three Widows Cirque.* How had Ulma introduced herself? *Ulma of Three Widows.* This was her town! An obvious conclusion now Jag thought about it. The similarity of their accents and clothing, the fact she hadn't been locked in the stable with them. He stole a look back at Gillian. She nodded, confirming she'd come to the same conclusion.

"Ulma." She mouthed the word at him.

He nodded curtly. But if they'd been with Ulma, why had these people attacked? Was Ulma some kind of outcast, or had she set them up? Unfortunately, Jag had no time to dwell on this new information. Evenly spaced in the wall were half-moon-shaped access points to the stadium. The villagers were streaming in through them. Jag and Gillian followed Anthony to a much larger door framed by ornate painted patterns of gold and silver stars. Eight men waited for them at the entrance, four on each side. They wore uniform black trousers and white tunics, and each had a long iron sword in a sheathe at their belts. As Anthony led them through the doorway, the men fell in line with them, flanking them protectively. They made their way up a broad, semi-lit passageway with steps rising every few yards ahead. Finally, they reached the end of the tunnel, which opened into the interior of the stadium. Sunlight blazed in through yet another half-moon doorway.

Anthony held up his arm, spreading his palm, and the group halted. "Now, we wait until the tenth bell. It won't be long."

They stood motionless and in total silence. Butterflies frolicked in Jag's stomach. What awaited them on the other side of that entrance? He pinched himself. How could he escape this most vivid of nightmares? Why had Ulma led them into a trap? Or had she? Could there be another explanation? He looked at Gillian. She stood in front of the stooped figure of Tiny. She smiled bravely, but, surely, she was worried, too?

"Just a few more moments, I think. It must be nearly time now," Anthony said. Then, almost as an aside, he added, "Young lady, young man, you may use this time to admire the collection of some—just *some*, mind you—of the weapons we have liberated from our enemies in recent skirmishes."

He reached out for a candle that helped light the corridor and used it to ignite the wicks of two very large candles positioned in the middle of a large storage area. When lit, they revealed a big stone chamber that was full almost to the point of overflowing with weapons of all types and sizes. Most were of the medieval variety, the kind Jag would have expected, such as swords, pikes, knives, battle axes, and slingshots. But there were others, too…some that looked like guns made of wood with twisted metal frames. Other items looked like grenades, and there was a whole assortment of objects he wouldn't have even guessed were weapons. Then he froze as he caught a glimpse of something very familiar towards the back of the chamber. He arched his neck to get a better view around the guard, but he couldn't get the angle he needed.

The loud resonance of a gong broke the silence.

"Here we go; it is time! Slowly and carefully, everyone. There will be many eyes on us when we enter. Forward." Anthony began to move towards the entrance.

"One moment, please," Jag called out.

He jumped out of the line and hopped towards the chamber, his guard, reacting quickly, snagged him by his shoulder and dragged him backward. But not before Jag confirmed the identity of one of the unlikeliest of the "weapons" on display. It was a large, well-used cricket bat. A bat he had witnessed strike many a cricket ball many a yard. A bat that belonged to Freddie Patel.

# Chapter 6

Gillian was convinced Jonathan had taken leave of his senses. As the guards dragged him back into line, he shouted at her and gesticulated wildly. What had he seen? Gillian stared into the cave, looking for something familiar, and her gaze fell on the bat.

"Freddie!" she yelled and moved towards the cave.

One of the guards yanked her back. Where was Freddie now? Could they have killed him? Clearly, that was what Jag thought—he appeared completely distraught. But there was no time to think about it, as they were marched through the final arched doorway and entered the interior of the stadium.

A crescendo of noise greeted them. The large crowd rose from their bench seats and delivered an overwhelming mixture of boos, cheers, whistles, and clapping. The Cirque was almost at capacity. Gillian and her group entered halfway up one of the terraces, but the door led straight onto a raised platform, putting them in clear view of everyone. It looked like a family occasion. There were a lot of children among the adults, and some families had brought smaller farmyard animals with them. A pair of cockerels escaped their owners in one section and were causing much hilarity as they repeatedly took off, flapped maniacally, and crash-landed back into the crowd.

A guard ushered Gillian and Jag to the front of the platform and told them to sit on a narrow, wooden bench. As she sat, she tried to steal a quick look at Jonathan. He sat hunched forward; his head buried in his arms.

"Please be okay, Freddie," she whispered to herself.

In the middle of the Cirque was an inner-circle, in which stood what looked like a church pulpit, except it was much taller and completely round in design. Opposite them on the other side of the Cirque was another raised platform, similar to theirs in size but much grander. There were about thirty people on it, and Grey Eyes sat front and centre of the group looking very regal in his white robes. Similarly, well-turned-out gentry surrounded him. Obviously, that was the VIP area. Gillian scanned the faces of those occupying the seats adjacent to Grey Eyes. Then she saw her, sitting three chairs away from him, pouting and looking very fed up. Ulma was dressed the part for the VIP area, but her fine robes didn't look right on her.

A nervous-looking Anthony made his way down a long set of steps that swept from their platform to the very edges of the inner-circle. He walked quickly across to the pulpit and ascended a spiral staircase until he stood high above the ground. He spun slowly around to engage the multitude. The noise lessened as he held his arms aloft.

"Good people of Three Widows, be advised that the tenth bell has sounded…"

"Yeah, we all heard it! So, get on with it!" shouted a wag from near the top of the terraces.

There was much laughter, and Anthony looked rather flustered.

"Good people, it falls to me in my role as Speaker to advise you of the purpose of this Cirque. As most of you know, last night, our reconnaissance team led by Marcus set out to the Valley border to check the welfare of Ulma. She had been on Cirque business and was delayed on her return."

"She probably wanted to avoid your speech," yelled the same heckler.

More laughter followed his statement.

Anthony coughed twice. "The details of her errand are not important here. What matters is that she came into contact with two strangers in foreign dress.

"In light of recent events, we trust no strangers who enter Mensa without first seeking approval from the regional elders," continued Anthony. "Ulma took them to be harmless and was leading them to Three Widows. Ulma made a clear error of judgement, a fact she now acknowledges."

Ulma looked far from having acknowledged anything. Her face was flushed a deep red, and her mouth was twisted in an angry-looking grimace.

"And so, pursuant to the laws and the constitution of the Great Cirque and of the Lesser Cirques of the six districts, including our own Three Widows, let us establish the purpose for which this pair of outsiders were entering the Three Widows Valley, and having done so, take whatever course of remedial action our Master, the town elder, Nikolas, sees fit."

A large hand patted Gillian gently on her head. She turned to see Tiny, his knees cramped under his chin. The chair he was sitting in was hopelessly inadequate for a person of his size. He grinned at her, and she smiled back at him.

"You will be okay, little flower."

The words formed in her head—she didn't hear them, but she knew they came from Tiny.

She looked back at him in astonishment. *Can you hear what I'm thinking?* He nodded and smiled.

The townspeople were losing patience with Anthony again as he continued his monologue. Boos accompanied shouts of, "We want Nikolas!"

Anthony, looking even more uncomfortable, sped through his last couple of lines. "Without further ado, I give you our Master and elder of Three Widows: Nikolas."

The villagers broke into applause as Anthony hurried off the pulpit, and Grey Eyes took his place. Nikolas. The elder turned around slowly, taking in his audience with those piercing grey eyes.

"Who will speak against the strangers?" he asked the whole assembly.

A man a few seats away from Ulma rose and responded. "I will, Master, if it pleases the Cirque."

"Thank you. The Cirque recognizes Addford as prosecutor in this matter."

The prosecutor took the staircase down to the outer-circle.

"And who will speak for the strangers?"

There was a general murmur in the crowd, but no one volunteered.

"Please, will someone of good standing take on this role? It is their constitutional right to have representation."

"Master, sir, I will speak for us." Gillian stood and raised her arm.

The crowd gasped. "For we have done nothing wrong, and I think I can explain things…at least, *some* things."

More murmurs and whispers came from the crowd.

Nikolas looked at her steadily, wearing just a hint of a smile. "Very well; the defendants elect to represent themselves. There is provision for this in the constitution."

For the first time since they'd entered the stadium, Jonathan looked alert. He sat up and gave Gillian a look of disbelief.

"Gillian is this a good idea?" he whispered. "We know nothing about these people, this place, or their rules and regulations."

But Gillian had made her mind up. "Would you rather have a complete stranger looking after our interests?" She made her way down alone, feeling very exposed, and came to a stop in the ring at the base of the pulpit. She had no idea what she should do next. Addford was striding round the perimeter of the Circle, looking up at the villagers. She started walking 'round in the same direction; the movement helped settle the butterflies that had started in her stomach.

"The floor is yours," announced Nikolas, pointing down at Addford.

Addford was a short, plump man and almost completely bald. He had large ears and a hawkish nose. He stopped walking and pointed one hand directly at Gillian.

"Who are you, and where is your allegiance?" he asked bullishly and turned on his heel as if he had already won the point.

Gillian refused to allow his manner to intimidate her. "I am Gillian of Pendleton, and my friend is Jonathan of Pendleton, and we have no allegiance," she said as loudly and confidently as she could manage.

The crowd reacted negatively, but she persevered.

"Before I say more, I'd like to know why we've been put on trial. I assume we are on trial?"

More grumbling erupted from the terraces. Addford ignored her question.

"You say your companion goes by the name of Jonathan, but when he first met Ulma, he told her his name was Ur-Jag. Can you explain this?"

"Yes, I think so," she responded, after thinking about it for a moment. "His given name is Jonathan, but I believe he and his friend decided he should change it to Jag—J-A-G—because those are his initials. I'm not sure where the Ur-jag came from... The only person I have heard call him that is Ulma."

"What friend?" asked Addford curtly.

Gillian frowned. "Excuse me?"

Addford had his hands placed on his well-padded hips. "You said 'Jag and his friend decided to change it to Jag.' Who is this friend?"

"Oh, his friend from school."

"And is this friend with you?"

"No, well, maybe—it's possible."

More murmuring sounded from the crowd.

Addford looked up at the pulpit and addressed Nikolas. "Master, I believe we should introduce Exhibit A."

Without waiting for an answer, he spoke to a guard standing at the edge of the circle. "Please bring them in."

*They're going to show the bat,* thought Gillian. A guard opened a door at the Cirque level. A procession of twelve people entered the arena, led by an athletic young man who the crowd immediately cheered and started calling by name.

"Marcus! Marcus!"

But to Gillian, the most noticeable person walked at the back of the group. He was a giant with a shock of red hair and a bushy beard.

*Freckles,* she thought to herself. Yes, that had to be Tiny's brother. He had one of his hands placed on the shoulder of the guy walking in front of him. A guy with a hood over his head but identifiable by his rangy legs and a much-dishevelled and torn Pendleton school uniform.

"If you please, Freckles." Addford motioned the giant to remove the hood.

Freckles pulled the hood up and off, revealing Freddie Patel.

"Freddie!" exclaimed Gillian.

Dirt and blood caked his face, and his uniform was ripped to shreds.

He was blinking hard, trying to adjust to the bright morning light. There was a commotion above them. Jag had bolted for the staircase. His guards gave chase, but Nikolas raised his hand and called them off.

"Let him come!" he ordered.

They stopped their pursuit immediately, allowing Jag to walk down the staircase onto the Circle and up to his friend. When he got to within a few feet, he stopped and looked at Freddie.

Despite his injuries, Freddie grinned. "Jagmeister! Welcome to my nightmare! I'd give you a hug, but I'm tied up right now!" He lifted his wrists and showed him the rope that bound them.

A little awkwardly, Jag stepped up to Freddie and put his hand on his shoulder.

Freddie smiled and then looked across at Gillian. "Ms. Gillian, welcome to the party. I think this might be a good time to bury the hatchet. I think we have greater concerns right now."

"Hi, Freddie, it's great to see you," she said, returning his smile. "You look awful."

"Thanks...you, too!" said Freddie.

All three laughed. For a few seconds, they stood looking at each another.

"So, there we have it Master, Speaker, councillors, and good people of Three Widows! I think this joyful reunion is evidence enough that the three all know each other. They are doubtless working together in some heinous plot against Mensa and it's gentle, peace-loving inhabitants!"

Addford's booming voice brought Gillian and her friends back to the dilemma they were facing.

The people in the crowd were muttering to one another. Intermittent boos punctuated occasional calls of, "Jail them!"

Despite the mood of the crowd, Gillian felt much better now she knew Freddie was okay.

"Mr. Addford, you know nothing about us. Perhaps you will allow me to tell our story, and then people can judge us."

Addford tilted his head back and looked at Gillian down the length of his aquiline nose. "Oh, you want to play at being a lawyer, young lady? Keep in mind, the sooner we get this over with, the better."

Gillian looked up around her at the banked terraces and the occupants leaning forward in anticipation. What had she gotten herself into? She looked at Jag, and he shrugged. Freddie gave her a thumbs up. Behind him stood the prisoner party who had escorted Freddie in. For the most part, they looked like regular locals—though better armed and more modestly dressed. They were all young, even Freckles. The big guy sitting at the back of the group had a youthful air about him.

At the front, leaning on the handle of a broadsword, which he'd driven into the ground, was Marcus, watching her intently. She unintentionally made eye contact with him and was alarmed to feel her

47

legs weaken. He had to be Nikolas's son. The steel-e grey eyes were a dead giveaway, although they weren't as intense as his father's gaze was. Nevertheless, they were very engaging. Gillian made a mental note not to look in his direction again.

She took a long, deep breath and began. Speaking slowly, she described the events of the last twenty-four hours. She made no mention of Pinhorn and his cronies or of young Farley.

She told the crowd how they had entered the tunnel with the intention of walking to the other end. Once inside, they lost each other in the dark. She described how she had panicked and ran through the tunnel, desperate to find her friends and a way out. She had finally tumbled into daylight, hitting the ground hard. The tunnel she had exited had disappeared, and she found herself by the foot of a cliff. She also found the battered and unconscious Jag.

When she finished, she looked up at Nikolas. He had his hand on his chin. She then glanced across at Addford, who was walking round in a small circle, hands locked behind his neck. The crowd waited.

"So, there were just the three of you, is that right?"

She hesitated for a fraction of a second. "Correct."

Addford gave her an intense look. "That was a very unconvincing response," he said. Again, he did the strange tilting of his head. "There were others—admit it. This is a very serious matter, and we need the truth, girl, and quickly!"

"Okay, I should clarify, Mr. Addford. There were others at the tunnel entrance."

"There were others, and you chose not to mention them!" Addford shouted, his face growing red.

"But, Mr. Addford!"

"It's Councillor Addford to you, girl!" he shouted, his hands thumping his chest.

"And it's Ms. Gillian to you!" she responded, hands on hips, looking straight at him.

The crowd loved the exchange, cheering, clapping, and booing.

"Okay. Enough, enough," called Nikolas from above them. "I have heard enough. A little mutual respect would not be amiss here. But I am ready to pronounce judgment."

Gillian sucked in a breath. That was quick. Did the speediness with which he'd made his decision mean he planned to rule against them? There was a murmur of disappointment from the crowd; clearly, the townsfolk wanted more.

"Councillor Addford, thank you for your participation. You have a fine ear for the truth. You may return to your seat."

Addford acknowledged Nikolas, briefly touching his head and nodding. He strode back across the arena floor to the steps that lead back to the to the VIP are.

"Marcus, prepare your squad for the outcome. Gillian, Jag, and Freddie, please come before the chair."

The three walked over to the pulpit and stood alongside each other with Gillian in the centre. Marcus's guards formed a line directly behind them.

Nikolas leaned over the edge of his pulpit to address them. "If there is bitterness and anger in the air, it is justified," he said, looking at them one by one. "We are close to war—a war we cannot win. In the past six weeks, we have lost eight people to our enemies to the south. All but two of them were captured through the cunning of our foe. They have used spies and agents to infiltrate the valley population and have taken some of our most loved and revered residents. The agents have been of all ages and all appearances. We have learned to trust no one. You three have entered our domain without seeking permission from the authorities. Your story is remarkable—so remarkable I am tempted to believe it. However, as Councillor Addford so quickly ascertained, you have not been telling the truth, and further, you have not been telling us everything."

Nikolas paused for a moment. He looked at each of them. Gillian shifted beneath his steady gaze, but she kept her eyes glued on his, while Jag and Freddie looked away. The crowd had become silent.

"Now, you might have very good reasons for being limited with the truth, but you haven't given us any clue as to what those reasons are. I am responsible for the safety of the residents of the Three Widows Valley, and for the greater good of the those who live in the other towns and villages of Mensa, too."

He stepped back to the centre of the pulpit and once again addressed everyone.

"The only option left is to order a term of incarceration for the three of you."

Out of the corner of her eye, Gillian saw Jag drop his head. Freddie cursed.

The crowd began speaking to each other in hushed tones. One of Marcus's men, a fresh-faced lad with blond hair, walked around and in front of them carrying a rope.

"One moment, please," said Nikolas, raising his hand. "I want to show you something. Perhaps it will bring understanding. All who live here know of this."

As he spoke, Nikolas pushed down a panel on the side of the pulpit and reached into what appeared to be a hidden compartment. He pulled out a small object no more than six inches long and covered in a silk cloth. There was a buzz of excitement in the crowd as he stood the object on its end on the front of the pulpit and removed the silk cover. "Does this look familiar?"

Gillian looked up at it. It was lovely, but not something she had ever seen.

"It's the man on the clock!" Jag said. "One of the three painted on the clock face at home. The harvester!"

Gillian looked at him. What was he going on about?

"Wait! I know what he's talking about!" said Freddie. "In Jag's kitchen at home—that really cool clock!"

"But what does it mean?" exclaimed Gillian, her thoughts racing.

"Interesting. I wasn't expecting that, but Gillian," said Nikolas, "there's nothing about it that seems familiar?"

She looked hard at the metal figurine as Nikolas picked it up and held it aloft. The crowd began to clap. As she studied it more closely, she realized there *was* something familiar about it.

"Gillian?" Nikolas was now staring straight into her eyes.

She felt her lips move and heard her voice respond. "Alinea, Master, per hiter per armamento."

The clapping stopped. All eyes were once again on Gillian. She gaped in amazement. What had she just said?

"Varnun, Gillian, esteren Varnun…" Nikolas held the figurine towards her.

A burning sensation began on her leg just above her knee, near the hemline of her skirt. It was getting hotter by the second. She reached into her pocket, which was empty but had a small hole in it. Whatever was burning her must have fallen through the hole into the seam of her dress. She grabbed the hemline and pulled at it. The stitches broke easily.

Into her hand dropped the small figurine she had nearly lost on the railway line. She held it in front of her, studying it closely. The young girl with a sack over her shoulder and her other hand held out in front, as if dropping something. No, not dropping… Throwing! Of course! All these years she'd had this piece and never realized what it represented. A sower of seeds. The two figurines were related—the seed sower and the harvester. How could that be? What was going on?

The heat had levelled off; she was just able to hold it. She rotated it in her fingers. She could feel the buzz of an electro-magnetic field around it… And was she imagining things, or was the figurine growing? The crowd in the terraces nearest her were able to see the piece, and as it grew, it became more visible to more onlookers. The electric charge she could feel turned into a visible blue gas floating around the figure. Those who could see it were going wild with excitement.

After a few seconds, the charm had grown to about the same size as the harvester, which Nikolas continued to hold, his arm stretched out towards Gillian. Following her instincts, she raised her arm in the same manner as Nikolas. The blue gas field around the piece oscillated rapidly. Faster and faster it moved. She looked up at the harvester Nikolas held. It, too, was shrouded in an ethereal blue cloud. A huge blue flash lit the air, and an enormous cracking noise sounded, as if the very atmosphere about them was being torn. The gas field disappeared, and in its place from the head of the figure sped a blue line of jagged, fizzling electricity. It arced up toward the harvester and was met halfway there by a similar blue strike originating from Nikolas's. The meeting of the twin lines of blue electricity caused another loud bang. And then the two pieces were united, and Gillian felt an enormous surge of power feed into her fingertips, her hand, her arm, and then throughout her whole body. Energy coursed through every cell, giving her a feeling of invincibility.

She was linked to Nikolas; and for a few seconds she felt very vulnerable and exposed. Nikolas could look into her mind and know everything she knew and there was nothing she could do about it. But then his words formed in her mind, "No – I will not read you." Gillian felt a wave of relief. The two were made one by an electric blue arc of power that hissed, crackled, and sizzled. All those watching were spellbound.

Then Nikolas let his arm drop, and the power surge was gone. Gillian slowly lowered her arm. She held the figure in front of her. It was at least ten times bigger than it had been. This world has magic? She looked up again and couldn't believe what she was seeing. Every man, woman, and child in the Cirque—with the exception of Nikolas and her two friends—were on their knees, bowing towards her. They were chanting two words. "Clamus matiata, clamus matiata," repeating the phrase again and again.

'What just happened?" she asked, turning to Jag and Freddy.

The guys looked stunned, standing there looking at her in disbelief.

"I think they are congratulating you on your fireworks display!" Jag finally said.

"It's a bit more than that," Freddie said, nudging Jag with his shoulder. "Excuse me, blondie!" Freddie called out to the young lad who had been preparing the rope in front of them before Nikolas had stepped in.

Like everyone else, the man was paying homage to Gillian, but he looked up at Freddie's call.

"Trick," he shouted back.

"Yes, I know that," said Freddie, "and a good one, too, judging by the response it's getting."

"No, my name is Trick," said the blond-haired boy, standing up slowly as he spoke.

"Blimey," said Freddie, rolling his eyes, "what were the chances? What is it you are chanting?"

"Bringer of hope." The words, spoken in a deep voice, came from behind them. Nikolas had left the pulpit and walked over to join them. "Your icon is of the Turn. Its whereabouts have been unknown for many years. Thank you, Trick," he called over to the blond boy. "Would you be so good as to untie Freddie?"

"Master," replied Trick, scurrying across to Freddie with his pocketknife in hand.

"The icon is several hundred years old. It is known as a bracefire. Each allied region in the Turn have (or used to have) two bracefires representing their region. I held the harvester bracefire. In the right hands, a single bracefire can be a powerful tool. But when used in conjunction with its sibling, you can expect that power to be many times stronger. The harvester and seed sower are siblings. The people of Three Widows have been waiting many years for the return of the seed sower. You will forgive us if we are a little excited, but the reunification of the sower and harvester gives us a glimmer of hope. But this is rather presumptuous of me. Gillian, are you willing to give the bracefire back to the Mensan people?"

Gillian held the sower in front of her and turned it around slowly. She looked out at the assembled townspeople, all of whom had their eyes fixed on her.

"If it makes this many people this happy, I simply have to!" she said, smiling.

She walked towards Nikolas, but he stepped back.

"Thank you, but please hold on to it for the time being."

The pyrotechnics brought the hearing to an abrupt end. Gillian had no idea why, but the performance had brought the crowd 'round to her side. They continued to chant and bow in her direction.

Within seconds, they were reunited with their belongings. Ulma beamed as she carried Jag's pack across the circle.

She skipped the last two steps to Jag and whispered in his ear as she gave him his pack. "See, I can read people."

A petite girl in a yellow wrap-around dress brought Freddie's and Gillian's backpacks. And then one of the guards stepped forward and presented Freddie with his bat, which was looking in poor shape. He used it to play a practice shot, which earned him a cheer from the onlookers.

"If you will follow me, please?" Nikolas beckoned.

Gillian grabbed Jag's and Freddie's hands and hurried after Nikolas. They left the arena to the sound of the crowd's cheers ringing in their ears.

# Chapter 7

Jag was relieved to leave the crowd behind. He followed Nikolas, who was giving instructions to various officials as they walked through the narrow corridors of the Cirque.

Nikolas guided them to a small, windowless room located under the main stand. Marcus and some of his troops, Anthony, Ulma, Tiny, and Freckles—who were on guard duty—joined them.

The only source of light came from some well-used, tall white candles. There were rows of benches and a lectern at the front. The place looked like a mini-chapel. The girl in the yellow wrap-around dress walked among those in attendance, offering mugs of steaming-hot cider from a large wooden tray. Jag took one gratefully.

Nikolas stood at the lectern. "Gillian, Jag, and Freddie. Thank you for your participation in the Circle. I am sure you are wondering what happens next. I know finding your way home is uppermost in your minds, but it's not a simple process. I ask for your patience as we find a solution that works for everyone." Jag doubled over. The anxiety was beginning to take the form of a pain in his stomach.

Nikolas nodded sympathetically in his direction. "Please don't despair; we know people who have expertise in transitioning. Unfortunately, none of them are here.

"Please also understand this: I think the three of you have been delivered here for a reason—one over and above returning the bracefire. I cannot pretend to know what the reason might be, but in the Turn, most of the time, everything happens for a reason.

"We answer to a higher authority known as the Order of the Great Circle. They are governing in exile from an island to the west of the Wastes. There are ways of communicating with them…but it takes time.

"They will be extremely interested in this morning's event, and I expect them to respond immediately. That could be as early as the day after tomorrow. Accordingly, I am scheduling a follow-up meeting then. Until then, I am requesting that Marcus and Dell take care of you."

Freddie jumped up, "You're kidding, right? Look at me. I didn't inflict these cuts and bruises on myself. Now, you expect us to spend some *quality time* with those responsible?"

There was an uneasy silence, which Marcus finally broke.

"Let me formally introduce myself. I am Marcus, son of Nikolas. I led the troop to the Western Wastes border. We were out looking for my cousin Ulma, who was several hours late returning from an errand she was running." His deep voice was uncannily similar to Nikolas's.

"I was fine!" said Ulma, crossing her arms.

Marcus ignored the comment. "When we found her walking back towards the village in the company of two strangers, I was deeply concerned. It is precisely the sort of covert tactic our enemies have been using to get to their targets. So, we sprang a surprise attack to make sure you didn't have a chance to react.

"As we were setting up the trap, we heard someone shouting to the west, and that's how we first saw Freddie. I left Dell in charge of retrieving Ulma and set off with three others to arrest him."

Freddie stood and waved a clenched fist. "Arrest? I ran into a tunnel, got ejected from the exit, and found myself in a strange desert. Eventually, I spotted my friends and gave chase. I was no threat to anyone, and these guys ambushed me and gave me a going over."

Marcus looked at Freddie. "I am sorry for what happened; my troops and I were just doing what we have been tasked to do—protecting our realm. Soon enough, you will learn what we are up against. If it's any consolation, you have earned the respect of my troops with your defensive combat skills. Where did you learn to use that club like that?"

"It's not a club; it's a bat. A cricket bat."

Marcus gave Freddie a blank look.

"A world without cricket? What a nightmare!" said Freddie.

Jag couldn't have agreed more and nodded vigorously. Why was Gillian doing the eye-rolling thing?

"I would be happy to be your host," Marcus said. "When we are not fulfilling our role as militia, my brother Dell and I run the old farmhouse. It is the largest agricultural centre in Mensa. My cousins Ulma and Roy, plus Trick, Captain, Spike, Ink, and Williams all live and work there. We work hard, but it's a great group of people, and we know how to have fun, too. I'm thinking we might patch up our differences over some good, old-fashioned farm labouring."

"Thank you, Marcus. Freddie, you have every reason to be upset," said Nikolas. "But you are going to need to show some patience. Once you get past their rough exterior, my sons are quite nice people. Yes, even Marcus. The farm is a safe place for you to wait."

Gillian seemed content with the proposal. Actually, she seemed more than content, considering the way she kept smiling and darting glances in Marcus's direction. Her behaviour grated on Jag's nerves. Freddie looked at Gillian. She nodded, and Freddie turned to Jag. He considered the proposal for a few seconds. Bottom line, they needed help from someone...why not from Marcus and his team? Jag nodded at Freddie.

Freddie hesitated. "Your offer of hospitality is appreciated, and I'm sorry, but which one of you is Dell?"

A sandy-haired lad who had been sitting at the back of the room raised his hand awkwardly. "That would be me, and you are most welcome."

Freddie smiled and saluted the young farm owner.

"Very well," said Nikolas, clapping his hands. "As of this afternoon, you will be farmers!"

But Jag had concerns. "I have no farming skills. I've never been to a farm before; the doctor has said they are bad for my allergies. I'm good at algebra and trigonometry if you need any help in that area?"

Ulma, who was literally skipping with excitement, explained. "Farming, Jonathan Ur-Jag. There is but one profession in Three Widows—farming. Everyone—be they big or small, old or young—farms or performs a service that supports the farms."

"That's correct," said Nikolas. "The farmers of the Three Widows Valley are famed around the Turn. They supply food for the six regions and many places beyond. Or at least, they used to.

He walked over to Jag. "There's nothing to worry about, Jag. Dell, Marcus, and their team will help you find your way around the farm. We have no expectations of you, so you should have no concerns.

"Dell, Marcus, our lost friends are now your responsibility. Can I suggest the first thing you do is have them bathed and given new clothes? The smell coming off them rivals that of a Hag Stink Hole. Good luck, everyone."

*****

A few hours later, Jag, Freddie, and Gillian were sitting inside an enclosed carriage on some rather uncomfortable stuffed-cushion seats. Across from them on the opposite bench, sat Marcus, Ulma, and Williams. Up above them, Dell took the reins and coaxed the two horses harnessed to the carriage into an easy trot. Sitting alongside him on the box seat was the girl in the yellow dress. Dell yelled down the introductions—her name was Ink.

"Don't tell me, Ink, you're Dell's second cousin?" Freddie called up to her, shouting over the clomping of the horses' hooves and the creaking and groaning of the carriage.

"I'm his sister," she said, looking dead ahead.

Freddie laughed, as Dell used a short leather whip to encourage the horses to pick up the pace.

"Talk about keeping it in the family; are all of you townspeople related in some way?" he asked.

"Give it a rest, Freddie," Gillian said, her arms crossed. "You're not being funny."

"Actually, we are all very closely related, Freddie," Ulma said, batting her eyelashes. "That's why we Three Widows girls get so excited when foreign breeding stock stumbles into the village." She gazed at Jag and

Freddie; eyes wide.

This time, the Three Widows contingent laughed, as Freddie was left speechless, at least for the moment, and Jag looked down at his feet as hard as he could.

That set the tone for the journey, and the banter continued unabated, Freddie leading the way with a seemingly endless stream of gibberish. Gillian alternately admonished the "juvenile" Freddie and then, seemingly despite herself, joined in with comments. Williams, who was very short, seemed to have a permanent smile on his face, and he, too, joined in the fun, cracking jokes no one understood but which he delivered with such style and timing that everyone laughed with him, anyway.

Everyone except Jag, that was. He didn't really do humour. He'd heard his fair share of jokes but very seldom found them funny. Most were disturbing, with punchlines that were written at someone else's expense. He left the others to it and instead peered out of the window to see what he could learn about this strange land. They had left behind the structures that formed the town and now travelled along a dusty road. Several outriders trotted alongside their carriage, Trick and Captain among them. They all rode so confidently... Jag hoped there wouldn't come a time when they expected him to ride. Horses made him nervous; *how do you control a beast of that size?*

"Hey, Jag, why don't you join us up here? The view is great."

The question came from Ink, and he accepted, grateful to escape the lampooning going on around him.

Dell brought the horses to a halt, and Jag stepped out of the carriage and climbed the ladder. Ink grabbed his arm and helped him into the box seat. He sat to her left, so she was perched between Dell and himself. Ink extended the blanket she and Dell had wrapped around themselves, sharing it with Jag to help keep him warm.

They started off again, and Jag marvelled at what he saw. A variety of fields lined each side of the dirt road, presenting a stunning array of colourful plants in greens and reds and purples and golden yellows. He had never seen the like.

"What you see are crane, wheat, barley, arras beans, sprags, flair-cabbages, squash, water rootes, and mustard porters," Dell said, as if reading Jag's mind. "And that's just this part of the farm. We grow twenty-eight different vegetables, all told. We raise livestock, too—sheep, goats, steers, chickens, wye-hens, and dairy cows. We also have a limited number of swine, but we keep them mainly around the farm buildings. The townspeople love raising their own pigs. They produce more than enough meat for their needs, and they can sell off the surplus to make a little extra coin, too. We don't want to flood the market and bring the price down. It's a very large farm, stretching from Three Widows many miles north to the foothills of the Maria Mountains, covering the greater part of the North Three Widows Valley."

"Is it dangerous? In the fields, I mean. I'm thinking of the RagaRaga."

Dell shrugged. "Not really. They don t come over the border. There are Spindles who cross, but as you heard earlier, they are usually spies or agents, and they don't want to draw attention to themselves by attacking farmers. Besides, the Spindles still need us—or rather, they need the food we produce. Sadly, that may change soon."

Jag glanced at Dell, the young farm boss looked very serious.

"Spindles?" asked Jag.

Dell's gaze left the road ahead for a moment, and he looked at Jag, "You don't know of them? You really must be from somewhere very far away! Nikolas will, no doubt, fill you in at your meeting. It's better you hear everything from him. Enough for now that you know there are very dangerous people beyond our borders. Be happy Nikolas has assigned Tiny and Freckles to be your bodyguards. I pity the fool who tries to get past them to harm you or your friends."

"Ah, yes. That's what I understood, but I haven't seen them. Are they meeting us at the farm?"

Dell and Ink both laughed.

"Look directly behind us," Ink said, pulling the blanket tighter round her shoulders.

Jag twisted himself around as best he could without risking falling off the box seat and was amazed to see the two giants running behind them, their long strides enabling them to keep pace with the carriage.

"They must be getting exhausted!" Jag said. How fast were they going?

"So, you don't know much about Oze giants, either?" Dell said. "They have incredible stamina. They could keep going at this pace all day and most of the night, too."

"What about sleep?" Jag was fascinated.

"They don't sleep; at least, not the way we do. They don't go to bed and only lie down if they are sick."

Jag looked back at them again as Dell continued.

"They take cat naps frequently. Usually, for a few minutes at a time, sometimes for just a few seconds. They can do it any time, even when running. Look at them long enough and you will start noticing periods of time when their eyelids flutter. This signifies they are asleep... Very lightly, but asleep nonetheless."

Jag studied first Tiny's and then Freckles' eyes, but their heads were bobbing around, and the carriage was kicking up too much dust to see clearly.

"Do they ever talk?"

"No, they communicate through a mixture of telepathy and body language. If you are open to it, you'll start to understand them after a while...and learn how to respond. Some folk, like Nikolas, are naturals at picking up the giants' language, while others—like me—struggle!" Dell placed his hand on Ink's shoulder. "If you ever need a translator, Ink is the best!"

Ink smiled shyly at the compliment. "Well, I'd like to learn about you three," she said, glancing sideways at Jag. "Where are you really from? I've heard stories of the lost before, of course, and their claim to be from a different Turn. Is that your belief? Are you sure you are not from somewhere on this world that is unknown to us?"

Jag scratched his head. She'd asked a reasonable question, and before he gave a full answer, he needed time to review his notes and look for clues. "Well, we don't know what the connection—"

Jag nearly jumped off the box seat as a pair of legs swung up from below. The rest of Ulma came into view as she grabbed a running rail, which allowed her to stand up.

"We must be close," she said, now standing behind them on the narrowest of ledges, her balance impeccable.

"Just a few more moments," replied Dell without looking around.

Ulma glanced down at Jag. "Are you okay, Jonathan Ur-Jag?"

His heart still raced from her unexpected appearance. "Are you safe, standing like that? And how did you get up here?"

"I climbed out the window. Did you miss me?"

"No, I'm just terribly worried you're going to fall." Jag held tightly onto the side of the box, as if somehow, this precaution would keep Ulma secure.

Dell laughed. "Have no fear, Jag; I doubt I could shake her off this carriage if I tried. There is a reason Ulma is our lead scout; her agility is second to none. She can climb anything, balance on anything."

"Farm, ahead!" called Ink.

Jag looked to the horizon and saw a very large wooden building painted a brilliant white. The white picked up colours of the sky, landscape and crops surrounding it—green, red, and blue—giving it a mystical aura. Jag shivered, looking forward to the warmth they'd find inside.

## Chapter 8

Upon their arrival, Jag and his friends had no time to explore.

The house was huge. The rooms were large and well-appointed with comfortable furniture. Large, circular windows allowed daylight to stream into the building, which Jag found very uplifting. As Nikolas had suggested, they were to start with a bath. Williams, Ink, and Ulma led them up a winding staircase in the north wing of the building. At the top was a long passageway, off which were several bathrooms. All the rooms were inter-connected via adjoining doors. Jag worried that there were no locks anywhere. Each bathroom contained a large wooden tub situated in the centre of the room. Jag, Freddie, and Gillian each chose a bathroom. A shiny pipe delivered hot water. Ink and Ulma insisted on preparing Jag's tub for him. He sat nervously on a stool in the corner of the room while the girls poured soap and various salts into the steaming water. Ink used a large wooden paddle to mix the contents. When they seemed satisfied, they both stepped back from the tub. Ink looked round at Jag and nodded.

"It's ready," Ulma said.

Both girls stood motionless, and Jag's cheeks burned. Surely, they weren't planning on standing there while he bathed?

"Oh, we forgot his towels!" Ink walked over to a cupboard, retrieved two plush-looking white towels, and then returned to her position next to Ulma.

"Oh, and his new clothes!" added Ulma. She picked up a pile of freshly laundered clothing that had been left on a bench by the door, and she re-joined Ink.

The two stood like statues, holding out towels and clothing in front of them.

Jag stood up and looked down at his dishevelled uniform. He would not take it off in their presence. Both girls began giggling.

"Jonathan Ur-jag, we are teasing you! We are not so primitive as you think!" said Ulma.

Ink and Ulma placed the items on the stool, and they turned to leave the room. They both looked around and smiled at him as they headed for the door. Ulma winked. Jag didn't know what to say; all sorts of conflicting thoughts were going through his head—although their antics unnerved him, there was something flattering about being the object of their attention.

With no warning, the adjoining door that led to Freddie's bathroom flew open, crashing into the panelled wall with a resounding bang. In strode Freddie, fresh from his bath, steam emanating from his exposed skin, swinging his towel helicopter style above his head. He wore nothing but the briefest pair of white underpants. "Hey, Jagmeister, check out Mensan underwear! They don't waste money on unnecessary material— Oh, hello, girls."

The girls' laughter instantly changed to panicked screams as they fled the room. Freddie bellowed with laughter, and this time, Jag got the joke and laughed with him.

The girls had left him two sets of farm outfits, which were made of the same sackcloth most of the villagers wore, and two pairs of the moccasin-like shoes that appeared to be the footwear of choice around those parts. Freddie returned to his bathroom, and Jag dressed quickly. The uniforms were full length and comfortable and warm. The moccasins, too, were easy on the feet and surprisingly tough.

*****

The three classmates took supper in a communal dining room. It was the largest room at the farm, furnished with ten trestle tables and long benches. Dell ushered them to the head table. He sat at one end and Marcus at the other. Jag, Freddie, and Gillian sat randomly on the benches, mixing with the friends they had already made and making acquaintance with workers they hadn't met previously. Many of those sitting at other tables took time out to come and see the "lost three."

Jag felt like a minor celebrity. Everyone wanted to meet him, to shake his hand, and ask a few questions. He didn't like the attention, but he sensed it was important he do his part to keep their hosts happy. Freddie, on the other hand, appeared in his element, shaking hands, slapping backs, and hugging anyone who came near him. His burgeoning reputation was further fuelled by the rumour he had been running around the bathrooms and the adjacent dormitories completely naked. Freddie said nothing to dispel the rumour.

Those in attendance treated Gillian very differently. Everyone appeared in awe of her. Jag watched as people approached her slowly, stopped a few feet away, whispered the salutation Jag had first heard at the Circle—clamus matiata—and then backed off slowly, head still bowed. If this newfound prestige was worrying her, she didn't let it show.

She sat next to Marcus, and when she wasn't eating or acknowledging those who came to pay her their respects, she was deep in conversation with the troop captain.

"Excuse me, Your Majesty, but would you mind passing the salt?" Freddie asked her at one point.

Gillian either ignored him or hadn't heard him because she continued her dialogue with Marcus. Strange but Jag felt quite comfortable with Gillian spending every moment talking with Marcus, but he noticed that Freddie seemed to be annoyed by it.

*****

The boys spent the night in the men's dormitory. Roughly thirty beds filled the long, narrow room, of which about twenty were occupied that night. Freddie, who was in a bed two away from Jag, was under the blankets and asleep before Jag had taken off his moccasins.

So many things were racing through his mind Jag feared he would never sleep. He lay on his back, staring at the ceiling. He regretted the fact he hadn't had time alone with his friends. They urgently needed to pool their knowledge and work out how they could get home. Memories flashed through his mind—Kevin Pinhorn's face snarling at him; the pitch darkness of the railway tunnel, the glowing light that had led him through the transition, the timekeeper with his sun dial, the Oze giants running behind the carriage. He had an urge to fetch his journal and re-visit his notes. So much had happened, but he sensed there were patterns and links to be identified, too. He desperately needed some answers—some foundations on which to build an understanding of what was happening to them.

His head was spinning.

"Here, drink of this."

Although the dorm was in darkness, Jag recognized Trick's voice. Jag could just make out the shadow of the man's hand offering a small cup.

"Anika?" asked Jag.

"No, we call this *lizartu* or more commonly *lights out*," whispered Trick. "It will help you sleep."

"I don't think anything will help me sleep right now."

"It's made of herbs unique to this region. It's healthy, and it will ready you for tomorrow."

Jag didn't want to spend the rest of the night wide awake with his brain racing. He accepted the cup and drank the contents. "Hmm, actually, that tastes rather nice; it reminds me of the herbal tea my mother likes. How long before it makes me feel…?"

Before Jag could finish his question, he was sound asleep.

"Wake up, Mr. Ur-Jag, it's farm time!" Williams was jumping and up and down at the foot Jag's mattress. "You'll need to get a good brekkie down you if you are to get through the day!"

The little farm hand had a broad smile on his face. Why did everyone seem to like him so much? He was just plain annoying.

"It's my custom to spend ten minutes, lying awake planning my day," Jag said. "What time is it, anyway?" He looked for his watch on the small locker adjacent to his bed.

"And it's my custom to jump up and down on the bed of anyone who is late getting up. It's actually in my job description; I insisted on it."

Jag frowned. He hadn't seen his watch since he'd run into the tunnel. He glared at Williams. "Please stop. You're going to make me sick."

Williams laughed, leaped off the bed, and ran across the room to the bed of another hapless victim.

*****

Freddie and Gillian were already in the dining hall tucking into eggs and bacon when Jag caught up with them.

"Blimey, we must be in a different universe. Jonathan Abbot Glover has arrived late!" quipped Freddie, smiling at Jag.

Jag edged onto the end of the bench. "Well, no one seems to have a watch or clock or anything here, so it's a bit challenging."

"How did you sleep, Jonathan?" asked Gillian.

It felt like the first time she had spoken to him in ages. Where was Marcus?

"Like the dead," Jag said. "Trick gave me a potion…something called 'lights out'. And that's pretty much what you experience when you drink it."

His two friends smiled.

"Late for breakfast, cracking jokes—whatever next?" Freddie asked.

"Hopefully, a cure for my allergies, since we're about to spend the day on the farm."

*****

After breakfast, they met Dell in the courtyard at the front of the building. Standing with him were Ulma and Ink. Dell was in his element, cutting an imposing figure as the farm boss.

"Okay, gang, Nikolas instructed me to put you to work. So today, you are going to shadow your buddies here; you know them, and they know their stuff. I don't know how long you will be with us, so learn everything you can. There's no room for passengers here!"

Jag shuffled his feet uneasily.

"Freddie, you will be on dairy duty with Ink," Dell went on.

Ink had her hair in ponytails, making her look even younger than she usually did. She stepped forward and took Freddie's arm, leading him away towards what Jag guessed were the cow sheds.

Dell pointed at Jag. "You will help Ulma feed the livestock."

Jag looked at Dell blankly. "Do you have an instruction manual?"

Before Dell could respond, Ulma caught Jag's arm. "Don't worry, Jonathan Ur-Jag, I will take care of you."

Dell and Gillian smiled.

"Gillian, you can ride, correct?" Dell asked.

"Well, I'm not an expert, but I've done some riding back home."

"Good, so you are going to join Marcus and me on fence duty. Marcus has already been out on the northern border for an hour; we need to catch up."

Roy walked two ponies over to them, and Dell helped Gillian into the saddle before deftly mounting the larger of the two ponies.

"Later, guys," said Dell, as he coaxed his pony in the direction of the main gate.

Gillian's pony tossed his head a couple of times and swung around in a tight circle. Jag instinctively covered his eyes, but after a brief struggle, Gillian brought the animal under control, and she followed Dell out onto the open road.

Ulma and Jag started the feeding routine by picking up two very large, round wheelie bins from a storage barn. Husks of corn filled the bins, and the fumes they gave off made Jag's stomach churn.

"You get used to it after a while, Jonathan Ur-Jag," said Ulma, as they approached the henhouse. "This reek, on the other hand...!"

"Yuck, no!" Jag pushed his bin into the enclosure. He stopped to bury his face in his hands. The stench was overwhelming. The noise level, too, was a challenge to his ears.

"How many chickens are there in here?" he asked, trying to avoid breathing through his nose. The barn was enormous, and there were hens everywhere. No cages—free-range pandemonium.

"I don't really know," said Ulma, leaning into her bin to grab more corn. "Lots, I would say." She threw an armful in front of her, and hundreds of loudly squawking chickens came running at them.

Jag instinctively ducked down behind the bin.

"Come on, Jonathan Ur-jag. They are not going to hurt you! Watch me."

Jag peered around his bin at Ulma as she pushed her bin a few yards, dispatched an armful of cobs, and then moved on a few more yards before repeating the process. He stood up and copied her technique as best he could. After a while, he got use to the hens flapping and running around him and found a feeding rhythm that somehow worked. By the time they reached the exit door at the other end of the barn, he was relieved but also feeling quite good about himself.

Ulma slapped him on the back. "Good work, Farmer Ur-Jag! I knew you had it in you. Now for the lambs..."

It took the better part of the day to feed all the animals. But with each passing hour, Jag found his confidence increasing. Ulma was a good companion, too; she enjoyed the work, and he felt comfortable in her presence.

The pigs, kept in a large enclosure about a mile away from the farmhouse, were their last call. They used a donkey and cart to transport the slops that made up the pigs' unique diet. Not for the first time that day, Jag wondered if these people had anything resembling a tractor.

Ulma hopped up onto the enclosure wall and beckoned Jag to join her. He managed to pull himself up onto the wall but with none of the Mensan girl's easy athleticism. He twisted himself 'round slowly so the two of them sat together with their legs dangling down. Ulma had untied a bag she wore fastened to her belt. She took out two large crusts of bread and some dark-yellow wedges of hard cheese. She split the simple food into two piles on her lap and gave Jag one of the servings.

For a while, they nibbled at the bread and cheese in silence and watched the pigs stretch out in the afternoon sun ready for a post-meal nap. Jag felt almost relaxed in that quiet moment. The day had been a lot better than he had anticipated. He'd suffered no allergy problems, the animals had all been interesting in different ways, and Ulma had been okay to work with. In fact, it wasn't too much of a stretch to say, for the most part, he enjoyed her company, and he wouldn't mind if they teamed up again the next day.

"So, how long have you liked her?" asked Ulma out of the blue.

Jag choked on a piece of crust he was chewing and nearly fell off the wall. "What? Liked who?"

"Come on, Jonathan Ur-Jag, I have eyes! And she likes you, too, I think, although, she is a bit distracted at the moment by Magnificent Marcus. But that happens to every girl when they first meet him. She'll get over him once she knows him better."

"I don't know what you are talking about," said Jag, his cheeks burning.

"Yes, you do, lost boy!" She glanced at him sideways and flashed her white teeth.

"I don't have feelings for any girl. Are you talking about Gillian? I definitely don't feel anything for her."

"Definitely?" said Ulma, refastening the empty food bag to her belt. "Definitely... Well, that means it must be true."

Jag's face heated up again. Why did he always blush like that? The conversation was making him feel very uncomfortable. "Can we talk about something else?"

Ulma scratched her head. "Yes, okay, let's talk about Freddie. Does he have a girlfriend?"

"I don't know anything about this subject. Can we talk about the farm? I'm very interested to know how it is financially structured. I'm also keen to know more about Mensa's trading partners."

"Oh, why did you not say so? I am an expert in those areas."

"Oh, good. Perhaps you could begin by giving me an overview of—"

"Jonathan Ur-Jag! I know nothing of these matters. I am a simple farm worker. What do I care about such things? You need to speak to Dell or Nikolas."

Jag sat open mouthed. If she didn't know anything about Mensan economics, why had she claimed she was an expert?

"Let's talk about your book," said Ulma. "Do you always have it with you?"

"Yes, I never know when I might need it. If l don't record something when it happens, there is a risk I might forget something important."

"What did you write about me? Something nice I hope?"

"Just a few facts, I think," said Jag. He hesitated for a moment and then reached into his backpack and retrieved his journal. "I don't see any harm in you having a look. There are no secrets in here."

He handed Ulma the book, and she took it, although she appeared reluctant to do so. She opened it and placed it on her lap, a look of concentration on her face.

Jag looked over to help her find the correct pages. "It's upside down."

"Yes, I know that!" Ulma said tersely, quickly turning the book the correct way.

Jag peered over her shoulder again. Ulma was staring hard at his notes. "You are looking at some run scoring analysis I conducted on the Pendleton Under 16 cricket team."

"Yes, that interests me a lot."

"You play cricket here? I had no idea."

Ulma thrust the book back at him, an angry look on her face. "No, we don't play cricket here."

"Oh, I understand now; you're not a very good reader."

"No, I can't read at all." Jag took a deep breath.

"That's amazing. I've never met anyone your age who couldn't read!"

His observation did nothing to lighten Ulma's sudden dark mood.

"No, I can't read at all, but so what? Not many farm workers can. Why do we need to be able to read? What use is it in our work?"

"Well, actually…" Jag had several ideas of how reading might help a farm worker.

"Can you castrate a pig?" interrupted Ulma. "No, all those books but you can't castrate a pig? What's the point in reading if it doesn't help you do your work?" Ulma crossed her arms and looked away from Jag.

He opened his mouth to speak and then stopped. An uneasy silence filled the space between them. Jag put the journal into his backpack and turned his attention to a piglet that was playfully butting one of the sleeping swine below them. Ulma swung her legs 'round, slid off the wall, and started off in the direction of the farmhouse. Jag followed her as quickly as he could. She moved so fast.

"I'm sorry," he called after her. "It's just that I've never met anyone who was illiterate before, and I find it rather interesting."

Ulma turned abruptly. "Ur-Jag, for a clever person, you are very stupid." She stormed off in the direction of the house.

Jag considered following her and trying to fix the situation, although he wasn't sure how. But then he remembered they had left the donkey and cart by the pig enclosure, and he doubled back to fetch them. He'd deal with the situation between Ulma and himself later. Maybe...

*****

At supper that evening, everyone was in high spirits, except for Jag. It seemed Gillian had had a wonderful day, assisting Marcus and Dell with mending various parts of the farm's perimeter fence. Freddie had learned how to milk three different animals and had even found time to learn the basics of cheese production. Ulma was in great form, talking and joking with her friends, but she completely ignored Jag, which made him feel very uncomfortable.

"So, what did you do to upset Ulma?" Freddie whispered to Jag as they finished off their apple pie and cream.

Jag related the conversation he had with Ulma, and Freddie howled with laughter, clapping Jag on the back. Luckily for Jag, his friend's actions didn't draw any attention—the farmhands were growing accustomed to Freddie's loud outbursts.

"It's not funny, Freddie. I've upset her, and now she's ignoring me."

"It's a good thing you don't care about her then!"

Jag used his fingers to poke Freddie in the ribs.

"All right, all right. I'm sorry," said Freddie, rubbing his ribcage. "Heck, those fingers of yours are lethal. Worth remembering if you are ever in a tight spot."

Jag stared down at his empty dessert plate. Freddie put his hand on Jag's shoulder.

"You know, you are quite the babe magnet, buddy! The girls are falling all over each other to get to you."

Jag didn't look up. "You said something like that back at school, but it doesn't make any sense. You're saying the more they like you, the ruder they are?"

"Well, kind of, yes."

"What's the point of that? What happens if one of them *really* likes you? I mean, how rude can they get with you?"

"Ah, I think we're moving into new territory. Don't worry about it, Jag. It'll be fine tomorrow. Just stay clear of the subject of books and reading. If I know girls as well as I think I do, she'll be over it in the morning, like it never happened."

"Hey, Freddie! Sing the milk maid song I taught you today!" shouted

Ink from the far side of the table. "People, you have to hear this! Freddie takes singing to a different dimension!"

Everyone cheered.

"Oh, if you insist, then," said Freddie, standing up. He started singing his new song, loud and proud and rarely in tune.

"Oh, no," said Jag quietly to himself and covered his ears.

The evening seemed to go on forever. After Freddie had finished, several of the locals took turns at leading a singalong. A very animated Williams played a crazy fiddle accompanied by two of his friends—one on bass and the other thumping a hand-held drum. Jag wasn't in the mood. Everyone was up and dancing when he left the room. He glanced around one last time as he reached the door and saw Gillian and Marcus and Ulma and a lad Jag didn't recognize, dancing together. Ulma was watching him depart over the shoulder of her partner, but Jag did not acknowledge her.

The impromptu party must have gone on until late because no one else turned in for several hours. Trick wasn't there to give Jag more lights out. He lay on his back, looking at the ceiling. Had they all gone mad? Here they were, having a party, while their families and friends back home would surely be desperately worried about them by now. They had been gone three nights. The police must have become involved; they were probably on the news. Of course, Pinhorn and his cronies would have to give an account of what had happened, though Jag doubted any of them would tell the truth...not even to the police. But what about Gillian's friends? Had Gillian told them where she was going? He couldn't remember. He was sure that one way or another, the authorities would end up at the tunnel. They would of course search the tunnel and the surrounding area. But what would they find? Would it be a regular tunnel for them, or would they be transitioned into this strange, new world? Jag had a vision of a posse of Pendleton policemen wielding truncheons emerging from a cliff into the Western Wastes. With these jumbled thoughts bouncing around his head Jag eventually fell into a light, troubled sleep.

*****

Jag awoke to a violent disturbance on his bed.

"Good morning! Good morning, Mr. Ur-Jag! You are late again!" yelled Williams, bouncing around on Jag's feet.

"No, Williams, pick on someone else!"

"Good idea!" replied Williams, jumping off Jag's bed and onto Freddie's.

Apparently, he'd overslept, too.

But Freddie was ready for their human alarm clock. He threw his pillow at Williams with such force that it knocked the young joker clean off the bed and onto the floor. Williams did not complain. He leaped to his feet, laughed, and scampered out of the dorm.

As they entered the dining hall for breakfast, they passed Ulma. She was on her way out, and she nodded at Freddie but walked past Jag as if he wasn't there. Jag looked at his friend and arched his eyebrows.

"Okay, she's a tough one," said Freddie as they clambered onto the bench, "but by breakfast tomorrow—you'll see."

After breakfast, they made their way to the meeting point in the courtyard. Jag wondered if Ulma would be there. But when they arrived, the only people waiting for them were Trick, Roy, and Williams.

"Good day, lost people!" said Williams. "Unfortunately, Dell has been delayed, but the good news is, he's put me in charge! I thought we'd start the day with some cow tipping..."

"All right, Williams, that's enough already," said Roy. "Actually, he's right about Dell being delayed. Apparently, an urgent message has just arrived from Three Widows. Dell is looking it over now. It came on the flyer, so it must be important."

Jag frowned. The flyer? What was that?

"Where are Ulma and Marcus?" asked Gillian.

"Out there somewhere, working on the perimeter fence again."

Gillian's face fell. Obviously, she was disappointed. "Oh, so, what are we doing today?" she asked.

"You'll know in two minutes; here comes the boss."

Dell had left the house and was striding towards them.

He was still a few yards away when he called orders. "Williams, get yourself some transport, find Marcus and Ulma, and have them return to the house immediately."

Without a word, Williams sped off in the direction of the stable.

"Trick, are Tiny and Freckles still working the lumberyard?"

Trick nodded.

"Good, go bring them back as fast as you can."

Trick made for the main gate. What had the giant brothers been doing all this time? Jag hadn't seen them since their journey to the farm.

"Roy, please gather Ink and the rest of our troops. Sorry, but I'm going to have to leave you in charge of things again."

"Understood." Roy headed off back towards the house.

Then Dell turned his attention to Jag, Gillian, and Freddie. "Sorry for the short notice, but you have to head back to Three Widows immediately. You'll be traveling ahead of the others. Go pick up your belongings and then meet me at the front gate. Nikolas has sent the fastest transport we have to speed the process."

"Can we ask what's happened?" said Gillian. "Does it relate to our going home?"

"Word has come from Nikolas that the Great Cirque has responded much faster than we expected. Also, there are reports of many incidents taking place throughout the six regions of the Great Circle realm."

"Incidents?" asked Freddie.

"Go get ready for your journey. Don't leave anything behind." Dell looked at Gillian.

She had her hand in her pocket, no doubt clasping the bracefire. Jag hadn't seen it since the Cirque. She'd kept it out of sight. She nodded in acknowledgement to Dell.

Freddie and Gillian set off to their respective dormitories to fetch their remaining items. Jag had everything he owned in his backpack. Since being reunited with it at the Cirque, he'd kept it close by him at all times. He was not going to lose his stuff again.

He followed Dell across the courtyard to the main gate, eager to see what the flyer was. They must have cars here, after all, or something even more amazing. But when they reached the gate, the only thing waiting for them was an old trap harnessed to a donkey. When Jag saw the donkey, he did a doubletake.

"Oh, no!" he said.

The donkey stretched his neck forward and brayed loudly at him. Had Jag needed further confirmation of the beast's identity, the familiar sign with its white lettering that hung around the donkey's neck provided it.

Dell produced two carrots from his pocket, and David ate them noisily. Jag examined the trap; there was barely room for the three of them on the bench seat, let alone a driver.

"I don't mean to sound rude, Dell, but you said this was a fast means of transport?" said Jag.

For a moment, a smile replaced Dell's serious look. "He's the best option available. David is from a rare line of donkeys famed for speed. The Asher nomads originally bred them for wars long past. Well, you'll see for yourself shortly."

As he spoke, Freddie and Gillian arrived with their packs. Gillian whooped when she saw David and put her arm around his neck and hugged him.

Freddie looked on with a grin. "You know this chap?" He patted David's flank.

"We're old roommates," replied Gillian.

"Okay, guys, climb on. We need to get you going."

Jag and his friends eased themselves onto the trap and sat, holding their backpacks on their laps. It was a tight fit.

"So, who's driving, and what if we get lost?" asked Jag anxiously.

"No driver required, and you won't get lost," replied Dell.

He bent down and whispered in David's ear then looked up. "Just hold on tight; it will be bumpy. David knows where to go. Don't stop for anything until you reach Nikolas's residence." He waved his arm and yelled, "Via, David, Via!"

The donkey lurched forward with such a punch of acceleration that all three of them grabbed the seat to keep from falling off. They held on tightly as David went into racing mode. The cold, northerly wind cut into exposed skin. Behind them, David's effort left a billowing cloud of dust.

# Chapter 9

Jag slid down his chair until he attained the optimum angle for staring at the ceiling.

*This is a very comfortable room,* he thought to himself. He and his friends were in the front chamber of Nikolas's residence, awaiting their meeting with the town master. It was late Monday morning, three days since they had found themselves in the Western Wastes. The journey back from the farm had been hair raising. David had started off fast and had got faster still as he warmed to the task. His little legs moved at an extraordinary rate. They arrived at their destination in record time—though they were all shaken up by the wild ride.

A tall, stooping, old man had greeted them at the front door. He introduced himself as Mit and explained that "the master" was already meeting with another group, but they were expected and would not have to wait long. He had a rather distracting habit of tugging at his right earlobe whenever he finished a sentence.

"Are you his butler?" asked Freddie.

The question earned him a glare from Gillian.

"No, I am the master's bodyguard," replied the old man with a tug of his ear.

Freddie had slapped his leg and burst out laughing. Jag's jaw dropped. Gillian gave Freddie her most lethal stare.

"Freddie, enough! Jonathan, chill. Mit doesn't mean it—he's being ironic—and who could blame him in the face of such a rude question? Mr. Mit, I apologize for my friend's lack of manners."

"Oh, not at all," said the old man. "I get that a lot. It doesn't worry me at all. Now then, you all look half frozen. Take a seat by the fire, and I'll fetch you something warm to drink."

The room was grand. It had a high ceiling and four large, circular windows at the front, allowing an extensive view of the main Three Widows thoroughfare. The floor was constructed of blue-grey slate paving slabs, on which lay a dozen or more throw rugs. In the centre of the room was a big, open hearth, in which a roaring fire blazed. The logs that fuelled it crackled and spat as the flames consumed the timber. They needed a fire tonight. The fresh, northerly wind that had blown in on their journey back from the old farmhouse had caused the temperature to plummet.

He opened his journal and jotted a few keywords.

The Great Cirque.
Bracefires.
Gillian—Three Widows connection.
The sower.
The harvester.
Jag—Three Widows connection.
The timekeeper.
Freddie?
RagaRaga.
The Tunnel.

He looked across at his two companions. They were sitting comfortably with their mugs of cocoa, eyes fixed on the fire.

"You know this is the first time we have been alone together for some while, and we should use the time effectively," Jag said.

"Regarding?" asked Gillian, without looking away from the fire.

Jag raised his voice. "We need to figure out what has happened to us and how we get home. Aren't you concerned about our families and how worried they will be by now?"

"We are, Jag," answered Freddie, "but what can we do about it? The whole thing is so whacky that it's impossible to know where we should even start. In the meantime, our only option is to play the game and hope Nikolas or one of his Cirque friends can find the exit door for us."

"We can't rely on them," said Jag. "How do we know we can trust them? What if we have been taken in by the bad side. How do we know the RagaRaga are the bad guys? We need to exchange ideas and try to apply logic to the situation."

"Oh, come on," said Gillian, slapping her hands together hard enough to make Jag and Freddie jump, "the Mensans have looked after us pretty well after a sticky start. They could have killed us by now if they had wanted to."

Jag looked at Gillian steadily, engaging her in an uncomfortable but necessary moment of eye contact. "Do you think their top priority is to see us get home? No, they see us as a miracle sent from the heavens to help win a war. They will not let us go anywhere until the threat is over."

"What can Gillian and I do to help?" said Freddie, standing up.

"I think it's possible that between the three of us, we may have a better understanding of the situation than we realize. For a start, there are several links between our world and this world."

Gillian and Freddie looked at him but said nothing.

"Gillian's bracefire, for example. I assume it first came into Gillian's possession in Pendleton? But it is linked to this world, too."

"That's an understatement if I ever heard one!" said Freddie.

"Fair enough," said Gillian. "The charm or bracefire, as they call it, was given to me by my father. It's usually attached to my bracelet, but it fell off when I was following you down the railway line."

"Another coincidence? Do you know where your father bought it?" asked Jag.

"No. He originally gave me the bracelet along with three charms as a birthday gift. He gave me a new charm every birthday. It became a nice tradition."

"Then there's Gillian's ability to speak Mensan."

"Can't help you there, either," said Gillian. "I've no idea how I obtained that ability or what I was saying."

"I have a link, too," Jag said. "The timekeeper mosaic above the tunnel entrance—the same character is on our clock at home."

Freddie and Gillian looked at him blankly.

"Oh, I never got the chance to tell you. The clock that features the harvester also depicts a juggling jester and a timekeeper. Three medieval characters."

"Yes, painted onto the face of the clock," said Freddie. "And you saw the same timekeeper above the tunnel entrance?"

Jag nodded.

Freddie stroked his chin. "That is freaky. It's as if the timekeeper was a signpost for you, leading to a surprise destination? Blimey! What about the third figure in the painting. The Juggler?"

The three of them exchanged looks. Before they could discuss the situation further, Mit stepped into the room.

"The Master will see you now," he said and beckoned them to follow him.

Just a few steps down the corridor the old man stopped and after a cursory knock opened a large door. He stepped in and said something Jag couldn't make out.

The voice that responded was loud and clear. "Thank you, Mit, thank you very much, yes, show them in, haste is the word today," said Nikolas.

Mit stepped to one side, and Gillian led the way into Nikolas's office.

It was a large room. In the middle, three men—Nikolas, flanked by Anthony, and Addford—sat at a round table. The walls were fitted with shelves, on which were stacked hundreds of ancient-looking books. More of the large, circular windows lined the wall on the north side of the room. They looked out towards neighbouring buildings, and beyond them, Jag could see the high peaks of the Maria Mountains.

Nikolas looked tall, even sitting down. He sat opposite the door they had just entered. He beckoned Mit over, passed him some paperwork, and exchanged a few quiet words. Mit nodded and left the room. Anthony was shuffling through a pile of papers as if he had lost something. Addford was looking down at the placemat in front of him. Nikolas waved his hands at Gillian.

"Yes, I know what you are thinking right now, but please give me a moment to explain. Addford is very much on our side. And when I say *our*, I mean *your* side."

Gillian stood motionless, hands on hips, glaring first at Nikolas and then Addford.

"Is this your way of asking for our help? Are we on trial again? This man would have had us locked up for the rest of our days if he'd had his way!"

She dragged away the chair Freddie offered, scraping the floor with the legs.

"My child," Nikolas said in a calm voice, "Addford has no issue with you. At the Cirque, he was playing a part someone of education and good standing had to play. He played the role well, too, because in attacking you, he brought your strengths to the fore. You are a spirited and gifted young lady. Addford?"

The prosecutor nodded in acknowledgement. "Thank you, Master, I appreciate your support." He spoke slowly and calmly, in stark contrast to the way he had delivered his withering verbal assault at the Cirque.

"Gillian, Freddie, Jag, please accept my apologies for the way I went after you at the Cirque. As the Master stated, sometimes, we have to assume roles."

"Are you telling me the trial was just a charade?" asked Gillian.

"No, no, not all," interjected Nikolas. "It was real, and had we concluded you were enemies of the Cirque, you would have been dealt with accordingly. It's just that a few of us were already convinced your arrival here was a great gift to the people of the six regions, and I include myself and Addford in that number. Come now, Gillian, please join us at this circle. Time, time, time is ebbing away."

Gillian puffed her cheeks and returned her chair to the table.

Nikolas jumped up and strode to the nearest of the windows.

He gazed out at the thoroughfare for a few seconds. Then he turned around to address the table.

"If time were not so pressing, I would like nothing more than to share the fascinating history of Mensa and the regions beyond.

"However, time is against us, so I am going to give you the bare-bones details on three topics you need to understand—our geography, our political system, and a brief history of the man who is responsible for creating the predicament we find ourselves in."

He reached into a drawer fitted to the underneath of the table and produced a large rolled parchment.

"Anthony, if you please." Nikolas passed the roll to his protegee.

Anthony unfurled the scroll and attached it to a frame built into the bookcase at the end of the room.

"You've been asking where you are; maybe this will help a little. Behold, the Turn," said Nikolas.

Jag and his friends leaned forward. They were looking at a map. Jag tried to match it with parts of the globe he knew but could come up with nothing.

"The Turn?" Gillian asked. "We keep hearing the word, but what is it?"

"If I'm not mistaken, it is our equivalent of what you three would call the world or Earth."

"It's not like any part of the world I've ever seen on a map," said Freddie. "Do you mind if I take a closer look?"

"Of course not," replied Nikolas, motioning them to the map.

Jag, Freddie, and Gillian walked over to the frame. Jag opened his notebook and did his best to draw a copy of the map.

"May I?" said Nikolas. He picked up a thin cane.

Jag and his friends moved to one side.

Nikolas positioned the pointer at a large black dot near the centre. "This is Three Widows, which is in the central area of the region of Mensa. Mensa is the northernmost of six regions that together form an alliance known as the Great Circle." Nikolas ran his pointer around the borders of the six regions.

"It looks more like a square than a circle," said Freddie, scratching his head.

"Ah, yes, indeed, Freddie, geographically speaking, you are right. But in this context, the Circle or Cirque—the words are interchangeable—relates to an ideology.

"Long ago, inspired by one of our great leaders, the residents of the six regions agreed on a shared vision of the future. They realized each region had its own strengths. By working together, they formed an entity that was much stronger than any individual part. No doubt, you can guess what Mensa contributed?"

"Well, judging by what we have been working with for the last three days, farm produce," answered Freddie.

"Indeed." Nikolas nodded. "But more precisely, staple foods. Meat, all kinds of vegetables, fruit, etc.

"To our southern border lies Samatra. It enjoys a warmer climate and has more hills and rivers. It specialized in the more exotic produce, such as citrus fruits, herbs and spices, fine wines, and rich cheeses.

"Below Samatra is Gonk. Home of the industrialists and the great scientific minds. They manufacture machinery and equipment. Unfortunately, they also started making advanced weapons."

Between Gonk and the southern sea is Amos Line." A melancholy look came over Nikolas's face. "Oh, Amos Line, jewel of the south. The

Amos are the most wonderful people—they inhabited the most wonderful lands. Theirs was a place of art, of music, of dancing, of laughter. Folk travelled there from all around the Turn." Nikolas ran his cane down the length of the Western Wastes. "The Western Wastes, you have already had a taste of, and I'm sure you were not impressed, but there was a time when this region had a significant population. They were known as the Dory. The Dory were a nomadic people who never set up permanent homes, preferring to move and stay wherever their business interests took them. They performed a vital role for the Great Circle, moving goods within it and importing and exporting to and from outlying lands. 'If you need something, ask a Dory,' the expression went, and it was true. They were a most resourceful people, always alert to money-making opportunities. Marvellous traders, with haggling skills second to none."

"You are talking about much of this in the past tense," said Gillian as she returned to her chair.

"Yes, Gillian, I am. Today, the regions of the Western Wastes, Samatra, and Amos Line are pretty much devoid of people. The citizens were driven out by a tyrant, which brings me to the last region, Brunella. The fairest of them all, with hills, rivers, fertile valleys, and two great forests.

"And at the centre of the region, cradled in a valley between two large hills, is Ely, the seat of Great Cirque. The Perfect Circle. It was founded by Brunella, the First Princess, then perfected through the ages by successive governments, each administration respectful of the constitution laid down by the First Princess. Each subsequent Princess enabled the Cirque; she did not govern it. Every Cirque was composed of elected representatives from the six regions. Fair representation for all—a system that everyone trusted in—a system that worked."

Nikolas fell silent, his head nodding towards the floor.

The room remained quiet for several seconds.

"I take it something went horribly wrong?" said Jag.

There were a few more moments of silence, and then Nikolas responded slowly, "Yes, Jag. I'm afraid it did."

The elder took a long, slow breath and continued. "Do you know the expression 'one bad apple spoils the bunch'?" he asked, putting the cane back into its holder.

"Yes, we have that same expression back home," replied Gillian.

"Well, the wonder is that the Cirque worked for so many years without breaking down or being corrupted. Yes, there were those who sought to destroy it for their own interests. There were leaders who were weak or incompetent. But the Circle had been so well thought out and implemented that it was robust enough to fend off or absorb these challenges."

Nikolas walked to the window. Outside, a large group of riders approached. All the men wore the uniform of the Three Widows militia.

"Our good people from the farm are arriving," said Nikolas. "I have to make this quick.

"Even during the best years of the Cirque, we had enemies. They have always been around. These spoilers came from without our alliance; the Hags and Spindles were the chief culprits. These are rogue states that have no interest in democratic circles, preferring instead to plunder and pillage those who work. The Spindles, in particular are a dangerous foe. In common with the other rogues' states, they have a large, unruly army. But they are particularly good at subterfuge. Their leaders place 'sleepers' all around the Turn. Sometimes for years. These operatives blend in with the locals and seek to earn their trust. Then they activate them and …. you can guess the rest. Brilliant actors – evil human beings. They have forever been a thorn in our side, but when the Cirque was established, the alliance set up organized militias who worked together to defend the people of the six regions. They were good at their jobs. Just a few years after the creation of the militias, we saw very few raids.

"The six regions enjoyed a peaceful existence, which was to last for many decades. But about twenty years ago, there was an increase in the raids again, and Gonk bore the brunt of the attacks. Apparently, the raiders were after the machinery and weapons Gonk produced.

Each region had two elected Cirque representatives. The senior was a Lord who was elected for life. He focused on central governmental issues developing legislation affecting all six regions. The Lords spent most of their time in Ely. The junior representative was usually an elder from one of the towns or villages of each region. Their job was to represent the region's local interests. They lived locally but travelled to Brunella to participate in scheduled Great Circle meetings.

"Gonk's elected representatives at the time were Lord Tarbus and elder Leprade. Tarbus, the senior, was a gentle, old man who had been in the Circle for many years. Some argued he had become too old and frail for the job. Chief among his critics was Leprade, the junior representative. Leprade was dynamic and young and had a reputation as a brilliant engineer, inventor, and strategist.

"The defence of the regions was always top of the Great Circle agenda. When the raids on Gonk became disproportionally high, Leprade went to the Great Circle and demanded additional militia. The Circle agreed and re-assigned some twenty percent of the militia pool to their defence. It was a fair offer, and that should have brought an end to it. But Leprade wanted more. When he didn't get it, he told the Cirque that from then on, they would take care of their own defence.

"On his return to Gonk, Leprade promoted a junior officer called Catchpole into a new role as head of the Gonk militia. He is a tall, wiry man with a crooked smile who has long been in Leprade's pocket.

"It was a marriage made in hell. Leprade's intellect coupled with the ruthless efficiency of Catchpole was a toxic mix. The two hatched a plan that was far more ambitious than simply securing their borders. Catchpole received permission to neutralize any outsiders found in or around the outer regions of Gonk. Within a few days, innocent people started to disappear or were found dead in the most unlikely places. The last straw was Catchpole shooting six Dory traders to death as they slept. By all accounts they had been in the Wastes when Catchpole murdered them.

"News of the atrocity spread fast. But Leprade did nothing to address the crime. Instead, he publicly praised Catchpole for the leadership and heroism he had shown as commander of the Gonk militia.

"Tarbus ordered Leprade to arrest Catchpole or resign. The same afternoon, four hooded men dressed in black dragged the Lord from his residence. They tied him up with rope, slung him over the back of a pony, and rode off with him. He was never seen again. Many of the townsfolk witnessed the kidnapping, and the residents became paralyzed with fear.

"That was how it started. The Dory Cirque representatives were understandably outraged and other regions backed them. Things escalated quickly. At the direction of the Grand Cirque, a militia was formed in Amos Line and dispatched to Gonk to restore order and arrest the rebel ringleaders. The allied militia was far too small and inadequately armed to take on the tech-savvy Gonk rebels. What Leprade's forces lacked in numbers, they made up for with clinical organization, ruthlessness, and futuristic weapons, many of which had Leprade had invented. The allied militia were still two miles short of the town when the rebels ambushed and slaughtered them. It was a bloodbath."

Nikolas looked at his outstretched fingers and sighed. "If only we had acted then. We could have put down this rebellion and restored order in Gonk. But one of the drawbacks of being a democracy is that the government can be slow to react. Inclusion, consultation, and agreement are great ideals, but weeks—yes *weeks*—passed while the five other regions argued about what type of strategy would put an end to the uprising.

"Leprade, meanwhile, was moving fast. His small group of followers grew rapidly. Some folks supported Leprade's call for independence; others, he coerced into joining him. His most loyal supporters ran a campaign of terror against anyone who resisted the takeover. And then from seemingly out of nowhere, he produced an army—one you have already heard about—the RagaRaga.

"The RagaRaga were mobilized and crossed the Brunella border, marching directly on Ely. Such was the surprise and the speed of the attack that there was little in the way of resistance. The only blessing was that The Great Circle, their close followers and their supporters escaped before Catchpole and his forces invaded. They fled north and west in a bid for survival. With the help of the Mensans they eventually crossed the Western Wastes and then set sail in a small fleet of boats to the island of

Espanada. They set themselves up as a government in exile on the island. But distance and sea made it very difficult for them to govern the six regions.

"Leprade moved into the abandoned Ely. He declared himself the new ruler of the six regions, lumping them together under one name, Lepradia—such humility. He set up Catchpole as his number two. Catchpole transitioned himself from battlefield commander to Chief Interrogator—a job he relished. To be picked up and interrogated by Catchpole was a virtual death sentence. Of those captured, just a handful tasted freedom again but not before they were completely broken, mentally and physically.

"Leprade demanded the leaders of the old regions recognize his new central government and that each pledge their allegiance or suffer the consequences. None of the regions complied, and Leprade ordered their 'liberation'.

"Amos Line fought valiantly but though they are a wonderful people, they are not warriors, nor could they match the technologically advanced weapons of the Lepradians. Many of the Amos fled to the Western Wastes, where the Dory people gave them aid. The Dory had already decided to leave the Wastes. They were the one region who had a sizable number of boats at their disposal. Refugees started appearing from the north, too…a few from Gonk and many from Samatra, which had not been yet been attacked but whose people saw the writing on the wall."

Nikolas walked back to the map. "So, the only regions that didn't evacuate their land were Mensa and Gonk," he said, tapping the map. "All the Dory left, and they took with them large numbers of Samatrans and Amos. Many Brunellans who weren't directly associated with the seat at Ely also fled. The Cirque lost about eighty percent of its population. It was on the brink of complete collapse.

"But Leprade made one mistake. He was in such a rush to take his high seat in Ely, he neglected to secure the surrender of the Gonk Cirque loyalists who remained.

"Instead, he left a power vacuum in his old town. Out of nowhere, a lowly apprentice engineer emerged as a new leader for those who remained. His name is Owlspin, and he was barely old enough to shave. But he is a natural leader who strengthened the alliance with Mensa.

"Thanks to Owlspin and the Gonk Cirque loyalists, Leprade has been held at bay for nearly twenty years. They have proved to be a real headache for the RagaRaga and their masters. However, Leprade has upped his game. He has thrown more of his resources into the fight, and crucially, he has enticed the Hags and the Spindles to join him in a rebel alliance. The numbers are now in his favour. Unless something changes, it is only a matter of time before he takes control of all six regions."

Nikolas stood silently and looked at Jag, then Freddie, then Gillian. Again, he waited.

Finally, Freddie broke the silence "Where do we fit into all this? I'm very sorry you're facing a battle with these bad guys, but I'm not sure what we can do to help or whether we should be helping."

"Ah, thank you for asking, Freddie. Oh, and by the way, catch!" Nikolas tossed a small leather pouch to Freddie.

Freddie caught it and stared at it a moment. "Oh, boy! Is this what I think it is?"

Nikolas nodded at him, wearing that half smile he seemed to reserve for certain important moments.

"I'm not sure about this at all. It's the harvester, right? I've seen what this can do! Pretty dangerous," said Freddie.

"In the wrong hands, yes, and ironically, in the right hands, too. But your hands do not fall into either of those categories, Freddie, so you will make an excellent custodian!"

Freddie held the pouch out in front of him, a look of confusion etched upon his face.

"You need to guard that with your life until you meet the person you should give it to. You will know when that moment is at hand."

"I will?" Freddie asked. "So, I have to take it somewhere?"

Jag guessed the answer before Nikolas could respond. "To the island place, right?"

"Espanada, yes," said Nikolas, "along with Gillian and her bracefire."

"If the bracefires belong to the regions they represent, why are they being sent to Espanada?" asked Gillian.

"At times of war, all power is centralized. There is an ancient table in the Grand Cirque that houses all the bracefires. When the bracefires are fitted to the table, they feed off each other to create power. Sibling bracefires have yet more power. Unfortunately, several of the bracefires are lost or are out of reach. Until you arrived with the sower, the alliance had no sibling pairs—hence, the excitement at the Three Widows Cirque.

"Finally, there is one vacant slot in the middle of the table. We are not sure what form the corresponding bracefire takes, if indeed it is a bracefire, but there are legends that speak of a master icon that generates power beyond measure. As you can imagine, we would like to get our hands on that one."

Nikolas crossed the room to one of the bookshelves. He picked up an old tome and blew on it once, sending a cloud of dust into the air. Then he walked over to where Jag sat and placed it on the table in front of him.

"This is an abridged version of Henry Shollick's excellent *History of the Robert Circle*," said Nikolas. "Look after it, Jag; it is precious...one of only three left that we know of. I encourage you to read it whenever you have time during the next few days and share the stories with your friends. I have marked the more important chapters. If you read nothing else, read them. They will answer many questions you may have."

Jag opened the book and started thumbing through the pages.

"Why us?" Gillian said, looking at the elder. "We aren't from here, and we are too young. We have no special powers. I don't get it."

Nikolas smiled but said nothing.

"Oh, come on! You want us to help, but you won't tell us anything. We need to know," Gillian protested.

Nikolas looked directly back at her. "I understand your frustration, Gillian, but if there are things I don't talk about, it is for your—and Mensa's—protection. More will be revealed to you when the time is right."

Gillian crossed her arms and looked over at Jag and Freddie. "Okay, you want us to deliver two bracefires to Espanada and give them to the 'right' person? That's all?"

Nikolas shook his head. "It may not be quite that simple."

"No, I've heard enough," said Gillian. "Freddie's right; it's not our war. If you won't show us the way home, we will find someone who will."

"The folks who may be able to help you reside in Espanada. I'm offering you a way of getting there," said Nikolas.

Jag sensed Nikolas's stare.

"And if they can't?" asked Freddie.

Nikolas hesitated. "If they can't, you would be well advised to help us, because you will be fighting for the future of your new home."

The words hit Jag like a thunderbolt. His legs flexed, sending his backpack flying. Both Freddie and Gillian looked over at him. He reached down to pick up a piece of cardboard that had fallen out of his pack. The room remained silent as he opened the message. Wait, hadn't he thrown it out? No, this one was different, as yet unopened. How was that possible? He started shaking as he quickly unfolded it. The handwriting in blue ink was his mother's—no doubt about that—and she'd written just two words in capital block letters:

TRUST NIKOLAS

"You okay?" asked Freddie.

Jag looked at his two friends. He took a long, slow breath then nodded. "I think we should do as Nikolas directs us."

"Why?" said Gillian.

He held up the message for his friends to see.

"Because my mother says so."

*****

Nikolas, Addford, and Anthony left the room to allow Jag and his friends to discuss the situation in private. Jag somewhat sheepishly came clean about the history of the secret messages his mum had been leaving for him since he started school. The he filled Freddie and Gillian in about the note that had motivated Jag to join Freddie on the tunnel adventure.

Freddie and Gillian appeared stunned.

"So, putting aside the mystery of how the notes found their way into your backpack, you are one hundred percent certain she wrote them?" said Gillian.

"Yes, it's definitely her writing," said Jag.

"Which means she is somehow involved in this?"

Jag ran his hands through his hair. Gillian was right; Mum couldn't have written the notes without having some kind of connection with the Turn. Plus, the timekeeper—the one depicted on the tunnel entrance—and the harvester—the one Nikolas had held at the Cirque—were the same characters as those painted on the clock in Jag's kitchen. The clock also featured a third figure, a juggling joker. Where did that fit in, if at all? Where had the clock come from? It had always been there. How he wished he'd asked his mother where she got if from.

"It's all a very strange," Freddie said, "but your mother is smart, and if she sent a message to us somehow, that's good enough for me."

Gillian closed her eyes and tilted her head back. A few seconds passed. She nodded. Jag sighed. They would put themselves at Nikolas's disposal.

# Chapter 10

Jag led his friends to Madam Nan's restaurant garden. Part-time militia members filled most available seats, finishing their lunches. Noise levels were high with excited chatter and the clink and clank of utensils meeting metal plates. Thirty of them would be employed, in some capacity, to assist with the protection of Jag and his friends on their journey to the Western Sea. A much smaller number would crew the boat bound for Espanada. All were aware of the reports of enemy activity close to the Mensa borders. But right now, there was an almost partylike atmosphere as the team members enjoyed the complimentary food and drink.

On his way out of Nikolas's residence, Jag had joined the throng of people checking the lists Mit had posted on the information board near the front door. They contained the names and roles of those Nikolas and his advisors had selected.

Many arrived from the farm or other parts of the village only to find they were not required. Among them were Roy, Trick, and Williams. All three were unhappy about being excluded. Nonetheless, they accepted an invite to Madam Nan's for the send-off meal. Nikolas had already stated he would not be coming with them. He said his first duty was the protection of Three Widows. Jag suspected there were other factors, but he didn't question the man. He was interested in the other selections, and while not surprised Williams was excluded, Jag was sorry Roy and Trick weren't coming. Marcus, with Dell as backup, would lead the taskforce. Ulma, Ink, and Spike also made the cut, along with the two Oze giants.

The elder had arranged for Jag and his friends to eat in a private room adjacent to Madame Nan's kitchen. Gillian had just discovered that Addford had been included in the list of those chosen for the expedition.

"Special Consultant! What can he possibly add to the group?" she protested, tapping her empty plate with her knife. "He's clearly not athletic enough to be a foot soldier or bright enough to be a leader."

"I'm sure Nikolas has his reasons," answered Freddie.

"Indeed, I do." Nikolas had slipped unnoticed into the room. "Don't look so shocked. I need to discuss one matter with the three of you alone. Jag, this is off the record."

Jag returned his journal and pen to his backpack.

"Thank you. You will meet many fine people in Espanada. Lord Mora, acting chair of the Great Cirque, is a marvellous man. I also believe the other remaining Cirque members are trustworthy. I think the same may be said of another group who reside within the walls of the Grand Cirque. They are called the Fade. They have no affiliation with us or any other political group; they have their own beliefs, but we have much in common and have benefitted from their assistance when a common interest is at stake.

"But the fact is, Espanada has been compromised; there is an enemy agent who has found a way of tapping into our communications, and he or she could hasten a terrible defeat for us if they are not identified and stopped."

"How can you be sure they've been infiltrated?" asked Gillian.

"We share our militia movements and other strategic activities with Espanada, and the messages have always remained secure. About a year ago, things started going wrong. Our enemies were anticipating our moves far too quickly. It could not be a coincidence. To check, we sent two pieces of false information and then watched what happened. Sure enough, they acted on the misinformation we planted. I believe the agent is hiding in plain sight.

"Unfortunately, this agent will know you are coming and will do whatever it takes to relieve you of the bracefires. Be careful, and trust no one."

Freddie raised his hands above his head. "So, I have this bracefire thing that I'll be giving to someone, and supposedly, I'll know who this someone is when the time comes, but at the same time, I can't trust anyone because there is an unidentified spy in town?"

"Yes, that about sums it up. And the same applies to Gillian's bracefire," said the elder.

Freddie buried his head in his hands and sighed loudly.

"Freddie has a point. Is there no one we can trust there?" asked Gillian.

"I'm afraid you will need to work that out for yourselves when you get there. But you do have one thing going for you—the loyal support of those taking this journey with you. I will vouch for any of them. Use them, use their knowledge. But above all, trust them."

"Even Addford?" asked Gillian, scowling.

"Especially Addford; that's why he is traveling with you. Speaking of which, I have to meet some of those who are not going. I owe it to them to explain why they weren't selected. First up is Williams. And you think you have problems!"

Nikolas stood as if to leave but hesitated for a moment and reached into a pocket and retrieved a small leather pouch. "One last thing," he said, untying the lace that kept the contents safe. "It would honour my people if you would each wear one of these." He held out three loop necklaces that were of the style worn by many of the residents of Mensa.

"They might even help you. These loops are symbols of the circle that is so important to us. They are made of Marian silver, mined from our great mountains to the north." He put the first one around Gillian's neck.

"These are not given lightly," he added. "We are putting a lot of trust in you. They also have power, or more accurately, they are capable of receiving power and passing it on to the wearer. You would be well advised to wear them at all times. May the wisdom of Brunella go with you."

*****

Three hours later, Jag and Freddie were sitting in a carriage at the main cross-roads to the west of Three Widows while Marcus checked the rest of the convoy. Gillian was working her way over to them after exchanging a few last-minute farewells. A couple of hundred townsfolk had come out to see them off. It seemed they all wanted to have a last word with the heroine who had returned the missing bracefire to them and her two friends and wish them well. All those traveling were either mounted on ponies or sitting in or on a carriage or trailer. The only exceptions were the Oze giants. They would travel on foot as was their custom. Freckles was at the rear of the convoy and Tiny at the front, where he was holding Marcus's pony.

"Blimey, look at that!" cried Freddie, pointing a little ahead of them.

Jag looked. Marcus was in a very passionate embrace with a pretty girl in a flowing blue dress.

"Who is she?" Freddie yelled up to Dell.

Dell glanced down from the box seat, where he'd been making sure the reins were correctly adjusted. "Oh, that's Libby. She is promised to Marcus," he said.

"They're engaged?" Jag asked, raising his eyebrows.

"Betrothed, yes. They won't marry for a year or two yet, but that's the plan."

Freddie started laughing. "Well, don't tell Gillian, because I have this nagging suspicion she doesn't know about that arrangement."

"Don't tell Gillian what?" Gillian opened the carriage door and hoisted herself up the step.

Freddie fell silent and turned to look out the carriage window.

"Oh, nothing, really," said Jag. "Freddie was just pointing out that the chap you would like to be your boyfriend is snogging his future wife."

Jag pointed at the young couple, who were showing no sign of ending their farewell moment.

"I'm thinking he didn't tell you he was engaged?" Jag asked.

He looked at Freddie. He was covering his face with his hands while pretending to be looking out the window Gillian's jaw tightened, and she clasped her fingers together so hard her knuckles whitened. She said nothing. Jag joined Freddie in staring hard out the window.

*****

The journey west to the Mensa border was largely uneventful. Jag was interested in the countryside, which he had missed on their journey to Three Widows.. The landscape was pleasant—mostly flat but with the occasional gentle, rolling hill. Much of it had been developed as agricultural farmland, featuring crops or grazing animals. They also skirted several small hamlets. The residents came running out to see them as they passed, and Ink distributed a newsletter and briefly updated them on events. The convoy came to a halt at the stream that marked the beginning of the Western Wastes. Everyone drank their fill of the fresh mountain water and re-filled their canteens. There would be no more drinkable water until they reached their destination. Jag thought back to the last time he had been here, only a few days ago, but it seemed like forever. Gillian and he had been desperately thirsty that day. He had sat cross legged with Ulma and Gillian, trying to make sense of what was happening. He had been convinced he was dreaming. He was now convinced it wasn't a dream. But if not, then what? He looked at the last page of his journal which he had been using to record all the possibilities as and when they occurred to him. Parallel universe? Black hole? Government experiment? Mental breakdown – madness? Religious event (Death? Re-birth?).

But they were just random ideas/concepts. There was zero evidence to support any of them.

Freddie was enjoying himself in the water, scooping large amounts of the cool, refreshing liquid and pouring it straight down his throat. Gillian was deep in conversation with Ink, who had a comforting arm clasped over Gillian's shoulder. Jag wondered what they were discussing.

"Okay, let's get going!" Marcus called out in a booming voice. "Scouts to the front, please."

Jag, Freddie, and Gillian returned quickly to their carriage.

Ulma and Spike trotted past them on their small ponies.

Spike grinned and waved as he passed the carriage. Ulma cast a quick look in their direction but gave no acknowledgement. Marcus had briefed them on the plan for the journey. From this point on, the Ulma and Spike would forge ahead of the convoy to scout the area for enemies. The Cirque alliance were keen to get to the boat unnoticed and even more importantly without stumbling headlong into a squadron of RagaRaga.

"Is she still mad at you, Jag?" asked Freddie, slapping Jag on the leg.

"I think so. You know girls are strange," Jag replied.

"Ha!" shouted Gillian without turning her gaze from the other window.

It was the first sound the boys had heard her emit since they left Three Widows. Freddie looked at Jag and raised his eyebrows. Jag shrugged.

"Okay, guys," Dell called down from the box seat, "you know the drill from here on; silence until Marcus gives the all clear."

Jag remembered the instruction from the briefing, but he couldn't see the point. Surely, anyone coming their way would hear the noise created by hooves and rattling carriages long before a voice would give them away? He hadn't raised any question at the briefing. As the party moved on, the silence added to the suspense. The riders closest to the carriage who had been laughing and joking just a few minutes before looked nervous now, their eyes constantly moving as they scanned the horizon. The convoy travelled in ten-minute cycles. They waited as the scouts moved ahead and then returned to confirm that the next section was clear. It was a slow, tedious business. They had planned to reach the sea just before sundown, so Jag used the descending sun as a gauge on how far they had to go. After two hours, he spotted a gull. He pointed it out to Freddie. His friend nodded. They were approaching the sea.

With no warning, the carriage jolted to a halt. Jag sat forward. What was up? The sound of whispered conversations filtered into the carriage. He risked poking his head out of the window. Marcus was standing just in front of them, and Addford, Spike, and Ulma were beside him. They were all nodding. Then Marcus came to the window as Jag quickly drew his head back in again.

"Okay, guys," he said quietly, "we have a problem. The good news is that we are very close to where the boat is hidden. The bad news is that Ulma and Spike have spotted several units of RagaRaga in the same area. It looks like they were expecting us."

Jag's stomach sank. Freddie and Gillian both sat up straight and exchanged worried looks.

"Here is the plan. It's risky, but Nikolas made it very clear we have to get you on that boat. We are almost certain our plans have been leaked. In which case, the RagaRaga will be expecting you to be traveling in this carriage. We're going to use it as a decoy. Spike is going to lead a group of our ten fastest riders, along with the carriage, down to the beach in plain sight of the RagaRaga. Assuming they take the bait, Spike's team will break south on the beach and lead the RagaRaga off as far as he can before turning east back into the wilds. This will give us time to go down, extract the boat from its hiding place, and get you onto the water."

"Who will be in the carriage?" asked Jag.

"Nobody. But they won't know that until they catch Spike."

"And I don't plan on them catching us," added Spike, who happened to be walking past them at that moment.

*****

As directed by Marcus, Jag lay on his front and slid slowly through the long grass towards the edge of a bluff. He looked down, and there they were—around thirty dark-haired men wearing black shirts, over which they wore what looked like dark metallic vests. There was no mistaking what each of them carried in their hands—long, vicious-looking spears. Blood raced through Jag's veins. The rumble of Spike and his diversion group entering the beach sounded from over to Jag's left. Some of the RagaRaga had horns, and they started blowing them loudly. Spike led his riders ninety degrees to the left, so they were running parallel to the sea. The RagaRaga had no horses, but they started chasing Spike's squadron on foot. Jag had never seen anyone run so fast. Three of the quickest arched their arms back as they ran and then thrust them forward, releasing their spears at the fleeing riders and carriage. Fortunately, they didn't have the strength to cover the distance, and the spears fell short of their targets, embedding themselves into the sand. Spike's riders rode at full gallop, a cloud of sand kicked up behind them, the RagaRaga in hot pursuit disappearing into the cloud. It was difficult to make out whether they were narrowing the gap. Looking down below, it seemed Marcus's plan was working; the enemy had all joined the chase, leaving no one beneath the bluff. Marcus confirmed this by looking left to right at Jag and his friends then raising a closed fist with his thumb up. At this signal, they all clambered out of their hiding places and crouched at the edge of the bluff. They would have to follow the line of the bluff south to get down to the beach. It was dangerously steep where they were now. Addford trotted back down the road to pass on the all clear to the Oze giants. The big men had remained on the track with the ponies, as they were too large to hide at the top of the bluff. The troop started making their way down the edge of the drop, starting with those at the lowest position.

Jag was at the top. He took one last look up the beach from his position. The sun was dipping fast, and a spectacular sunset was developing. There were reds, oranges, and yellows refracted by distant clouds that on any other day would have lifted his spirits. And then he saw them marching down along the water's edge, coming from the north. There must have been two hundred, maybe three hundred RagaRaga, all of them armed with swords, crossbows, or spears. He turned to alert Marcus, but their leader was already on his way down. Jag had to risk raising his voice.

"Marcus! Marcus!"

Marcus turned back towards him, and Jag, in his excitement, lost his footing. He stumbled backward. His legs churned, treading on air, as he plummeted downwards to the beach far below.

He bounced once off a ledge halfway down, which sent him ricocheting off the face of the cliff in a slow spin. He took another glancing blow a few yards farther down, and then he slammed into the sand with a gut-wrenching crunch. Every nerve in his body was screaming. Groaning, he tried to focus, determined not to black out yet again. He lay there for several minutes, wondering if he'd ever be able to walk again. and then he saw her moccasins, and her ankles, and her sun-kissed brown legs.

"Come, Jonathan Ur-Jag, you have to get up fast. I can't carry you, and the RagaRaga will be here very shortly."

She went down on her haunches, pressing a bottle to his lips. Ah, that sweet, bubbly draft, Anika. He took several gulps—much more than the first time she'd administered it to him. It hit him with a jolt; where he previously experienced pain, he now had a tingling sensation. Ulma moved away from the cliff face and signalled to someone above. She ran back, and with her help he was able to stand, but he was giddy and staggered around. He wanted to ask her how she had reached him so fast, but he had no voice.

"Jonathan Ur-Jag, the RagaRaga saw you falling. They are coming for us; we walk, or we die!"

Jag stumbled forward. Ulma took his arm, and he managed another step and then another.

"We don't have too far to go. I know a place we can hide until they pass," said Ulma. She took his hand and led him south down the beach.

Ratta-tat-tat, ratta-tat-tat. He heard them now; they had drums. Fast-paced drums. They were coming quickly...

They hobbled on as fast as Jag could manage. The drums grew louder. How far away were they? He didn't dare look back.

Ratta-tat-tat, ratta-tat-tat.

The beach tapered to a point at the end of the bay. Ulma changed their direction. A small wave lapped over Jag's feet, soaking into his farm shoes. The water was not too cold, but what was Ulma doing? She was leading them straight into the ocean.

"Take off your backpack and hold it over your head."

Jag still couldn't speak, something to do with the impact of his fall, but she must have read his expression.

"Just do it. Unless you want your precious book to be soaked."

He managed to free his arms from the straps and with her help balance it on his head. The waves were coming in up to his waist now. Was she planning on them swimming away? His leg rammed into a large rock; its apex rose just above the water. He stepped up onto it. Then next to it was another and another like a series of stepping-stones. She guided them from rock to rock.

"Here we are. We are safe here. You cannot see this place from the beach."

They stood on a large, flat boulder a few inches above the water, and Jag sank to a sitting position.

Jag looked toward the shore, and to his horror saw the front end of the RagaRaga patrol at the point where Ulma had re-directed them into the sea.

"You sure they can't see us?" croaked Jag.

"Jonathan Ur-Jag, I have spent many hours here hiding from these evil beasts. Even at midday you can't see this part of the rocks from the shore. Also, the RagaRaga don't like the seawater, so they would never walk out here."

The drumming stopped, and the patrol went totally silent. The soldier leading the line stood motionless, his torso and his head tilted to the side. Ulma held her finger against her lips. Jag nodded. For a minute, nothing happened, then the lead soldier stood up straight and pointed south. The drummers started up again, and they started marching towards the next bay.

"How many?" asked Jag, his voice a little stronger.

"Many, Jonathan Ur-Jag, but I am more concerned about the drumming."

"Yes, they are frightening."

"No, what I mean is, they play the drums as a celebration…if they have won a battle or been successful on a mission. Look…"

The dying embers from the evening's sunset provided just enough light to silhouette the endless line of troops. He had counted two hundred soldiers and could see no end. Four RagaRaga carried a long stretcher between them, and on it lay a heavily bound captive. Rope almost completely covered the prisoner, and he had a bag over his head. Jag squinted hard. The victim's muscular arm looked familiar, and there was just enough light for him to make out a tattoo of a black bull on the man's biceps.

Jag couldn't think straight for a few minutes.

Ulma was studying him. "You know the prisoner?" she asked. "The fat boy?"

He nodded. "He attacked my friends and me…back home."

Ulma craned her neck and stared intently at the passing troop. "We've been watching him for a while."

"What?" said Jag. This was all too much.

He started readying himself to head back up the beach to join his friends.

"Hold on." she whispered, pointing south down the beach, "the RagaRaga who went after Spike and his group are coming back. We go nowhere until they pass."

They kept their heads down as the patrol reached the point where Jag and Ulma had entered the water. The warriors were all staring hard in different directions. Jag's stomach knotted as the RagaRaga skirted the line of the rocks upon which he and Ulma hid. However, Ulma was right; the soldiers gave no indication of being able to see them, even when they were just yards away.

Ulma pointed north and out to sea. Following her direction, he spotted the shadowy shape of the Mensan boat riding the surf as it fought its way over the breakers. The forms of two giants at either end of the boat were all the confirmation he needed.

"What the heck? They're leaving without me!" Jag stood up, prepared to call out to his friends.

"Jonathan Ur-Jag, stop!" Ulma said forcefully. "It was known you would be separated from your friends on this trip."

"Known by who and how?" asked Jag.

"Nikolas instructed me to give you this at this time," she said, reaching into her pocket and handing him a folded letter with a large letter N on the front.

He quickly broke the seal and read aloud:

"Dear Jag,

"If you are reading this, then you have been separated from your friends. This was foreseen.

"Gillian and Freddie need to go to Espanada and deliver the bracefires to the inner-circle of the Great Cirque. As you witnessed, the bracefires have great power. This linked pair will strengthen the Cirque's hand immeasurably. But it is unlikely to be enough to turn the tide of the upcoming conflict.

"Jag, we need your help, too. Ulma will escort you to Fabrice in the region of Gonk. There, you will meet Lord Owlspin. He is our friend and ally, and you may trust him. Without his leadership and the bravery of the Gonk people, the six regions would already be subject to Leprade's rule.

"It was revealed that you have a connection with a cipher we need to obtain. You will go to Gonk, and Owlspin will give you your next instructions."

"What sort of task? What's a cipher? What is happening?" Jag folded the note and stuffed it into his backpack. "How does this help get the three of us home?"

"I am sorry, Jonathan, I do not have the answers. But we need to start now," Ulma said as she negotiated the first of the rocks that marked their way back to the beach.

Jag followed her as quickly as he could. He was still in a world of pain from his fall. He remembered seeing Gonk on the map when Nikolas had given them a geography lesson. It looked some distance from Three Widows. But the scale of the map was questionable at best. What he could say with some certainty, was that his friends were headed in the completely opposite direction.

# Chapter 11

Tiny and Freckles each had a large paddle and were using them to power the boat through the breakers rolling onto the beach. Once they had passed the break point, they picked up the pace. The swell was deceptively large, and a swooshing sensation filled Gillian's stomach as the boat pitched and rolled on the angry sea. While they'd helped dig the boat out from its hiding place both Freddie and she had demanded they find Jag. Their leader had refused, promising an explanation once they were at sea.

She looked back at the disappearing shoreline; the RagaRaga—quite a lot of them—were still in clear view, although they appeared to be moving off down the beach.

"Don't worry, they won't follow us," said Marcus, edging his way past Addford and Ink who were sitting behind Gillian. "They don't have a boat, and they're not keen on water anyway." He perched down on his haunches in front of Gillian and Freddie.

Gillian avoided eye contact. "I'm more concerned about Jag and Ulma. What will they do now? Return to Three Widows?"

Marcus looked down for a moment. "Nikolas believes Jag has a different role to play. He will be tracking the second group of Raga with Ulma and then paying a visit to Gonk."

"What!" both Gillian and Freddie yelled together.

"This is not Jag's war," said Freddie. "I seriously doubt he'll be anything other than a hindrance to Ulma. Why would he want to go to Gonk? Isn't that where all the fighting is going on?"

Gillian had so many questions coming into her head she didn't know where to start.

"That's ridiculous! How could Nikolas have known there would be a second group of RagaRaga?" she said slamming her fist into the palm of her other hand.

"Actually, you have an interest in that RagaRaga unit. They have a captive we believe you know," said Marcus.

Gillian's mind was racing.

"In fact, he's been tough to track. He wandered around the Western Wastes, seemingly with no idea where he was heading. He has a tattoo of a bull on his arm."

For a moment, Gillian and Freddie were speechless.

"Pinhorn. How long have you known about him?" asked Gillian, anger rising in her voice again.

"About the same length of time you have neglected to mention that he was with you," replied Marcus firmly.

"But he wasn't with us. He's no friend of ours. In fact, he was chasing us down the tunnel with the intention of hurting us," said Freddie.

"And you didn't think that was worth mentioning to us?" said Marcus.

Gillian opened her mouth to reply but realized she didn't have an answer.

*****

The day had been fairly mild, but with nightfall temperatures plummeted. Gillian was wearing all the clothes she possessed. Although the farmworkers' outfits were well insulated, she'd need a set of thermal underwear and a parka to ward off the damp cold that was causing her to shiver so much now. Freddie wrapped a blanket around her shoulders and pulled her gently towards him.

"Now, I don't want you getting any ideas, madam," he said quietly. "This is per my old Boy Scout survival manual...and only because neither of us fancies a dose of hypothermia."

Gillian laughed.

"But if it keeps our commanding officer from seeking your warmth, then that is a bonus!"

"Ha!" replied Gillian. "No amount of suffering would induce me to allow him anywhere near me. I hope he freezes his nuts off!" She rested her head in the space between his shoulder and his neck.

The temperature dropped still further as they moved away from the land. The pitching and rolling worsened, too. A pretty miserable night lay ahead of them. At the briefing back in Three Widows, Marcus had estimated it would take them approximately thirteen hours to make the crossing. The Hag and the Spindle pirates generally only attacked their prey during daylight, so it made sense to use all ten hours of darkness. Freddie, of course, fell asleep and managed to stay asleep. Addford was not much of a sailor and spent most of the next few hours with his head over the side of the boat. Gillian felt sorry for him and tried to talk to him, but he appeared to be focusing all his efforts on trying to ward off unrelenting waves of nausea. Dell and Marcus shared the rudder duties in half-hour shifts. The two men spent much of the time deep in conversation, pointing animatedly at the night sky. After a few minutes, she realized they were navigating by the stars.

The stars! This was the first time they had been clearly visible since she and her friends had arrived on the Turn. She scanned the sky from horizon to horizon. They were spectacularly beautiful, sparkling like brilliant diamonds against a background of dark velvet. But she didn't recognize any of the constellations. She was no astronomer but vaguely recalled learning that different formations were visible from different parts of the world. While the unfamiliar night sky didn't mean they weren't still on Earth, it definitely made it more unlikely. Jonathan would probably know.

Poor Jonathan! Every time she thought of him, she became racked with guilt. They shouldn't have left him behind; they should have refused to leave the mainland without him. Nikolas had pre-planned this. They were being used. She had mixed feelings about Freddie. She respected his unyielding loyalty to his friend, but Freddie hadn't fought that hard against leaving Jag behind. How odd that they had given in so easily... Was there something else at work here?

The night dragged on, and Gillian fell into a stupor, too tired to stay awake and too cold and uncomfortable to stay asleep. At one point, she thought she was hallucinating. A small sphere came into her view and remained floating there for several seconds, bobbing around in front of her eyes. It didn't alarm her in any way; in fact, she found its presence rather comforting. She felt as though it was observing her, making sure she was okay. Was it a bubble? She reached out to touch it, but it was too quick for her, accelerating away over the sea. She closed her eyes and fell asleep.

Someone tapped Gillian on her shoulder, and she jumped. Blinking to clear her vision, she looked up at Ink.

"Take one box and one bottle." Ink lowered a container full of boxes and cartons.

Gillian did so and raised her brow, giving Ink a questioning look. The boxes were hot! How had she pulled off such a trick? No way could you cook anything on an open deck in these conditions.

"You don't have angel fire where you come from?" Ink asked. She lifted the box, and underneath it was a recess where small blue and red flames danced around, heating the metal plate above. "The flames are created by mixing two minerals together—Cale and Rion. The flames themselves are not hot, so there is no danger of setting the boat alight! All the heat is generated above them. The box contains pork meal, prepared by Madam Nan herself!" Ink produced a pin from her belt, and she pierced the top of the bottle. Steam rushed out of the hole with a screeching noise. "Hot lemon elixir. It'll warm you up in seconds and make you feel a whole lot better!"

"Thanks, Ink. I don't think we should wake Freddie; he's in a better place right now!"

Freddie had slid off Gillian as soon as he'd fallen asleep and lay curled up on the deck, half under the bench. "I'm not sure Addford is going to want to eat right now, either."

They both stifled their laughter as they looked at the forlorn Three Widows prosecutor. He was sitting with his head between his knees.

Ink was right. Madam Nan's pork dish was hot and delicious, and the spice-infused meat was tender and full of flavour. On the side, there were creamy mashed potatoes, fresh carrots, and peas. The hot lemon elixir set Gillian's whole body tingling as it spread much needed warmth. By the time the warming effects of the nourishment began to wear off, she spotted the first welcome hint of the approaching new day on the eastern horizon.

Tiny and Freckles were astonishing. They never let up on the paddles at all, driving them through the water, port and starboard, in perfect time. Tiny's face gave nothing away. She wondered if they enjoyed rowing non-stop for thirteen hours.

Yes, little flower, we love to work. Tiny and Freckles are very happy paddlers.

Again, Tiny's unexpected response to her thought gave her a jolt. Gillian laughed, half in embarrassment. She was going to have learn how to control her thoughts around these Oze giants!

"We're about two hours away," shouted Marcus.

Things were improving, thought Gillian. The swell had subsided considerably, and the first rays of the morning sun were now catching the boat, bathing them in a silver glow.

"Okay," Marcus continued, "we're on the most dangerous part of the journey now, and I need everyone's help."

"Hey, Freddie, wake up!" Gillian said and shook the sleeping boy's shoulder.

He sat up with a start, banging his head against the underside of the bench. He pulled himself up groggily and sat on the bench next to Gillian. "I was playing a nice game of cricket," he muttered.

"We need to watch for hostile boats. They can come from any direction, and they move fast. The islanders around here are expert sailors. The quicker we spot them, the better chance we have to outrun them. I want everyone to scan the horizon, and shout if you spot anything."

"How do we know if they're hostile?" asked Freddie, wiping the sleep out of his eyes. "Boy, am I hungry."

"Assume any boat you see is hostile. Dell and I will take it from there," replied Marcus.

"So that includes the three behind us?" Freddie pointed over Marcus's shoulder.

"Freddie, I am deadly serious; there are some very bad—"

Freddie continued to point and mouthed the word, "Look."

Marcus turned around and did a doubletake. Gillian looked up to see three large sailboats. They were tracking the line of their boat's wash.

"By Brunella!" yelled Marcus. "Tiny, Freckles, pick it up if you can. Dell, Freddie, let's get some sail up; we're going to need it. Ink, make sure everyone's armed."

Dell had a telescope trained on the pursuers.

"Hag boarding ships—this is not going to be a lot of fun," he shouted.

"The rat strikes again! No way is this meeting a coincidence!" said Marcus.

Ink held out a small dirk to Gillian.

"What's that?" she asked.

"We will need to fight if we can't outrun them; the Hag are savages," said Ink, offering her a longer knife.

"I don't know how to fight. There's not much call for it where we come from," said Gillian, her eyes tearing up. How did they end up in this nightmare? Why couldn't she wake up?

Freddie seemed relatively calm. He pulled out and inspected several different weapons from the box. For a moment Gillian thought he was going to stick with his cricket bat, but then he found a cast iron catapult and several boxes of ball bearings.

"Ah, these might be worth a go!" he said, nodding.

Freddie gathered up the items and then clambered over the benches to the stern of the boat, where Marcus was steering.

"The sails?" he asked Marcus.

"It's no good, Freddie," said Marcus in a low voice. "They have twice our speed-with or without sails. "

"So, what's the plan?"

"We're going to attack them."

Dell dropped the telescope. "Have you gone mad?"

"If anyone can offer a better alternative, I'm all ears,' said Marcus. "We can't negotiate, and we can't outrun them. Our only option is to fight, so let us at least fight them on our own terms."

Gillian looked over Marcus's shoulder. In the short time since Freddie had spotted them, the three Hag boarding ships had halved the distance to their target.

"We let them chase us until they are five hundred yards off. Then we swing around and go straight at the lead boat. They won't be expecting it, and that's why we might have a chance. We are going to take their boat from them."

"How many Hag will be on each boat?" Freddie stared back at their pursuers.

"They usually have a crew of about twenty," replied Dell, "and it's likely that all are experienced fighters. I know those odds don't sound good, but we do have a couple of Oze giants on our team. That evens things up a bit."

Gillian frowned. What about the bracefires and the extraordinary power generated by the two when they were linked? Couldn't they use them somehow?

"We are going to ram straight into the bow of the lead boat. Their deck will be several feet higher than ours, but I think Tiny and I can find a way up. We'll take care of any initial resistance. We'll fix a rope—you will need to get across as quickly as possible—and Freckles will help you. Dell first, then Ink, followed by Gillian, Addford, Freddie, and Freckles."

There was no time for further discussion. They lined up as directed by Marcus. The chasing ships were very close now. Each boat was several times larger than theirs. Large, rectangular white sails embroidered with a big, ornate letter H swept them along. Gillian could make out the Hag soldiers now; they were lined up on either side of the boats. Most of them had beards and wore pointed, steel helmets and red tunics. Each held a long spear. As they drew closer, their voices carried over the water.

"Aye Aye Aye! Aye Aye Aye!"

Gillian's mouth went dry at the sound of their blood-chilling war cry, and she began shaking violently. She clasped the handle of the dagger Ink had given her. The weapon was totally inadequate.

"Okay, we go at five hundred," yelled Marcus. "We're at nine hundred, eight hundred…"

The lead boat grew bigger and bigger as it closed down on them. Gillian half covered her eyes.

"Seven hundred, six hundred. Okay, steady and about—hard to port!" cried Marcus, pulling the rudder as far as he could to his right.

At the same time, Tiny thrust his paddle straight down into the sea on the port side while Freckles stroked faster on the starboard side. The boat pitched and groaned but obediently carved its way into an abrupt U-turn. The change in momentum almost knocked Gillian off her feet. Addford did fall, but luckily, he landed on the deck. Freddie helped him to his feet.

Once in line, Tiny and Freckles drove their paddles hard into the green sea, and the little boat accelerated through the water. They were on course for a very fast head-on collision with the lead chaser. The Hags yelled, no doubt surprised at the sudden manoeuvre, but there was no time for any adjustment. There was an almighty crack and a sickening thud as bow met bow. Everyone in the Mensan boat flew forward onto the deck. Pandemonium reigned. The front of the boat lifted out of the water by about thirty degrees. As Gillian scrambled to try to get to her feet, Marcus and Tiny jumped onto the pirate boat. The lifting of their bow had made the jump relatively easy. Seconds later, their boat lurched back and then made a grinding sound as it rubbed against the hull of the larger boat on its descent. Gillian couldn't see the fight on the pirate boat—the Hag deck was too high—but she heard the clash of weapons and the yelling and shouting of combat.

A rope lowered from the Hag deck. Dell caught it, pulled it tight, and started shimmying his way up.

A flash of light caught Gillian's eye. There it was again—that bubble or sphere or whatever it was. The glowing orb hovered just above where Marcus had dropped the rope. Did anyone else see it? Why hadn't she asked them earlier?

Dell finally yanked himself onto the pirate deck out of sight. She couldn't do that! A well-trained gymnast would struggle with that stunt, and she was no gymnast. She looked around, but the sphere had disappeared. Ink followed Dell, and she made it look even easier. She pulled herself up the rope and swung herself over the top rail. She was out of sight in seconds. It was Gillian's turn, but there was no way.

A large hand rested gently on her shoulder.

I will help, Little Flower.

The words formed in her head. This was the first time Freckles had communicated with her. His voice was distinct from his brother's...slightly higher pitched but with the same warm glow.

He wrapped his arm around her waist, reached up with his other hand, and grabbed the rope. He pulled against the rope and with extraordinary strength lifted them both clear off the deck. She clung to him, which freed him to use both hands, and he reached up as far as he could. She could just about clasp the deck of the pirate boat with the tips of her fingers. The movement of the two boats made this very precarious. She released her grip on Freckles so she could pull herself up. The deck of the Hag boat was fractured and from it, pin sharp splinters impaled themselves in her fingers. Trying to blank out the pain, Gillian edged herself over to the pirate vessel just as a large Hag pirate came into view. He peered down at her and raised an axe high above him. She was sure the blow was destined for her exposed fingers, but there was nothing she could do. He grinned toothlessly at her, and Gillian closed her eyes. But his axe never swung forward. She heard a loud crack and opened her eyes to see a ball bearing planted in his forehead. He staggered and toppled forward over the edge of his boat. As he fell, his body caught her a glancing blow. The impact almost took her down with him, but she managed to cling to the ship as her attacker hit the water below. Adrenalin coursing through her veins, she pulled herself up and rolled onto the deck.

The scene was mayhem. Clouds of smoke from torches that the Hag were carrying made visibility hard, but there were battles going on everywhere. Tiny had two of the pirates in headlocks. He walked them slowly to the edge of the boat and threw them both overboard. Marcus and Ink were in a confrontation with four Hag pirates brandishing cutlass-shaped swords. They had the Mensans trapped against a wheelhouse. Their swords flashed in the early morning sun as they delivered a withering attack. Marcus wielded his broadsword, catching them with skilfully delivered counterblows. Alongside him, Ink used her speed and agility to avoid the vicious blades, but she was struggling. Still hyped up from her dramatic boarding, Gillian ran headlong into the fracas. She drove her dirk into the shoulder of the tallest Hag. He yelled out in pain and swung around, Gillian lost her grip on her weapon, which remained embedded in the infuriated Hag. He swung his cutlass at her and cut her forearm as she staggered backward. She fell onto her back as he brought the sword around, ready to strike her with a fatal blow. But Ink drove a short blade into his chest, and he collapsed in a heap. At the same time, Marcus swung a large arc with his broadsword and knocked the cutlasses out of the hands of two of the assailants. They both fell to their knees, seeking mercy, and the fourth pirate ran off, looking for an easier battle.

"Off the boat!" roared Marcus. "Maybe your friends will pick you up!"

The remaining two pirates crawled to the edge of the boat and tumbled into the water.

Out of the corner of her eye, Gillian saw Addford staggering along the deck, the smoke blinding him. Nearby, Freddie had assumed a semi-crouched stance with his catapult held out at arm's length in one hand and a bearing ready to fire in the delivery pouch.

Freddie looked her way. "To me, to me, watch out!"

She ran towards him. A projectile whistled past her ear, followed by a thud and a sharp yelp. She turned to see a Hag bent double on the deck; a spear dropped in front of him. She ran over to her classmate.

"That's twice you've extended my life in five minutes, Fast Freddie!" she said.

"I'll send you the bill," said Freddie.

Marcus appeared out of the smoke. "Well done, you two! Are you okay?" He spoke between gulps for breath. "I think we've got it, just waiting for Ink to check in."

As he finished the words Ink emerged from below deck.

"We're clear below Marcus," said Ink.

The Mensans whooped and cheered. Freddie pumped his fist, and Gillian smiled with relief. Tiny and Freckles whistled quietly to themselves as they cleared the debris off the deck.

"Okay, this isn't over, guys," yelled Marcus. He was watching the other two boats, which, having initially overshot their target, were now doubling back towards them. "Dell, can you sail this thing?"

'I'm on it," shouted his brother as he worked on the rigging.

Gillian looked over to the right. Two of the crewmembers they had thrown into the sea had managed to board the Mensan boat and were trying to raise the mast. Several more were treading water, waving to their comrades for help.

"Won't they switch their attention to rescuing their survivors?" she asked.

"Don't count on it,' said Marcus. "They'd sell their own mothers for half a silver piece."

Their mainsail flapped loosely for a few seconds. Dell was working the wheel as fast as he could. The boat edged around in place, going nowhere, and the sails continued to flap uselessly. They were very vulnerable with the two remaining Hag boats bearing down on them fast. The slow tack finally put them in position, and right on time, the south-westerly breeze picked up. The mainsail billowed out. A split second later, they were skimming along at high speed. Once again, they cheered. Addford, who had finally managed to stand up, grinned and slapped Dell on the back.

Gillian made her way to the front of the boat, where Freddie had been helping Dell and Ink work the ropes.

"I didn't know you had sailing experience. When did you learn how to crew a sail boat?"

"About five minutes ago!" Freddie laughed.

They were on a heading that would take them to the left of the two remaining pirate vessels.

"Great job, Dell! Hold this line steady," yelled Marcus. He was rifling through documents he had brought up from the lower deck.

"Do you think we're safe now?" Gillian asked Freddie, her hands clasped together, as if in prayer.

"Unless they have some way of stopping us, we're going to run past them at high speed. They will have to make U-turns and then tack around to chase us. It will take them forever."

A few minutes later, the boats flashed past each other. There was no question of repeating the ramming strategy, thought Gillian. At this combined speed, the impact would surely destroy all boats involved.

"Yes!" shouted Freddie, grabbing Gillian's shoulders.

At that precise moment, they heard a loud boom from behind them. They all looked around. A projectile hurtled in their direction, powering towards them on a low trajectory and passing about fifty feet above them with an ear-piercing screech. It hit the water about two hundred yards ahead of them. At the point of impact, the sea water exploded upward, an eruption of boiling vapor and steam. The shock generated a wave that grew larger by the millisecond as it raced away from the explosion in an expanding circle. Gillian and Freddie stared as it approached their boat. There was no way to avoid it. The wave grew...ten feet high, twenty, forty, eighty...

The wave met their ship, and they found themselves riding up the face as if they were in an express elevator. The angle was so steep, Gillian was convinced the boat was going to topple backward. She grabbed hold of Freddie as they reached the apex of the wave. For a full second, it felt like they were weightless, balanced on top of the wave. Then slowly the bow started dipping, revealing a near-vertical drop. They accelerated into a sickeningly fast freefall. When they hit the trough on the other side, the boat shuddered as the front end became immersed in water. A deafening cracking noise pierced the air. Sea water gushed at them from every direction.

"Whoa!" yelled Freddie.

A fracture ran across the width of the boat, dividing the deck in two. They jumped over it and raced to join the rest of their crew. Dell and Ink were sitting down, recovering from the impact of the fall. Addford stood holding on to a rail, his face ashen.

Two more spheres arrived. They darted around like early morning bees, hovering in front of a crew member's face before racing away at high speed to observe another. She was about to say something to Freddie when Tiny's voice formed in her head.

Yes, Little Flower, they are watching us.

"Who?" she blurted out. "Who's watching us?"

"What are you talking about?" asked Freddie.

Friends.

Marcus ran up the steps. "It's bad," he said. "We've got water coming in from several places. We're going down."

Addford stepped forward. "Marcus, we have to get Gillian and Freddie to Espanada; the rest of us are expendable."

"Agreed," said Marcus, "all our resources need to be prioritized accordingly."

"Rubbish," called out Freddie. "The priority is to save everyone!"

"Agreed," said Gillian. As she spoke, the boat lurched alarmingly to starboard.

"We only have one option. Tiny, Freckles, are you capable of swimming to shore and taking these two with you?" Marcus asked.

The giant brothers exchanged looks and then silent words. Gillian did her best to listen in, but they communicated too quickly.

Ink, however, followed their conversation and jumped into the discussion.

"It's about twenty miles."

Another minute passed, and then Ink nodded at the giants and updated the others. "They think they can do it, but they are not sure."

"Fair enough," said Marcus. "Tiny, you will look after Freddie. Freckles, you take care of Gillian. You have one objective and one only; get them to Espanada. The rest of us will be decoys. The longer we can keep swimming and avoid being picked up by the Hags, the more time we buy our bracefire holders to make good their escape."

"Look to stern. To stern!" yelled Dell.

Gillian swung her head around and almost choked when she saw the Hag boats just a hundred yards away. How had they avoided the tidal wave? The pirates had lowered their sails.

Gillian scowled. Probably waiting for our boat to sink so they can move in and pluck a few high-value targets from the sea.

There was another loud crack, and the deck lurched, knocking Gillian off her feet. The hull of their boat was almost vertical. The only thing preventing her from sliding off the boat was her vice-like grip of the rail. Freddie was clinging to the same rail. Addford wasn't so lucky. He slid the length of the deck before being swallowed by the sea. Frothy seawater bubbled over the submerged bow. She could feel the vibration of water rushing beneath her feet. They had seconds left.

Freckles had somehow managed to traverse the deck, and he gripped her shoulder. Tiny had performed a similar manoeuvre to secure Freddie. Everyone else seemed to have disappeared.

"Fade Spheres!" yelled Ink. "Fade Spheres, praise be, Brunella!"

Gillian couldn't see Ink, but her voice came from somewhere above. Then Gillian saw the cause of Ink's excitement. Hovering just above them was a giant bubble, similar to the orbs she had seen earlier but much bigger.

*Little Flower, trust Freckles.* The Oze giant tied his feet to the railing with a piece of rope, then he gently lifted Gillian, using his tied foot for leverage.

Freddie's legs dangled from above her. From the waist up, his body was inside the bubble. Tiny stood below, pushing Freddie upward by his feet. Freddie was sucked in, and Tiny dived away, making a large splash beneath them. The deck rocked violently. The boat accelerated downward. Freckles gave one more push on the soles of Gillian's feet, and her head and torso squeezed through the skin of the bubble. Freddie grabbed her arms and pulled her all the way in. As soon as her legs and feet were inside, the bubble re-sealed. She lay flat on the inside of the strange craft, listening to Freddie as he tried to catch his breath.

They were ascending rapidly. Below them, Tiny had located Addford who was struggling to stay afloat. Tiny swam over to the town official and hooked his arm round the man's torso. Then he slowly dragged Addford away from what little of the boat remained above water. One of the large bubbles floated down to sea level, and in a show of strength, Tiny hauled the bedraggled Addford up and into the orb. There was a loud roar of compressed air escaping the doomed vessel as it disappeared. The rope Freckles had used to secure his feet when he'd helped Gillian was still tied to the boat, and the other end was snagged around his ankle. Swimming on his back, he tried in vain to free his foot. Then in an instant he was gone, dragged down into the deep by the sinking boat.

Gillian screamed, "Freckles!"

But there was nothing she could do for him. Air bubbles rose from the point at which he had gone down. At first, they were large and frequent, but as time passed, they grew smaller and less frequent and then smaller yet, until eventually, there were no more.

# Chapter 12

Jag, hands on his knees, looked up at Ulma. "I'm completely knackered." They were standing in a clearing located in an area of dense woodland. The forest marked the border between the Western Wastes and Samatra.

Twenty-four hours had passed since they had laid low in the rocky outcrop and watched the RagaRaga pass by with Pinhorn. Ulma hadn't allowed any delay once they had passed. She'd led them briskly southward, following the coastline. They had walked through the night, stopping only for a few minutes' rest each hour. Their only sustenance was bread and sharp cheese, the kind Ulma had shared with him back at the farm. Ulma also had a flask of Anika water, which they had sipped sparingly.

Jag's fall from the bluff had left him with a few injuries. His ribs were severely bruised, and he had numerous cuts and grazes. The shock and the adrenaline rush from subsequent near encounters with the RagaRaga had masked the pain. But once things calmed down, he was in a lot of trouble. At their first rest stop, Ulma had found a secluded spot in among some large dunes. She'd dropped a liberal dose of Anika onto some floss and carefully rubbed it into his cuts and grazes. She had a surprisingly gentle touch for such a dynamic girl. Her half smile suggested she had finally got over the reading incident back at the farm.

After they'd followed the coastline for several hours, the light had returned to the east as night slowly gave way to morning.

Ulma had pointed at a single large palm tree standing close to the water's edge. "The Lonely Tree."

She'd made a sharp left onto a very old, indistinct trail. Ahead of them lay the rugged, barren landscape of the southern half of the Western Wastes. Ulma had pushed them even harder, encouraging and cajoling Jag whenever he had showed signs his energy was flagging. Around midday he had seen the first trees lining the trail ahead. They were a welcome sight after the hours of brutal, featureless landscape. They stood like sentinels on either side of the path, guiding Jag and Ulma out of the Wastes. As they'd progressed, the trees had become taller and stood closer together, losing their sentinel-like effect. They encroached onto the path and had slowed Ulma and Jag's progress. The trees became a forest. Jag and Ulma climbed higher and higher—so high the altitude change made Jag's ears start popping. There were birds on the upper branches of the trees. Their melodic calls were comforting. Ulma, who had been decidedly edgy from the moment they'd left the rocks, had finally appeared to be more relaxed.

Eventually, they'd found the clearing they stood in now, a small oasis of grassland within the densely packed woodlands.

"We sleep here tonight," Ulma declared.

Jag puffed out his cheeks in relief. He was exhausted and ready to keel over. He'd never walked so far in his life.

"I have only a few morsels of food left. From here on, we start living off the land." Ulma crouched next to Jag, rubbing two sticks together.

"Oh, dear, that's a bit worrying," Jag replied. "I've never had to do that before."

"Jonathan Ur-Jag!" exclaimed Ulma. "Do you have any idea how many times I've been in this situation before? This is what I do! Also, we are in a region famous for its food. We will eat like Cirque Lords while we are within the borders of Samatra. You wait here and keep the fire going—no bigger than it is now, though, unless you would like the RagaRaga to join us for supper."

Jag had several concerns about this plan - he didn't want to be left alone in this place, for one. But before he could open his mouth to speak, she was gone, gliding silently into the darkening forest.

As she disappeared, so did his relaxed mood. He became acutely aware of his surroundings. The RagaRaga could walk into the clearing without notice, and he would be helpless. Then what would happen? Would they kill him straight away or save him for an even worse fate? He remembered seeing Pinhorn bound in all that rope, totally at their mercy. Jag actually felt sorry for him. As the light faded, the birdsong halted, and other noises emanated from the forest, many of them disturbing. He peered into the dark shadows cast by the trees, hoping to see Ulma returning. Were those eyes he caught a glimpse of? Two sets of eyes? He closed his eyes tightly, then looked again, but they were gone. A shiver ran up his spine. There was definitely an animal out there, breaking forest debris underfoot. Or could it be Ulma?

He closed his eyes again. He had to stay calm. Eventually, after an hour of misery, he dug into his backpack and retrieved his journal. A good distraction.

"Time to update," he said. Soon, he lost himself in thought as he listed all that had happened since his previous update.

Had Freddie and Gillian reached Espanada yet? Surely, they must have done. Marcus had described the island as being an overnight trip away, in which case, they would have arrived there that morning. How would they contact him to let him know if they had found a way back? There were no phones here. How did people communicate over long distances? He put his journal to one side. It wasn't helping.

His head was full of all sorts of worries again, riding the edge of a full-blown panic attack. He had been through this many times before, though not recently. Sometimes, he ended up having to take an emergency trip to the doctor. He couldn't afford to have a breakdown now; he had to keep it together.

He reached into his pack and pulled out the book from Nikolas. Reading would be a good distraction! Jag remembered the elder's advice and rather than start at the beginning, leafed through the pages until he found the first bookmark.

"Hey, O' learned one, would you read it aloud? Maybe while I prepare supper?"

Jag nearly jumped out of his skin. Ulma stood next to him, her arms full of supplies. She had a small rabbit, which she had already half prepared, several root vegetables, and a variety of bushy green plants.

"Ulma, you scared me. I'm hungry, but I'm not sure about the rabbit. It looks, err, it looks too much like a rabbit!"

Ulma scowled at him. "You are very lucky. Samatra rabbit is famous throughout the Turn! Of course, it looks like rabbit! What did you expect? I suppose where you come from food is all cut to size and wrapped up in a nice package?"

"Well, actually..." Jonathan gave her a sideways look.

"Okay, Jonathan Ur-Jag! Enough of your fantasy world. Read the story while I cook a meal you will never forget!" said Ulma. She twirled her knife skilfully as she started peeling the potatoes.

Jag angled the book towards the fire so he could see the small, dark print. Nikolas had put six markers in the volume. Jag opened the page at the first and began reading.

"The Orphan.

"Before the founding of the Great Cirque and the establishment of the six regions there was no central or local authority in the fertile valley that lay south of the Maria Mountains. There were no militias to protect the residents and no government departments to coordinate and promote adherence to fair trading. There were no healing guilds to pool medical knowledge and develop strategies against deadly illnesses. Accordingly, the farmers were forced to make a living without protection and with limited resources. They lived and worked in small hamlets consisting of four or five dwellings, each trusting to luck or to their deities that they would not fall victim to one of the many ways of dying young.

"Ten-year-old Robert lived with his parents in the smallest of a four-house hamlet grouped together in the central valley. His father worked as a hand on a pig farm, typical of the area. As a hand, his father was on the lowest rung of the social and economic ladder, had no assets of his own—the small shack their family called home belonged to his employer—and he could not save enough from his meagre earnings to set out on his own.

"It was a brutally hard life. Robert couldn't remember a time when he was not hungry. The winter months, in particular, were tough. The weather was cold, and their small home inadequately insulated to keep the three of them warm. All the villagers lived in daily fear of the raiding parties that came from afar to rob and pillage what little they had. But there was one thing they feared more—the plague. It was a frequent visitor in those days, brought to their region by rats migrating from the south. Highly contagious, the disease wiped out whole families and sometimes entire communities. Once a victim was infected, the disease ran its course quickly; from the first symptoms of discolouration of the skin until the patient died would rarely take more than two days. However, those two days brought indescribable suffering to the victim. Robert was soon to witness this first hand. The area he lived in took a major hit during one of the outbreaks. He could only watch and cry helplessly as the cruel disease took both his parents. When they were finally at rest, Robert waited for his turn, checking his skin every few hours. But no lesions appeared. Against all the odds, he never caught the virus. But for a ten-year-old orphan living in his circumstances, the outlook was still bleak. His father's employer quickly reclaimed the house in which Robert had been raised, so he was homeless and penniless. He was too young to have any value as a worker, and he looked set for a life of begging, abuse, and, in all likelihood, a premature death. He decided to leave the area and take his chances somewhere else. He was standing at the crossroads near his old house, wondering which direction he should go, when a distantly related uncle by the name of Brough came by on his horse. Brough was a huge man. He pulled up his mount and though he knew about the passing of Robert's parents asked him for all the details. Brough nodded once when Robert had finished, offered no sympathy, and asked him no further questions.

" 'I can give you shelter for three days, four at the most. But after that, you are on your own. Hop up!' Brough said, patting the horse's hindquarters.

"The shelter turned out to be one his uncle's pigpens, but Robert wasn't complaining—it was better than the alternative. His uncle even gave Robert scraps from the family's table. He was wise enough to know that his best chance of survival was to impress his uncle by working as hard as he could in the hope the man might extend Robert's stay or perhaps even employ him indefinitely. For three days, he worked himself to the point of exhaustion. He assumed all the duties required of a pig hand, using the knowledge he had gained when helping his father. His uncle's son, Boniface, a skinny, blond-haired teenager who was responsible for tending the swine, was delighted with Robert's contribution. In fact, Robert was such an effective worker that Boniface was confident Robert was more than capable of handling all the daily tasks alone. Boniface took full advantage. After Robert's second day, his cousin told Robert to cover for him and disappeared for an hour. The next day, Boniface's absences grew longer and more frequent. Then, on the fourth day, Robert's uncle arrived unexpectedly to see how things were going. When he discovered his son had neglected his work and had gone off, he was apoplectic with rage. He cursed his son and hurled the pigs' feed tray across the yard. And though it was no fault of Robert's, his uncle slapped him hard about the face three times, causing him to fall to the ground, his cheeks and jaw stinging sharply.

"The next morning, Uncle Brough awoke Robert before dawn. He scampered quickly from the sty to find his uncle standing there, his large body silhouetted against the early dawn sky. Behind him stood Boniface, head bowed contritely. He appeared to be holding something.

"Uncle Brough fumbled for words, sounding uncomfortable and apologetic. 'Well, boy, I'll not going to mince words here. You have to go. I know it's not your doing, but my good-for-nothing son has put me in a hole.' Without looking behind, his uncle swung his arm backward and caught Boniface a glancing blow to the head.

"Boniface cried out in pain.

"Uncle Brough continued. 'I had hoped that the lazy git would use you effectively to grow the stock. I should have known better.

" 'I tell no lie when I say I considered throwing him out and offering you his place in the family. But blood speaks strongest, and so, that's the way of it. I know it will be hard, but you are strong and that will hold you in good stead—if luck be with you. Also, there is this…'

"There was a pause, then his uncle swung his arms back, and the knuckles of one large hand caught his cousin squarely on the mouth. Boniface emitted another yelp of pain.

" 'Pass it over, you imbecile!'

"His cousin stumbled forward and held out the object he had been holding. It was a small piglet no bigger than Robert's cupped hands. Robert took hold of the tiny pink creature and pressed it gently to his chest.

" 'She's a sow—the runt of the litter and still as likely to die as not. I was going to give her to the dogs last night, and then I thought of you. Raymond across the way will give you a little milk if you approach him right. But don't return here looking for handouts; we have barely enough to sustain us as it is.'

"Ejected from his uncle's farm, Robert sought help from Raymond. Luckily, it turned out his Uncle's neighbour was a kind man. He not only gave Robert a skin full of warm milk but let him sleep in the barn with the three dairy cattle. Once again, Robert set to work, determined to prove his worth to his new benefactor. He put all his energy into the running of the small farm. Raymond and his son, Drake, lived alone; they, too, had lost their family to plague. Every minute Robert wasn't helping with the farm duties, he focused on nursing the piglet. He fashioned a piece of tree bark into a funnel and used it to direct drips of milk into the piglet's mouth. Day by day it grew, at first very slowly, but as time passed its growth rate accelerated. Soon, it was a healthy piglet and then a fine-looking pig. Its food consumption rate became an issue—there wasn't much to go around for the three of them and little in the way of scraps. Raymond offered to take the pig to market and sell it to the butcher so they could realize its value before it ate them out of house and home. But young Robert had other plans and after some discussion persuaded Raymond to support him. When the time came, the two of them took the sow back to his uncle's house. The giant pig man roared his approval when he saw how well Robert had grown the pig. He summoned his son from the lower field and had Boniface look at the strapping sow. Then Uncle Brough slapped his son hard on the back of the head, admonishing him for not being more like Robert. Boniface glared at Robert with ill-concealed hatred, but Robert ignored his cousin. His uncle offered to buy back the pig, but Robert looked him in the eye and said no. Raymond took two paces back as Robert proceeded to negotiate a deal with his uncle. After ten minutes of haggling, Robert got the exact terms he had promised Raymond in their earlier discussion.

"Robert was very fond of his first pig. She even ended up with a name—though this had more to do with Drake's poor letter skills than anything Robert instigated. Drake used to brand the pigs on his father's farm. The process was very simple: first letter of owner's name followed by sequential number. Raymond's animals had always been marked with a *D* in honour of Drake. They would use *R* for Robert's stock. But Drake mistakenly used the letter *I* instead of the number *1*. Brough saw the branding on Robert's first pig and roared with laughter.

" 'RI—it sounds like Rye!' he said.

"The name stuck with her for the rest of her days.

"When the time was right, they bred Rye with his uncle's best boar, and she was soon expecting her first litter. As agreed, Brough supplied additional food, which he sent 'round to Raymond's farm. The sow yielded twelve piglets, all of which survived. For his part of the bargain, Robert gave Brough the first three picks of the litter.

"Within eighteen months, Robert had a successful business on his hands. He'd paid off his uncle and was able to breed his own stock. The first piglets grew large and strong and were ready for market, and the money started coming in. It became so successful that within two years Raymond re-structured the farm's operation to the exclusive production of swine.

"These should have been happy days for Raymond, but his health started to fail. He knew his days were numbered, and his main concern was to ensure Drake's well-being. Raymond summoned Robert and put a proposal to him—a share in the ownership of the farm in exchange for his word he would look after Drake. The three reached an agreement that ownership of the property would be passed on and split between Drake and Robert. The old man died of a fever a few weeks later. On his death bed Raymond insisted he was ready to go, but both boys were grief stricken at his passing. Robert owed the old man so much. He was true to his word and looked after Drake as if he were a younger brother. Robert was determined to comply with the old man's wish. The years passed, and everything went well. The farm continued to grow and was strengthened by an alliance with his Uncle Brough whose fortunes were similarly on the up.

"Then one autumn day, tragedy struck. Robert and Drake were due to ride over to a nearby crop farm to discuss a deal on animal feed. Just as they were about to leave, one of the hands brought word that their lower field was flooding, and the pigs were on the verge of drowning. Robert had to stay and deal with the crisis. He fully trusted Drake to negotiate a good deal for them and sent him on alone.

"Robert received the bad news from his Uncle Brough. A group of twelve mounted raiders attacked the farm Drake had been visiting. They killed everyone. An arrow had struck Drake, piercing his skull and burying itself in the back of his head. He died instantly.

"Robert was devastated and racked with guilt. Raymond had asked only one thing of Robert, and he had failed. He told his uncle about the promise he had given Raymond.

" 'Oh, come now, boy! Drake was a grown man. It wasn't Raymond's intention that you molly coddle the boy for the rest of your days. I've never known these raids to take place in broad daylight before. You had no way of knowing. Had you been there as you intended, you'd be dead now, too.'

"That night they shared a large flagon of rough cider as they discussed what measures they could take to defend themselves. This was the third such attack that year and the first in daylight. They concluded they needed guards. Brough said two should do the trick. Robert had suggested they needed more, reminding his uncle that a dozen or more armed men often made up the groups of raiders.

" 'Ah, now,' said his uncle, grinning, 'that'd be a waste of our hard-earned coin. How many guards does Woakes have? Or Frimley? Or Jacob? None and none and none again—three farms, all near enough the same size as ours, none with guards though. These raiders ain't stupid; they want reward but at the lowest risk. They have a choice, and though we'd only have two guards, it's two more than our neighbours. They are not going to bother with us when our neighbours' belongings are much easier for the taking. We don't need enough guards to defeat the raiders; we just need more guards than our neighbours.

" 'And there is one thing more, my boy. Long term, you need sons! Not girls, though, and not sons as act like girls, either!' said his uncle, becoming very angry and banging the table they were sitting at with his fists. 'Not like my poor excuse for a son. Why didn't I kick him out that time and take you in his place? Make sure you got the right sow mind. You need quality in your breeding stock. She should be tall and strong and should have a temper about her, too—that's very important; temper feeds the aggression, and aggression keeps you on top and safe...'

"In the end, they hired two reformed raiders and put them to work dressed in distinctive uniforms. For several months his uncle was proven right. Though there were frequent raids in their valley, neither Robert's nor Brough's farms were hit. Both continued to grow, and they both became increasingly wealthy. Eventually, other farms followed their example and brought in their own security. Brough and Robert simply responded by hiring more guards to ensure they were the best defended and continued to do so every time their neighbours upped their numbers.

"It was about this time that Robert first went to the mountains. Running the farm was hard work, and once in a while, a few hours in a different environment refreshed and re-energized him. For several months he had this strange feeling the mountains to the north were calling him. So, one morning he set off alone on his pony and traversed the rough terrain to the north that led to the foothills. His original intention had been to climb to the top of the range and take a look at what lay beyond. However, once he reached the jagged hills that preceded the mountains, he realized the scale was a lot steeper than it appeared from his farm. To climb to the top would be a major undertaking. He contented himself with climbing some of the way up the southern-facing slope. He had gained several hundred feet on the granite slope when he found what looked like a man-made path winding its way through the large boulders and the fragmented scree. Curious, he followed the path. It took him deeper into the granite maze, finally ending in a circular opening. In the middle of the opening stood a man with bedraggled brown hair.

" 'Hello, Robert,' he said in a rough, broken voice. He took a step forward, his long grey robe flowing as he moved. 'My name is Timothy. Nice to meet you finally.'

*****

"Later that year, Robert found himself in the front room of a house in a nearby hamlet. The owner had established himself as an agent for security guards, and his clients were the farmers who were hiring an ever-increasing number of them. Brough and Robert had recently decided to bring two more guards on board. The owner was standing at the front door when Robert arrived, and he shook the man's hand.

" 'Ethel is not here today, Robert; I've hired a new young lady to negotiate contracts,' the man said.

"Robert acknowledged the information with a nod. He didn't care very much for Ethel anyway, so a new negotiator would be welcomed. He made his way over to the negotiating step. In front of him, deep in conversation with another farmer, stood a tall, slim girl dressed in a simple black robe. She had a pale complexion and green eyes. She was arguing with the farmer, and her body was swaying as she made her points.

"The movement was so graceful Robert started feeling giddy. He looked up at her face and was overwhelmed—he couldn't stop looking at her. Which is why he tripped over a discarded box and found himself staggering forward, out of control, his arms swinging in a vain attempt to correct his balance. He crashed into her, and they ended up in a tangle on the floor. She yelled at him, calling him out for being a complete idiot and adding several expletives for colour. She didn't move her head; her glorious green eyes were wide open with fury. He wanted to apologize, but it didn't seem like there was any point—clearly, she wasn't in a forgiving mood. After she had finished her outburst, he lay there looking at her for several seconds and finally asked in a shaky voice if she would care to marry him.

"The wedding of Robert and Maria took place a month later. They had a small ceremony attended by Maria's mother and uncle, Brough, and several of the most loyal hands from the two farms. Robert was still in a stupor; which he hadn't been able to shake since the moment he'd first set eyes on Maria. Brough thoroughly approved of the union, especially when, a few days before the ceremony, he witnessed Maria shouting at and seeing off a group of uninvited vendors.

"He laughed loudly and clapped Robert heartily on his back. 'Just as prescribed by Uncle Brough, my boy, just as prescribed!'

"At Brough's request, Robert didn't invite Boniface to the wedding. Brough had thrown Boniface out of the house.

" 'He'll still get the farm when I croak,' he told his friends. 'Those are the rules of my bloodline, but I see no reason why I should have to look at his pasty face in the meantime.'

"After the ceremony ended, Robert lifted his bride onto his favourite horse and hoisted himself up behind her. They rode about three hours north of the valley to the foothills of the mountains. Skilfully, he directed the horse up through a barely used pathway that zigzagged through rocks and scree, gaining elevation all the time. Finally, they reached an open space with a lookout to the south. They dismounted and walked to the edge of the clearing. The sun was beginning to set in the west, and the shards of sunlight that stretched their way across the valley reflected off rocks, river, trees, and grass, giving the valley a mystical ambience.

"Robert held his new wife closely. 'Maria, I have been lucky in life. On several occasions I have looked death in the face, fully accepting my fate. But each time I have somehow escaped its cold grip. I was once an orphan who should have been taken by the plague, but I survived, and from that point on, every time I needed luck, it found me. Now I am a man of wealth, and I am married to the most beautiful girl I have ever seen. I don't pretend to know what power has looked after me all these years, but I do know I am in its debt, and I need to repay it.

" 'I first came to this place many moons ago after my farm became successful. Something drew here, to this very spot. Look behind you, back towards the mountain. Do you see anything unusual?'

"Maria turned around and looked hard at the granite face of the mountain. She looked up, down, left, and right, then shook her head. "I don't see anything out of the ordinary.'

"Robert nodded. 'Neither did I the first time I was here. Okay, now close your right eye, and look again.'

"Maria did as he asked and was amazed to see, just above their heads on a rocky ledge, a large, circular stone with a hole in it. It looked like a giant letter O. She opened both eyes, and it vanished. She repeated the process, closing her eye again, and the symbol reappeared.

"Robert was smiling. 'Clever trick, huh? Come on, let's go!'

"There was a crack on the face to the left of the O. They used it to scramble up the face until they were level with the ledge and then stepped across onto it. They were standing right next to the giant O. It was about ten feet high, perfectly circular, and smoothly finished, in contrast to all the surrounding granite.

" 'This is the answer,' said Robert slowly. 'Everything I need to do starts here.

" 'I did not find this place. A man called Timothy revealed it to me. He was an amazing man—not of this Turn, I don't think. We spent many hours talking and discussing matters. He gave me hope, not for me, but for the Turn.'

"Maria moved to put her hand through the hole, but Robert stopped her quickly.

" 'No, you must not do that,' he said, pulling her back gently. 'There is something magical about this stone, but I believe it is also dangerous. It is an instrument that can be used for good or evil. I have already used it, though I cannot tell you why. But I know what I have to do to repay my debt. I have already spent many hours working on it. Timothy was my mentor. I have a plan—one I've already committed to paper and have hidden where no one will find it. I am not ready to execute yet. The next part of this story is where you come in. I need you to bear me a son, or better yet, two or three if you could manage?'

"He wrapped his arms around his new wife, and the two laughed together.

" 'I need them to help run and eventually take over the farm, and I'll need them to support my efforts to make this a better Turn. What I have planned is a huge undertaking and may take several lifetimes to achieve. Maria, give me sons, and we will set about making this part of the Turn a better place. We will create a central body that will include representation from all areas, for all people, be they rich or poor. The body will ensure sharing of resources for the common good. It will sponsor an armed militia that will put a stop to the raids that terrorize the people of the valley. It will train people in the way of medicine to eradicate the plague and other dreaded illnesses. Like this stone, the body will be circular—everyone will have a voice; there will be equality among the delegates. There will be leaders, of course, but they will be chosen by the people and held accountable to the people.'

"They turned and looked out at the valley below, which was bathed in an orange glow.

" 'This could be such a wonderful land; it just needs the right people to set it in the right direction. Those people are us, Maria—you and me and our children.'

"They gazed out across the valley. The sun was descending quickly beyond the ocean to the west. Evening was approaching. Long, shadowy fingers of darkness reached across the grasslands, breaking the natural contours of the land.

" 'I think we'd better get home,' whispered Robert."

Jag closed the book slowly.

The food was sizzling, and a delicious aroma filled the air. Ulma had two knives, which she always kept on her. She gave Jag the smaller one. She had created passable plates using bark from a fallen tree. Jag was hungry. Even for rabbit. Ulma served him a plateful, and he wolfed it down. Ulma laughed.

"Yes, okay, it was quite good," said Jag, wiping his mouth with his sleeve. "What did you think of the story?"

"Much of it I have heard before. It's a very old tale!" she replied a little dismissively. "But it shows you how you can achieve anything if you are determined enough."

"The mountains he explored, were they the Maria Mountains?" Jag asked.

"Yes. This story takes place before many of the towns, rivers, and mountains had names. I believe the Maria Mountains were named after his wife."

Jag thought about the story for a couple of minutes, gazing into the small fire, which was now giving them much-needed warmth. "I assume Robert was the founder of the Cirque movement?"

Ulma hesitated before answering. "Well, yes. I suppose he was, but things didn't happen the way he planned."

"What do you mean?"

"I'm sure if you continue with the book, you will find out."

"Too tired," said Jag. "I've never walked so far in my life. Do you think we can sleep safely here?"

"As safe as anywhere around here," Ulma replied, cleaning the plates and knives with some water from her canteen. "We should probably take turns doing watches, but I think we are both too tired. Tonight, we will take our chances."

There was plenty of loose grass available for bedding. They gathered enough to create a large sleeping area. The temperature was cooling rapidly, and they only had one blanket between them. They put on all their clothes and lay down on the improvised bed. Jag felt Ulma cozy up behind him, draping her arm around his waist, but he was too tired to object. He closed his eyes and sank into a deep sleep.

*****

At some point near dawn, the dreams started.

Robert was in them. He was trying to tell Jag something. But although his mouth opened and closed, he had no voice. Tears of frustration ran down his cheeks. Maria appeared from nowhere. She pushed Robert roughly out of the way saying, "Let me tell him; let me tell him."

But she said nothing. She walked gracefully up to Jag and positioned her face within a few inches of his. She looked into his eyes, and her face changed to Ulma's. Ulma stepped back, touching her cheek with one hand and placing the other on her hip.

"Which town are you of, and where is your allegiance?" she asked.

He tried to answer, but he had no voice, either. Ulma repeated the question with more than a hint of impatience, but still, he could not talk. The question came a third time, but now a man asked, speaking in a deep, baritone voice with a soft accent. Ulma called out, and Jag woke immediately. A tall, gaunt man dressed in black robes, a clerical collar, and a three-pointed hat towered over Jag, a shotgun aimed directly at Jag's forehead.

Ulma shifted her hand to within inches of her hunting knife.

"Make one more move, young lady, and I'll blow your friend's head to kingdom come."

# Chapter 13

"Yes. Nikolas sent me to look after him," said Ulma.

She and Jag were kneeling on their improvised bed with their hands on their heads. The tall man stood over them. He appeared tense, his nerves betrayed by a slight shake of the gun he still held trained on them. A small clay pipe dangled unlit from the corner of his mouth. As he spoke, he flipped it with his lips to the opposite corner and then back again.

He looked skyward for a moment, as if thinking. "Well, if what you say is true, I have no quarrel with you. I haven't seen him for several years, but Nikolas is a good man. It's a shame he didn't take over as High Lord and have Mora pack his bags, instead. We wouldn't be in the mess we find ourselves in today had he done so."

*I know that accent,* thought Jag. When the man talked, it was almost as if he were singing.

He looked at Jag.

"And you, young man, what is your story?" He poked the barrel of his gun against Jag's stomach. "You don't look like a Mensan."

"Well, I'm not Mensan. I don't come from anywhere."

The man laughed. "Well, I doubt that somehow, boyo. Everyone comes from somewhere. We've met a lot of different folk in the south lands—and returned a good few to their maker, praise be—but I don't recall any who came from nowhere."

"He is of the lost," said Ulma. "I can vouch for him. He has only been in the Turn a few days, but Nikolas regards him and his friends as important people in the effort to put down the rebellion."

The man spun his pipe across his mouth twice, and then reaching into his pocket, brought out a flint, which he used to spark a flame. He blew a long plume of grey-white smoke over their heads.

"Of the lost, eh? Interesting. Most interesting. Just a few days in, too? I expect you still have full memory of your past life?" He looked at Jag.

"Of course. Why wouldn't I?"

The man sighed. "Yes, you are new to the Turn. You may lower your hands. I don't believe you are a threat to us. Now, I imagine the pair of you are famished? Would you care to take breakfast with us?"

"No, not famished," said Ulma haughtily. "Hungry for breakfast, yes. But we have not wanted for nourishment. I have been providing for us as I always do when scouting."

"Please accept my apologies, young lady," exclaimed the man, executing a theatrical bow. "I didn't mean to patronize you. I'm sure you are a fine scout. I just thought we might enjoy a little breakfast and a bit of a natter. We would very much like to hear more of your journey and your plans."

Jag couldn't hold back the question any longer. "Who is 'we'?"

"Excuse me?" replied the man.

"You keep saying 'we,' but there's only you. Or are you one of those odd people who always refers to themselves as we?"

The man laughed loudly. "Well, there are plenty of people who think I'm odd, but not for that reason. Yes, I have a companion; he's in the woods foraging for our breakfast. He'll be back any moment now. I hope he found beetroot. I'm rather partial to beetroot, you know."

The man sat cross legged in front of the remnants of Ulma's fire from the previous night. He poked at the pile of ash with a small stick until it yielded two or three glowing embers. In a few minutes, the fire was burning nicely, and several small cans filled with water were heating up rapidly. He turned to face Jag and Ulma.

"They call me The Vicar," he said, touching his clerical collar. "I don't have a home as such. Nor do I have a church in which to preach. I am liberated from the shackles and chains of ownership and responsibility. I go where I please, when I please. This transient lifestyle also sits well with my vocation."

He awaited the inevitable question, and Jag obliged.

"What is your vocation?"

The Vicar narrowed his eyes. "To rid the Turn of every piece of evil that darkens it's precious soil."

Jag had no idea how to respond to that statement. Ulma remained silent, too, a slow nod her only acknowledgment.

"I didn't choose this job, you understand? It's a calling, if you like," he continued, staring straight ahead. "Yes, a calling. And right now, I'm getting a calling from my ruddy stomach, because it's wondering where its breakfast has got to!" He tilted his head back and roared with laughter.

His merriment was infectious, and Jag and Ulma found themselves laughing along with him. The Vicar jumped to his feet.

Cupping his hands around his mouth, he yelled, "Smedley! Smedley!"

Alarmed, Ulma jumped up next to him, her finger pressed against her closed mouth.

"It's perfectly okay, young lady. We had a thorough look around before we gave you your morning call. The RagaRaga have moved on."

Ulma seemed dubious, but there was to be no stopping The Vicar anyway, so she squatted down and diverted her attention to fire maintenance.

"Smedley, where are you.?" he bellowed again.

There was a disturbance in the long grass that bordered the southern end of the clearing. Ulma reacted lightning fast, jumping to her feet, knife in hand.

A small dog came bounding towards them. For the most part, he was hidden by the long grass, but every few strides he would jump high above even the tallest blades to check and adjust his direction. Within just a few seconds he was clear of the tall vegetation. He ran to The Vicar and sat down at his feet, panting hard. In front of his chest he carried a large basket, attached to him via a complicated-looking harness. Vegetables, plants, and mushrooms filled the basket.

"Good boy, Smedley!" The Vicar detached the basket from the harness and emptied the contents onto the ground in front of him for inspection. "Beetroots and parsnips, too, boy! Oh, you gem! We will eat like Cirque Lords this morning. Oh, how rude of me. Smedley, I'd like you to meet Ulma of Three Widows and Jag of...?"

"Pendleton." Jag filled the blank.

"Ah, thank you, Jag."

The brown and white-quartered terrier trotted over first to Ulma and then Jag. He tilted his head to one side and offered each of them his front right paw. They both grinned and shook the little dog's paw.

"What a remarkable animal," said Jag.

Ulma gave their new friend a hug.

"Yes, he has his moments. Great forager, as you have witnessed. Excellent pathfinder and keeps watch for me when I sleep. He also finished as runner up in the Gonk Regional Invitational Chess Competition two years running."

"He did?" exclaimed Jag.

"No! Of course not! That last one was a joke, boyo. Yes, he's smart, but at the end of the day he is still a dog." Once again, The Vicar opened his mouth wide and laughed.

He cooked them an excellent breakfast, using everything Smedley had collected. Jag surprised himself. He was eating unfamiliar food and eating it in large quantities. What would his mother say if she could see him now?

They learned over breakfast that a 'lady of his acquaintance' had given The Vicar the dog. He had trained the little guy to be his partner.

"He does his bit—he earns his keep," said The Vicar.

After they had eaten, Jag quizzed their new acquaintance.

"You said earlier that your job was to eliminate evil. What do you mean by that?"

The Vicar retrieved his pipe from his robe and lit it up. "I mean exactly that. Some would call me an assassin, but that suggests I am for hire. I'm not. I do the Lord's bidding and only that."

"How do you decide when someone needs to be eliminated?" Ulma asked.

"Oh, I just know. I can see evil, smell evil, taste evil. It never takes me more than five minutes to make a judgment. Justice is served very shortly thereafter."

"Your accent…which part of the Turn are you from?" asked Jag.

"The Turn? No, no, no. I'm not of the Turn, boyo. Like you, I'm from another place. They call it Wales."

With hindsight Jag realized it should have been obvious. The accent was a major clue, but there was something even more telling. He just didn't look like he was from the Turn. Jag started writing notes. What did this new knowledge mean? Good he had found someone who might be able to answer some of their questions. But not good the man appeared to have been here for many years… Not good at all. Did that mean there was no way back?

"Tell me about your life before the Turn and how you ended up here."

The Vicar removed his hat and ran his hand over his spikey grey hair. "I don't remember much of anything, Jag. You just forget, see? I know I've been here a very long time, but some days, I forget I ever lived anywhere else."

"Were you married? Did you have children? Family? A job? You must remember some of the big things." Jag pressed the man for more information.

"Actually," he replied, his face creased in concentration, "now that you mention it, one thing does come to mind." He paused, took a long draw on his pipe, and then released the smoke slowly. "I remember us beating England to win the Triple Crown at the Millennium. Best day of my life."

Jag sighed, stood up, and looked at The Vicar. "Rugby?" he asked incredulously.

The man had his eyes closed and was smiling contentedly.

"What is he talking about?" asked an obviously mystified Ulma. "What is rugby?"

"Rugby is a sport from back home," said Jag." He can't remember if he had a wife and kids, but he remembers a rugby game."

Ulma rolled her eyes.

"Have you ever tried to return?" Jag's initial optimism regarding The Vicar's store of knowledge was fast disappearing.

"No, I don't think so. As I said, my calling is here. And I…"

Jag waited for him to finish.

"Well, I vaguely remember that things weren't particularly good back home. I think it had something to do with this woman."

Jag was seeing a pattern. "Okay. Never mind that. But please, if you think of anything that might help my friends and me, let me know."

"Ah, indeed, young sir. You will be the first to know. The first, mind you."

"Thank you."

"You know I'm not the only one," The Vicar continued. "There are many more of us in the Turn."

"Really, where?"

"Why, all around. You have to keep your eyes and ears open, and you'll spot them. There are a lot in the islands."

"The islands?"

"Yes, out in the Western Sea there are a lot of islands. I wouldn't recommend visiting them, mind. Many of the islanders qualify for my termination list. And under no circumstances go anywhere near Spindle or Hag."

Jag thought about his two friends. "What about Espanada?" he asked.

"Espanada! That's a totally different matter. The home of the Great Circle in exile. The Lords are good people…usually. As are the people who associate with them. Usually. They have a fully trained militia to protect them. There are many Fade, too—they are unlike anyone you will meet back home. They have, for lack of a better word, powers. You might even call it magic. They can do extraordinary things. If anyone can show you the way back, it would be them."

"My friends are headed in the right direction then," said Jag.

"Oh, that's right, your friends are heading there. Yes, I'd like to hear your story."

"Well, you must walk with us while he tells you," said Ulma, "I want to reach Gonk by nightfall, so we have to get going."

The Vicar stood upright; eyes closed.

"Yes, why not? I can walk with you a while; I'd like to hear more. Also, if you will allow me, I will lead. I know the southland better than anyone. I will take you on paths the RagaRaga don't even know exist. I'll have you standing at the Gonk border by tea time."

Jag looked at Ulma, and she nodded.

"Right-e-o, let's break camp and be on our way," said The Vicar, extinguishing his pipe with his thumb and erupting into song.

Jag packed his few belongings into his backpack. Out of the corner of his eye he thought he saw movement on the edge of the clearing, close to where Smedley had returned from his breakfast hunt. Jag blinked and shook his head. He must be imagining things. He was with two survival experts and a trained hunting dog. If they saw nothing, then there was nothing to see.

When they first set off under The Vicar's leadership, Jag's limbs were still sore from the previous day's excursion. However, after a while he warmed up, and the aches and pains eased. The Vicar led them in a zigzag pattern. At various points he stopped and whispered into Smedley's ear. The little dog would race ahead for a few minutes, and then upon his return, he usually ran a circle round his master, which Jag learned was Smedley's way of saying, "All clear." However, on two occasions he returned and sat at The Vicar's feet. Smedley received a pat on the head, and The Vicar changed their direction to avoid whatever danger they would have encountered on their original path.

"It's not just the RagaRaga," The Vicar cautioned. "There're plenty of others we have to stay clear of, and the old villages are best avoided, too. A shame, really, because they were full of lovely dwellings."

He told how most of the residents had fled west when Leprade's armies had invaded. The Dory had left the Western Wastes. They had purchased a fleet of boats from the Crows, a trading partner from the South Seas, and were embarking on a journey into the unknown—north through the One-Way Channel.

"Where does the One-Way Channel lead to?" asked Jag, trying to recall the map Nikolas had shown them.

"Well, that's the thing," replied The Vicar, "there's a reason it's called One Way. Many have sailed into it heading north. But not a single one of them has ever returned. There are very strong currents that funnel north. So strong and so constant, there is no way you can sail back again."

"Why do people chance it?" Jag was intrigued.

"Desperation. If it's a choice between dropping into the channel or fighting the RagaRaga—or worse still, the Spindles—most would take a chance on the One-Way Channel."

Jag walked alongside the tall Welshman. "Did all the Dory and all the Samatrans leave the Turn?"

The Vicar stopped walking for a moment and stared ahead at the hill they were heading for. "Not all, but most. Same story with the wonderful people of Amos Line, too. Lovely folk but not fighters. Only the people of Gonk and Mensa and the outpost in Espanada are left, and it looks like their days are numbered."

The Vicar started moving again and picked up the pace. At one point, they skirted the outskirts of Light, formerly the capital of Samatra but now a ghost town. They came close enough for Jag to see some of the deserted homes. As The Vicar had said, obviously, they had once been beautiful. Each house was crafted from wood and local stones and were unique in shape and size. They had been painted to blend with the landscape. Jag would have liked to explore them, but The Vicar and Ulma said there was no way they could take the risk. On they walked without stopping for food or rest. Jag was getting hungry. At one point, Smedley disappeared into the woods, and when he came back, he held a bright-red apple in his mouth. He trotted up to Jag and lifted his chin, offering him the fruit, his tail wagging vigorously. Jag wiped it clean and bit into it. It was sweet and juicy with a light, earthy taste. The Vicar's craggy face broke into a broad grin as he watched Jag enjoy the best apple he had ever tasted.

"It's the soil, you see, boyo. It's rich and fertile. You'd struggle to grow anything that tasted less than marvellous in Samatra."

As they walked, Jag told his story. He gave The Vicar a detailed account of their journey, from the time the three of them had run into the tunnel right through to their close encounter with the RagaRaga at the rocky outcrop. The Vicar listened attentively, stopping Jag only once to defend the way the Mensans had treated them when they were first captured.

"There are a lot of evil people in the Turn, Jag. And they are masters of deception. Trust the wrong person, and it will cost you your life. No doubt, Ulma can tell you a few horror stories."

Ulma nodded.

Once Jag had finished, they fell silent, each deep in their own thoughts, their focus on walking. The Vicar picked up the pace again, and Jag struggled to keep up. He didn't complain. He kept going, one foot in front of the other. A few hours later, they entered another dense forest. It was packed with tall green pine trees, the branches of which formed a canopy. Occasionally, he would glimpse the shadow of a fast-moving creature above. The animals shrieked loudly as they passed by. Apes? He was shaking, and not because of the temperature. Smedley trotted alongside him, seemingly unaffected by the noise or the dark atmosphere.

At last the trees thinned out, and they were in open country. Despite the relief of clearing the woods, Jag had to keep stopping to attend to sore muscles and aching feet. The physical punishment he had been taking since his arrival in the Turn was beginning to catch up with him.

"I have to stop; I need a break." he muttered, coming to a halt and putting his hands on his knees.

The Vicar looked at him and placed his hand on Jag's shoulder. "Then you will no doubt be pleased to know we are at our destination."

"What?" said Jag and Ulma simultaneously.

The Vicar pointed ahead. "Well, near enough. See the tall trees yonder?"

"Pine Tree Row!" shouted Ulma. "It marks the border between Samatra and Gonk. We made it."

"Not quite," replied The Vicar. "There is one last hurdle to overcome. A trading route runs just in front of Pine Tree Row. It's used frequently by the RagaRaga to carry supplies and plunder to Brunella."

"So, how do we cross it without being spotted?" Jag asked.

"You will need to wait for dark," said the tall man.

His words reminded Jag The Vicar wouldn't be coming with them.

"I suggest we stop here, have some grub, and wait for sundown. I will help you cross the border safely," The Vicar added.

Jag didn't have a better suggestion and Ulma nodded and smiled.

"Very well." The Vicar crouched to equip Smedley with his food crate. He whispered a couple of words into his dog's ear, and Smedley bolted off back in the direction of the forest they had just passed through. Jag was grateful he did not have to follow him into those creepy woods.

"You two rest now. Smedley and I are tonight's chefs. How about you read another chapter of the history book you were telling me about? You can learn a lot from those old tomes."

Without answering, Jag retrieved the book from his pack and opened it at the second of Nikolas's markers. Ulma sat on the grass and pulled her knees under her chin, her eyes half closed. The Vicar hung the water tin over the fire and sat down next to her.

# Chapter 14

Jag read aloud:
"Sisters

"Radeem was the youngest of three sisters who lived with their father in a large, well-appointed farmhouse in the Mensa valley. Her father had risen from the depths of poverty to become one of the wealthiest and most respected men in the valley. Her family enjoyed all the privileges that such wealth brought.

"She ate four meals a day, received an education from a private tutor, and she had a bedroom filled with clothes and books and jewellery. Her sisters doted on her, and when she wasn't being tutored or at play with her friends, she enjoyed nothing better than to help around the farm.

"But Radeem didn't have the one thing she craved the most—the love of her father.

"He was affectionate with her sisters, but though he rarely vented his anger on her or struck her, he made no secret of his indifference to his third child. He talked to her only when there was no other option and cut short any attempt by her to talk with him. He never held her close when she was sick; he never comforted her when she was unhappy. It was as though she was invisible to him.

"When her sisters were young, their father read to them before bed. He was a good storyteller. But her father never allowed Radeem to join them. He sent her to bed and expected her to be asleep by the time he finished the story.

"Desperate to hear them, she regularly tiptoed out of her room and hunched down by the door to her sisters' room, her ear pressed against the thin panelling. His stories were sometimes set in the mountains to the north, or they took place on the great seas beyond their land where hardened seagoing folk battled each other for supremacy of their corner of the Turn. He also had stories based in the south lands, where exotic people lived a very different lifestyle. All his tales were full of wonder and magic.

"On special occasions he showed them his cipher, a wooden box that would only open upon a unique command. He let the girls try to guess the magic word, but despite their best efforts, the box remained solidly locked. The girls begged him to tell them what was inside the box, but he told them they had to earn the right to see by solving the problem.

"Her father never explained to her why he resented her, and she knew there was no point in asking him. When she turned twelve, her older sister Mathilda decided it was time Radeem knew the truth.

"Matilda started by reminding Radeem about their father's rags-to-riches journey. She described how he had been born into poverty and then lost both his parents when he was about her age. He not only survived the experience but worked his way to great success. He had been mature way beyond his years. He started his own farming business, which was an immediate winner. As the years passed, his farm became the largest in the valley. Soon he had more money than he knew what to do with. He met and married the most beautiful woman he had ever seen...their mother Maria.

"Then Mathilda told Radeem how their father's run of luck in life stopped abruptly. Soon after they were married, Maria fell pregnant. The young couple were overjoyed—yet again, it seemed good fortune had followed their father. But the baby was born too soon and was weak and feeble. He passed away after no more than a few hours. Maria also fared badly. She struggled with the delivery, and it took her several days to recover. They were shocked but determined not to give up.

"Their next attempt saw the birth of Matilda. Of course, they had wanted a boy, but they were more concerned about Maria's health after the delivery. It took several weeks for her to recover. For the first time, their father questioned the wisdom of further attempts. Yes, he was anxious for a son, but he did not want his beloved Maria to risk her life for his dream. Their mother was not to be put off though. She was determined to give him the son she had promised him. Another baby, another girl—their sister Kira. Once again, Mother did poorly during the birth and worse than before. For many hours it was touch and go as to whether she would live. She fought hard and eventually pulled through. Their father had seen enough; they would stop at two children. He reasoned that his daughters would marry one day, and their husbands could fill the roles of the missing sons.

"But their mother hadn't given up. Soon, she was expecting again. Their father was nervous at first, but Maria convinced him this was a strong pregnancy, and she knew for certain she was carrying a boy. Her confidence was infectious, and in time he, too, became convinced that finally he would have a healthy son. The baby, Matilda said, was Radeem. In delivering her, their mother became very ill again. Tragically, her determination to keep trying for a son finally cost her life.

"Their father refused to acknowledge Radeem's birth. For several months, he went off the rails. He took to the bottle and disappeared for weeks at a time. He made the occasional visit home, but he was constantly drunk and completely neglected his duties as a father and as owner and manager of his farm. When he was home, Matilda and Kira avoided him as much as possible, and he never asked to see his third child. Without his leadership the farm started to suffer. Fortunately for the family, Great Uncle Brough stepped in and took charge of the business and the household. Brough had helped their father when he was first orphaned, and as their father grew up, he had re-paid his uncle by helping him grow his small farm into a much larger and more profitable concern. Though he was now an old man, he still had remarkable energy. He ran the farm effectively and looked after the sisters as though they were his own daughters. They adored him; he was a big man and had a famous temper but with the girls he couldn't have been kinder or gentler. It was he who gave Radeem her name several weeks after she was born. He also filled her room with many of the lovely things she had.

"'I believe he paid a pretty penny to acquire the fiddle you play so exquisitely," Mathilda explained.

" 'Our father made one of his fleeting visits home when Brough happened to be at the farm. He was peeling potatoes at the sink and through the little window saw our father staggering towards the house. It was the first time he had seen him since our mother's funeral. Clearly, Uncle Brough had been waiting for this moment. He was standing by the front door when father stumbled across the threshold. He grabbed him by the collar and dragged him outside into the large stable. For about an hour all that could be heard was the roar of Brough's voice accompanied by a lot of banging and crashing. We feared for father's life, but no one dared go near the stable much less intervene. At last the sound of violence ceased, the door flew open, and Uncle Brough dragged our semi-conscious father across the yard to one of the water barrels. He hoisted him up and dumped him head first into the largest. Father was awake after that but unable to stop Brough pulling him out again before throwing him into the hay barn. Without looking around Brough walked back to the kitchen and continued peeling potatoes.

" 'He laid an extra place setting at supper that evening. We were not sure why because we didn't expect Father to come back. However, a few minutes into the meal he walked gingerly into the house. He was battered and bruised, but he was sober. Without looking up he sat down at the extra place setting. He took a little stew from a serving dish and put it in his bowl. To our surprise, Father thanked Brough, saying it was just what he'd needed...

" 'From that day forward, things improved considerably. Father gave up the drink and moved back into the farm. He immersed himself in his work and soon got into the groove again. He also started being a father to Kira and me.

" 'But he still couldn't find it in himself to forgive you. I don't know why.'

'"Why?" sobbed Radeem. 'What did I do wrong?'

"Her sister held her tight. 'I know it's not right, but I'm afraid it's true. Not even Uncle Brough can talk sense into him. We've all tried. But don't give up hope, Radeem; I know he will come around eventually.'

"Radeem's head was spinning. She had been a new born. What could she possibly have done to warrant such anger and resentment?

"'He was angry at himself for letting her become pregnant again. He was angry at our mother, too, for risking everything to give him the son he wanted. He was angry at fate for giving him such a charmed life only to crush him by taking away the one he loved the most.

"'Sometimes, people mad with grief need to find someone or something to blame for their loss. He was angry at himself, but that wasn't enough for him. In his warped mind, he blamed you.'

"The next morning, Matilda went to check on Radeem. But the eldest sister was shocked to find her bedroom empty—her bed had not been slept in. Trying hard not to panic, Matilda did a quick mental inventory. Some clothes were missing, and Radeem's sheepskin coat was not hanging in its usual place. Her fiddle, too, was gone! She couldn't have run away though, could she? Then Matilda saw the note.

"Radeem stood at the crossroads. Which direction should she go?

"She had no way of knowing that many years before, her father had found himself in the very same place with the exact same predicament. But there was no Brough to come to her rescue, and she had to get going. The first dapples of early morning sun were appearing. It wouldn't be long before her sisters found the note she had left. They would send out a search party, probably several.

"She opened her travel bag and retrieved the Cipher, which she had found in her father's hiding place. She wondered how long it would be before he noticed it was missing. She had a hunch about the secret word. She held the box in front of her on the palms of her hands and spoke the name she had in mind. The lid opened smoothly. She examined the contents and made a decision. She looked to the north. 'Later,' she whispered, and then she turned and looked south.

"She pulled her sheepskin jacket tight around her shoulders and linked the clasp at the neck to ensure she had maximum protection against the elements, and she started walking."

Jag closed the book and looked over at his two companions.

"Yes, it's a sad tale," commented The Vicar, "and it gets sadder."

"Oh, no, please don't tell me that," said Jag.

From the woods behind them came a loud howl.

"Smedley!" yelled The Vicar, jumping to his feet. In an instant he had grabbed his shotgun and was sprinting over the long grass in the direction of the pitiful sound.

"Stay here! Don't move an inch!" cried Ulma, wielding a knife in each hand. She took off at a dead run and caught up with The Vicar in seconds.

Panic erupted in every part of Jag's body. His instinct was to go after them, but Ulma had delivered her order for him to stay put with such conviction he felt obliged to comply. He stood still, rooted to the spot. He started shaking and felt sick. What was going on? What had happened to Smedley? Had he been attacked by the ape creatures?

Someone yelled from behind him, and he spun around. The shouts were coming from the direction of Pine Tree Row. He thought he saw someone on the horizon, but they ducked out of sight. Then he saw another person running in the same area, waving frantically.

"This way. Run!"

This time there was no mistaking the words. But who was it? Then it came to him—the Gonk people! They knew he was coming. He looked back at the forest. There was no sign of activity. Ulma and The Vicar must have gone deeper into the woods. Again, someone called from behind, and they sounded desperate. Jag squatted on his haunches and placed his hands over his face, trying to cut himself off from the mayhem surrounding him. Then came the sound of two rounds being discharged from The Vicar's shotgun. Ulma shouted, and then another two blasts of The Vicar's gun echoed in the distance. A moment later, Ulma emerged from the forest and sprinted towards him.

"Run, Jonathan, run! To the border!" she shouted breathlessly.

A second later, she fell flat on her face. Jag stared in horror. Had she been shot? "Oh, no," he said. She'd told him to run for the border, but he couldn't just leave her there. He started running back to where she had gone down, shouting her name, tears streaming down his face. He was running so fast he didn't see the three RagaRaga that blocked his route. He crashed into the tallest of the three, banging his head on the man's metal chest plate. Strong arms picked him up and threw him hard onto the ground. As he struggled for breath, the second trooper pointed a strange-looking device at him and fired a bolt of electricity. On impact, his whole body flexed in pain, and he lost any control he had of his muscles. He lay on the ground, his arms and legs flailing. The third trooper bent down and pressed his finger on Jags exposed arm. Something sharp—a needle?—buried into his flesh. Some kind of liquid entered his body, injected by the man who'd jabbed him with what Jag suspected was a syringe. A now-familiar feeling coursed through him. They were putting him to sleep. He had no time to ponder the irony. He disappeared into the nothingness yet again.

## Chapter 15

The town of Espanada was located on the most easterly point of the island. Most of the houses were made of white-washed stone and were shimmering in the early morning sun. Tiny waves lapped the shore along the town's two beaches. To the south was a natural harbour, in which half a dozen boats sat docked. But dominating the town through its sheer size, stood a large, circular building with a round tower located at its eastern edge. The tower rose high above the town.

Gillian was looking down at the picturesque harbour town, but her mind was elsewhere. She lay on her front, her face pressed against the cold, rubber-like membrane from which their bubble was constructed. Tears were still falling, smearing the inside of the membrane and causing her to repeatedly wipe it clear with her sleeve.

"We're descending," said Freddie.

It was the first time either of them had spoken since making their escape. Gillian didn't acknowledge him, but as she looked down, she could see the other two bubbles below, and they were now close enough that she could confirm the passengers—Marcus and Addford in the lower of the two and Dell and Ink in the other. No Giants. She had hoped she had missed something during the rescue and perhaps one or even both had been picked up. But she knew in her heart they'd lost Freckles. Even if Tiny had somehow managed to avoid drowning, how would he cope with the death of his brother? Fresh tears welled in her eyes.

Their strange craft angled its descent with precision. It was on track to land at the very top of the round tower. She couldn't see the others landing ahead, but their turn came quickly. They floated gently down until they were within a few inches of the stone rooftop. A man came into view. He looked like he was miming some sort of leg exercising routine. Neither Freddie nor Gillian could hear anything from outside the bubble.

"He wants us to stand up," said Freddie.

She got to her feet, the man struck the membrane with a small wooden implement, and the bubble burst. They dropped the remaining two inches to the roof. Gillian stumbled a couple steps but avoided falling over. She turned a slow circle, taking in their new surroundings. They were high up with spectacular views in every direction. The bubble buster stood in front of an open doorway, which appeared to lead to a narrow spiral staircase. Their three remaining friends were next to him. Ink tearfully ran forward and hugged both Gillian and Freddie, as did Dell. Marcus was leaning over the perimeter wall.

Addford didn't look at all well. His clothes were still wet, and he was shivering uncontrollably.

The bubble buster, in his dashing blue military uniform, stepped forward and took Gillian's hand gently in his. He raised it a little and leaned forward, kissing the back of her hand very softly. As he did so, his mop of dark hair flopped down in front of him, tickling her arm. He stepped back and bowed again. He flicked his hair back with his hand and greeted her.

"Gillian, welcome to the acting seat of the Great Circle. It is an enormous honour for us to receive you. I am Morgan, Deputy Commander of the Great Circle Guard."

"Thank you, Morgan, we're pleased and relieved to be here," replied Gillian, glancing sideways at Freddie to include him in her greeting.

Freddie stepped forward and shook Morgan's hand. "Freddie Patel…of Pendleton."

"Delighted to meet you, Freddie," said Morgan, slapping Freddie on the back. "I gather your journey here was something of an adventure?"

"You could say that," said Freddie dryly.

"But these brave Mensans delivered you unscathed," Morgan said, clapping his hands.

"They are not packages," said Marcus, swinging around. "Gillian and Freddie deserve great praise for their courage and character. They helped us take the Hag boat. Without their efforts none of us would have made it here."

"Agreed!" said Dell.

Ink nodded vigorously.

"Well, that's great to hear," the commander replied, nodding an acknowledgement.

"Morgan is there any news of Freckles and Tiny?" asked Gillian, her voice breaking.

"The Oze are very strong swimmers, Gillian, and the pickup point was only a few miles from Espanada. They should join—"

Dell cut in. "It's not that straightforward, Morgan. Freckles went down with one of the Hag boats. I believe his foot was tangled in the rigging."

Morgan looked shocked. "By Brunella, this is terrible news. Lord Mora will be angry at his loss, and Peter will be inconsolable…"

"Peter the Benevolent?" asked Ink. "He is here?"

"Indeed," said Morgan.

"How? When? Will we get to meet him?" Ink clasped her hands.

"Who?" asked both Gillian and Freddie at the same time.

"Okay, we're getting ahead of ourselves here," said Morgan, holding up his hands. "That's not my call. I am here to escort you down to the important people below. Lord Mora is awaiting your arrival. In fact, if I don't get you down to him in the next few minutes, I will be in trouble. He's a great man but not famous for his patience."

"Okay, Clayton," he said, addressing the soldier who had been standing just behind him, "lead the way down. We are heading for the outer-circle."

They followed Clayton through the door and onto the staircase. It was a long, treacherous descent; the stone steps were steep, uneven, and slippery. Gillian had not yet adjusted to being back on land and stumbled several times on the way down. Morgan was alert to the situation; he followed her closely, catching her each time she lost her balance.

To Gillian's great relief, Clayton finally led them out of the stairwell into a long stone corridor. The corridor led to a pair of large, semi-circular doorways that looked very similar to those Jag and Gillian had passed through at the Three Widows Circle. Morgan knocked hard on the left door three times. The door swung open and revealed a very large, round chamber. It had a vaulted ceiling and was divided into segments. Each segment contained numerous comfortable-looking chairs and ornately carved tables. The partitions that divided the segments were of different heights. Some rose only to floor level, some all the way up to the ceiling, and others in between. Gillian instinctively grasped the reason for the design. It gave the chamber the flexibility to act as one large room or to be divided up as required. At the centre of the chamber was a permanent-looking circular wall Gillian guessed housed the inner-circle chamber.

Clayton led them to the one partition that rose all the way to the ceiling. He knocked on what looked like a small door, and it swung open in the same manner as the previous door had. He stepped to one side, and Morgan slipped by him and, stooping to avoid banging his head, led them into the room.

Three men sat at yet another round table. Two were dressed in splendid white gowns similar to that worn by Nikolas, their robes decorated with small, coloured patterns. They both had short grey hair and craggy, sunburned faces. The third man also wore a gown, but his was grey and featured a large hood that hung forward, concealing his features.

The white-robed man farthest to the right looked at each of them slowly and then stood up to greet them before returning to his chair.

"Welcome, friends, to the Great Cirque in exile. I am Lord Mora, head of the Great Cirque. On my left is Lord Saracen who is the senior Cirque representative for the region of Brunella."

Saracen did not acknowledge them; he stared vacantly ahead of him.

"To his right is Adrian. Adrian—if he will forgive me for categorizing him—is the senior Fade currently residing with us."

Adrian held up his hands, palms pressed together, and nodded in acknowledgement. Gillian and Freddie responded by mirroring his movements.

Gillian briefly introduced Freddie and herself. The others had all met before.

Mora crossed his arms. "I appreciate that you are in need of refreshments and could no doubt use a bath and some sleep, too, but we are already behind the enemy and have to catch up. Nikolas has given his version of your story, but I should like to hear it directly from you if that is okay?"

"Yes, but please, before we get into all that, I have two questions. We…lost two people on our journey… Two people we care about, and I was wondering… " Gillian looked at Mora pleadingly.

He said nothing, so she continued.

"Is there any news on the whereabouts and well-being of our friend Jag? And the same question regarding the Oze giants, Tiny and Freckles? Are they—?" Gillian couldn't force herself to voice the words.

Saracen stood up. "Whither do they wander? You'll never know! I'll see to that!" he said.

"I'm not sure I follow you." Freddie frowned.

Saracen turned his head towards Gillian and fixed her with a manic gaze. "Don't test me with your pretties, brazen harlot!" he yelled at her.

Gillian's cheeks grew hot at this unexpected outburst. She opened her mouth to respond, but Freddie came to her defence, interrupting the Samatran Lord's verbal tirade.

"Whoa, you are out of order, Lord, Lord whatever your name is! We've been living a crazy nightmare and have every reason to ask questions about friends, all three of whom have been helping your cause."

Saracen's face had turned a nasty shade of purple and his bottom lip quivered. Clearly, he was not accustomed to people answering him back because he appeared temporarily speechless.

"Okay, thank you, all three of you." Lord Mora sought to calm the waters. "These are difficult times. We are all on edge, but please save your anger for those who deserve it. I believe we are all friends here. Please sit, Saracen."

Lord Saracen did not appear to be any calmer. He sat back down slowly and stared at Freddie again. Freddie returned the glare until Gillian tapped him on the arm, at which point he finally looked away.

After a few seconds passed, Lord Mora addressed Gillian's questions.

"Gillian, I am sorry, but the answer is no. We have people looking out for Tiny and Jag but have yet to receive news. As for Freckles…" He looked down.

Gillian's eyes burned, and she blinked back her tears. "Thank you," she said. She swallowed the lump in her throat then gave the assembled group her version of their story. For the first time, she included Pinhorn and his part in the drama.

It felt good to be giving a straightforward, truthful account finally.

"Thank you," Mora said when she had finished. He had an open, cleanshaven face; Gillian couldn't decide how she felt about him.

"I want to tell you what we are thinking," he said," but first, I'd be happy to tackle any questions you might have."

"I have one," said Freddie.

Mora nodded.

"What the heck were those amazing bubble things that rescued us from the sinking boat?"

Mora chuckled and extended his arm towards Adrian. "You have to thank my friend here for that. The Fade are not our allies; their philosophy will not allow them to take sides, but they are good people and will give aid to those who both need and deserve it. We asked them if they could assist with bringing you here safely. We were able to monitor your progress with seeing bubbles. These are tiny bubbles that can watch and send graphic representations of what is going on back to the Fade."

Gillian nodded. "Yes, I saw several when we were on the boat. It makes sense now! Thank you, Adrian."

Adrian nodded but said nothing.

Mora laughed again. "Fade aren't allowed to speak very much. In fact, when they first take the hood, they can't talk at all and must remain silent for five years. After they pass that landmark, they are allowed a limited number of words each day, which increases each anniversary. But the maximum is twenty, so they never waste words. There are a lot of people I know who could benefit from that discipline!"

Gillian and Freddie laughed with him.

"Nikolas said we might meet someone who can help us find our way home. Should we be talking to the Fade?" Freddie asked.

Saracen squirmed in his seat, clearly not happy with the questions and answers session, but after a slight pause, Mora answered.

"We are already talking to them. There are many factors involved. Bear in mind you were probably brought here for a reason, and it's unlikely you will be allowed to return unless that reason is satisfied, which could take a day, a week, a month, or even years."

Gillian dropped her head, as did Freddie. Ink, who was sitting behind Gillian, put a hand on her shoulder. There was a long silence.

Mora shook his head. "I'm sorry. I know it's not what you wanted to hear, but I want to be honest with you."

Gillian and Freddie looked up but said nothing

"Any questions from the Mensan crew?" Mora asked.

Marcus stood up. "What news of the enemy? We heard many rumours before we left Three Widows—none of them good."

"Thank you, Marcus," replied Mora. "What news, indeed? We, too, have been hearing all sorts of reports relating to their movements. Something is afoot; that much is certain, which is why I have called for an extraordinary inner-circle. What is more, each region will be represented—this will be a full meeting."

Obviously, this was the first time Saracen had heard about Mora's plan because he looked very surprised.

"But, Master—the missing! The missing!" Saracen picked up the pile of papers in front of him and threw them back down again.

"Thank you, Saracen; your concerns are noted. However, all regions will be represented. This matter concerns everyone, and everyone should have a voice." Mora looked around for Morgan. "Morgan, would you be so kind as to bring over the placard next to the door? Thank you. We have no easel; do you mind acting the easel?"

Morgan smiled. "Of course, My Lord." He held up the placard for all to see.

Mensa: Addford
Samatra: Mora
Gonk: Freddie
Amos Line: Gillian
Western Wilds: Rush
Brunella: Saracen

"Why are our names up there?" asked Freddie.

"Yes, why?" added a clearly unhappy Saracen.

Mora looked at Saracen. "Well, I did consider putting Gillian in as the Brunella rep. Then I thought the senior rep might take offense to being completely overlooked."

Saracen muttered something under his breath and then slumped in his seat like a sulking child.

Mora continued. "No, Saracen, I included our lost friends based on recognition of what occurred in Mensa. Gillian demonstrated she has a relationship with bracefires—there are very few who can trigger a bracefire event. We do not know why she has this gift, but her presence at the Cirque will increase the likelihood of other bracefires being triggered and strengthen the links between those that do fire up. We've included Freddie because of his association with her."

Mora stood up, picked up his documents, and started walking to the door.

"Morgan, please see that our guests are given the best accommodations available," he said over his shoulder. "Oh, and food and drink, of course. No doubt, they will wish to sleep awhile, but if they have any energy left, they may explore this wonderful building." He paused at the door. "They have freedom to go anywhere except the inner-circle. Oh, and the Fade's wing, of course. Most important of all, they must not leave the Cirque building. Word is out regarding the discovery of a bracefire—one that completes a pair. The people of Espanada have been living in fear of defeat for many years now. This is the first bit of good news they have had in a long time. Naturally, they want to see the parties responsible for the return of the bracefire. There is already a crowd forming at the main doors, and their enthusiasm could be dangerous."

He turned to leave and then stopped again. "How foolish of me; I neglected to mention the Grand Cirque will take place at first bell the day after tomorrow, which allows time for Rush to find her way here. See you then."

A few seconds later, Saracen, his eyes shifting around the room, picked up his belongings and silently followed after Mora. Then Adrian stood, nodded once, and headed for the door; his cloak was shredded, the hemline dragging across the floor. Gillian watched him, fascinated. The long cloak and his easy movement gave the illusion that he floated over the floor.

Freddie called after him. "Adrian, thanks for the bubble ride—easily the most extraordinary half hour of my life!"

Adrian glanced back and acknowledged Freddie with a very understated nod before disappearing through the door.

Freddie sat, hands on his head. "Wow," he said, "Gillian, this is completely mad!"

Once Saracen had left the room, the mood at the table lifted.

"What about that Saracen guy?" said Freddie, addressing the remainder of the group.

"Freddie...enough already," said Gillian. "We are guests here, and Saracen is one of our hosts."

"I thought he came from Brunella?" replied Freddie.

"You know what I mean," said Gillian, suppressing a much more volatile response.

Morgan stood up. "Guys, a word about Saracen," he said quietly. "Before the troubles started in Gonk he was a junior officer in the Brunella militia. He travelled a lot, often carrying missives around the Turn. I met him several times; he was just about the nicest person you can imagine. When the rebellion started, he saw action on the front lines. He was a brave, skilful soldier and was building a great reputation for himself. He was a fine scholar, too. He is without peer as a historian, and we use him a lot when working with the Fade. He became a Lord at a very young age but continued to work on covert operations. Then one night when scouting alone, a rebel patrol captured him. He ended up in a dungeon in the town he once called home. If that was not bad enough, he attracted the attention of Catchpole. For four years, Leprade's evil sidekick tortured Saracen. I won't go into details, but when Catchpole had finally finished with the poor man, he ordered a small troop to take him into the forests of Gonk and execute him. Catchpole wanted the Gonks to find Saracen's broken body. But fate intervened. There is a singular but very enigmatic man who wanders those parts. He doesn't have a lot of time for anyone he regards as evil—and anyone associated with Leprade falls squarely into that category. The four rebels were fitting a noose round Saracen's neck when four blasts of the vigilante's gun cut them down. The stranger then carried the unconscious Saracen to Fabrice, where the Gonks nursed him back to health. But the damage had been done. Saracen became a bitter, twisted shadow of his former self, and no one has been able to rescue his heart and mind from the dark prison Catchpole created for him."

Freddie had his hands over his head. "Me and my big mouth," he said quietly.

"Don't feel bad," said Morgan. "We all know what happened to him, and yet, we still find it difficult to avoid cussing at him. Lord Mora has been brilliant with him, giving him responsibilities and keeping him busy."

"The stranger who rescued him," asked Freddie, "what's his story?"

"Good question," replied Morgan, "There is a rumour that he is of the lost. He doesn't seem to have a name. Folks call him The Vicar."

Gillian was intrigued by the story of this stranger. Could he be from home? She glanced at Freddie. His expression mirrored her interest. But Morgan dropped the subject and began to get them organized for their stay.

"Ah, here come the details," he said.

Six extremely short people dressed in white tunics and baggy black trousers trotted into the room.

"There's one assigned to each of you, and they will look after you for the duration of your time here."

One of them—a girl with a shock of red hair—ran straight to Gillian. She bowed and introduced herself as Violet. Her blue eyes seemed impossibly large.

"Service?" she asked.

"I'm sorry?" replied Gillian.

"Service?" the little lady repeated.

Gillian looked around and realized her colleagues were going through the same exercise. The "Service?" question echoed 'round the room, and her friends all looked equally mystified. Then she caught sight of Morgan and Clayton. They were standing to one side, smiling broadly. Morgan clapped his hands to get everyone's attention.

"They are asking for their orders. Make a request, Gillian."

"Um…may I have a glass of water?" Gillian asked.

"Service!" shouted Violet and ran off on her errand as fast as her little legs would carry her. She was back in less than a minute with a draft of cold water.

Morgan held up a box.

"And best of all," he said, "if you don't need them or if they are being problematic, you can turn them off!"

He clicked a button on the remote, and Violet slouched over at the waist, her little arms hanging loosely in front of her.

"How cool is that?" exclaimed Freddie.

Laughter and chaos followed, as they learned how to use their robotic assistants. Freddie asked his detail, Donald, to go around the room tickling any legs he saw. It turned out that Donald's vision wasn't too brilliant, and he tried to tickle anything he bumped into. Marcus and Dell had only been using their remotes for a couple of minutes before they decided to explore their robots' combat potential. Using the remote controls, the men guided their robots' actions and experimented with different attack commands. Within a few seconds the details were in a full-on battle. By the time Morgan had managed to activate a master override cut-off switch on the brothers' details, the robots had suffered major damage; both were down to one arm, while Marcus's had lost her left leg below the knee, and Dell's had both his eyes gouged out.

Morgan waved at his subordinate. "Clayton, please pick up what remains of the two damaged details and take them down to engineering. "

Marcus and Dell were looking rather sheepish.

"Well, friends," said Morgan, standing, "you heard your options for the day. Please let me know what you want to do."

The six chattered amongst themselves. Addford requested a hot tub, some warm, dry clothes, a steaming bowl of soup, and a bed. Everyone else followed his example, and suddenly, they were all yawning hard.

Morgan cornered Gillian. "Okay, Gillian, I noticed you suffered quite a nasty nick on your arm. Was this from a Hag cutlass?"

Gillian put her hand on the wound. "Yes, but the cut is not too deep."

"Hmm, are you aware the Hag often coat the edges of their blades with poison? I'd be happy to take a look at that for you. Better safe than sorry."

"No, that won't be necessary," interjected Freddie. "If she'd been poisoned, we would know by now. She'd be rolling on the floor in agony with spit coming out of her mouth."

Gillian glanced briefly but sharply at Freddie. "Freddie, you're an idiot! I'm sorry, Morgan. Yes, thank you for the offer. It might be a sensible precaution."

Freddie sighed and turned his attention back to Donald's hair, which he was attempting to plait.

"Wonderful," said Morgan, flicking his hair back. "I'll contact you at the next bell.

Freddie looked theatrically round the room. What was wrong with him?

"Anyone else have a cut or graze that needs attention?" he said, looking in the direction of Ink. "Oh, Ink, what's that I see on your shoulder? Did you notice that before? Looks nasty, would you...?"

"No, I'm fine, thanks, Freddie. I took *ramicide* before we left; no poison is going to get the better of that fine Mensan herb."

Addford pushed himself up to a standing position and raised his hand. "Actually, young man, since you are volunteering, when I fell from the boat, I took quite a knock to my lower back, and I think I have a very nasty scrape in my abdominal region." He started shuffling towards Freddie, working at undoing his belt buckle.

"I've just remembered—I need to be somewhere," said a panicked Freddie as he ran out of the room.

# Chapter 16

Gillian was lying on her bed, wide awake and feeling terrible. In another bed across the room, Ink snored softly, having fallen asleep several hours before.

The frustration of being so tired but unable to sleep made things worse. Morgan had sent his apologies via yet another detail. He had been summoned by Lord Mora and did not expect to be free until very late. Morgan's message had stated he hoped to see her at breakfast; they still had much to discuss.

Before Ink had surrendered to her need for sleep, they had talked at length. Of all the Mensans, Ink was the only one who had not previously visited Espanada, yet she was very knowledgeable about the town and the people who lived there. Ink was jealous of Gillian's invitation to attend the Grand Cirque. The room was out of bounds to everyone except the six senior representatives of the regions and a few very select Fade who had specific roles to play within the chamber.

"You will get to see and touch the original Cirque table! I'm told it is something to behold. This is the table at which Brunella chaired the first Grand Cirque."

The girls also talked about the battle of the details and laughed at how Freddie had fled when Addford sought personal medical assistance.

"Poor Freddie!" said Gillian. "Now I know why people at school call him 'Fast Freddie'; I've never seen anyone move so quickly."

After that, Ink lay down and had fallen asleep in seconds. But Gillian had too much going on in her head to even attempt sleep. She lay there and stared at the ceiling, pained with guilt. She'd wanted to discuss her thoughts with Ink, but her young Mensan friend had been more interested in talking about Freddie and Morgan.

Gillian's biggest worry was Jonathan. The longer they went without seeing or hearing any news of him, the more concerned she became. What were they thinking, deserting him like that? Okay, he had Ulma with him, but the two of them were literally from different worlds. Also, their relationship had become strained, hadn't it? They could have demanded they pick the two of them up in the boat. Jonathan's best friend had let him down, too. She had no complaints about Freddie, but his actions in that regard were out of character. She lay on her back and lost herself in the eggshell-blue-painted ceiling. She spoke her thoughts aloud in the vain hope Ink might hear her and offer solace or ideas.

"The Turn is illogical. Nothing makes sense. How does time work here, where there are no clocks, just seemingly random bells? And how is it that the inhabitants can design and build highly complex machines like the details and yet lack even the most basic communication devices such as phones?"

Ink didn't stir. Gillian stopped talking aloud but continued with her thoughts. Freckles. She was responsible for his death. Had she not been there, he would have lived. But she was there, and he had spent the last few seconds of his life making sure she escaped. And for what? Nikolas had assigned her with two tasks—give bracefires to the correct person and identify the traitor who was leaking top-secret information to their enemies.

She'd arrived here, and so far, no one had come running over offering to relieve her of the bracefires. As for finding the imposter, how could she possibly do that? She had no clue where to start. Saracen's wild outbursts had seemed to indicate he could be a possibility, but then she'd learned the guy was a hero, albeit a mentally unbalanced one. That seemed to eliminate him. For now, anyway…

Unhappy, disturbing thoughts chased each other around her head. She slid out of bed and stood up. No point in trying to sleep. She looked over at the window. The drawn curtains allowed a tiny gap of sunlight to peep through. It must be around mid-afternoon.

"I'm going for a walk." She spoke aloud again, on the off-chance Ink might be awake enough to hear. Gillian thought about summoning Violet to use as a guide but decided it would be more liberating without her, and anyway, Gillian could always call her robotic assistant if she became lost.

As it turned out, she became disoriented within a few minutes of leaving her room. The corridors and staircases presented a huge directional challenge. There were so many, and they all looked alike—there were no signs or markers to help her find her way. She experimented with a couple of turns and realized she was already unsure about how to get back. *Thank goodness for Violet.* Gillian reached into her pocket for her remote, but the controller wasn't there. Her heart sank. She'd left it in her room.

She would have to find someone to help. But after she had walked the length of several passageways and ascended and descended two different staircases, she saw no one. There were numerous doors in the corridors, but none had numbers or any other kind of identification marks. Finally, she came across one with a green triangle painted on it. She placed her ear to the door and could hear someone talking. She thought about knocking and walking in meekly but then thought better of it.

*I need to be bold and self-confident,* she thought, and with that, she opened the door and strode inside. The room was much larger than she had anticipated, and books lined the walls. The library! Tables and chairs occupied the middle of the room, and a man in a white robe sat with his back to her, his head buried in a tome, from which he was reading aloud to himself. He stopped abruptly and looked back over his shoulder as if he'd sensed her presence. Gillian recognized him instantly. *Saracen.*

She froze as he leaped up from his chair and ran at her surprisingly fast. He grabbed her shirt by the collar and yanked her towards him. His eyes were wide open as he starred at her.

"Spy!" he yelled. "What are you doing in here, girl? What did you see me doing? Answer me, damn it! You are no hero! What did you hear?" His voice became louder with each word. His breath was putrid.

"Please, Lord Saracen, I haven't heard anything. I am lost," she said, trying to pull his hands off her.

She wanted to tell him she had heard his story, and she had great sympathy for him. But his grip tightened, and she could no longer breathe let alone speak. She was starting to black out. Then she heard a second voice.

"Oh, dear me, what's happening here now? Oh, Saracen, Saracen, Saracen. Do let go of the poor girl. What has she done to deserve this?"

"Spying on me, Master!" he replied. "She is trying to set me up!"

As he spoke, his grip eased, and she was able to get a little air into her lungs.

The second man continued, apparently unflustered. "Now then, Saracen. Let go and return to your chair. That's the way. Good chap, easy as you like."

Gillian gulped down air as Saracen fully released his grip.

She looked up to see an elderly man dressed in a monk's outfit leading Saracen back to his seat. Once Saracen had settled down, the monk put his arm round him and whispered in his ear. Saracen reacted by bursting into tears. The old man comforted him, wrapping his arms around him as Saracen continued to sob. This continued for a couple of minutes, then the old man looked towards the door.

"I say, Rhys, would you be so kind as to see Saracen back to his living quarters?"

"Of course, Master." The response came from the shorter of two young men also dressed in monk's garb. They must have been standing by the doorway the entire time.

Rhys helped Saracen back to his feet and led him out of the room.

The old man smiled at Gillian. "Well, well, you must be the young lady who retrieved one of the missing bracefires."

Gillian approached the old man and shook his hand. "Hello, my name is Gillian. Thank you so much," she said, returning his smile. "I'm not sure what would have happened if you hadn't arrived when you did."

"I'm very sorry about that, Gillian. I need to speak to Lord Mora about the situation. I'm not sure Saracen can be left unaccompanied anymore. It's not his fault. I don't know if you have been told about what happened to him?"

"Yes, I have," replied Gillian. "It's very sad. May I ask who you are?"

The old man laughed. "Yes, of course. My name is Peter, and this lad over here is my friend Duncan."

Duncan had an easy smile and long blond hair. "Hi there, pleased to meet you." He bowed his head to Gillian. "The Master does himself a disservice by naming me his friend, though that is most flattering. I am, along with many others here, one of his followers."

"Semantics, young man, semantics!" Peter laughed and clapped Duncan on the back. "Anyway, what is a young lady like yourself doing wondering around this rabbit warren without map or guide?" he asked, stroking his long greybeard.

Gillian explained how she decided to have a look around but had got lost and had then realized she'd left the remote to her robot assistant behind.

"You were very brave, relying on a Gonk experimental robot to come and find you," Peter said, laughing. "Perhaps we can help you find your way around. And when I say 'we,' I mean Duncan, because I'm not sure how far my old pins will go before, I have to be returned for emergency bed rest!"

They all laughed.

"Again, take that with a pinch of salt," Duncan added. "The Master is fitter than most men half his age."

*****

Gillian and Duncan found themselves sitting in the large dining room that was located above the front entrance of the Cirque. They snacked on pork pies and sausages and looked out onto the square through the largest of the three east-facing windows. A small crowd had gathered, and they were calling out, though it was not possible to hear their words. Duncan had taken Gillian on a grand tour of the Cirque building and had given her some useful navigational tricks. She had asked him if there was anywhere they could go that had a view of the sea, so he'd brought her to the dining hall, which overlooked the front entrance and the water beyond.

"It's okay; they can't see in through the windows. They are made of one-way glass," said Duncan.

But Gillian hadn't been thinking about the crowd outside. She was looking at the sea beyond the square. It was so vast. Where was Tiny? Could he really swim to the island? How would he even know which way to go?"

"You okay?" asked Duncan.

"Sorry, yes," said Gillian. "I think it's due to lack of sleep, but my mind is just drifting in every direction. Tell me about Peter. When Lord Mora told us he was here, my friend Ink got very excited. He seemed like a nice chap, and he definitely has a presence about him."

Duncan brushed away some pastry crumbs that clung to the area around his mouth and sipped on a bottle of water.

"Oh, he has a presence, all right," said Duncan. "He is an amazing man. His greatest achievement is his work with the Oze giants. Many years ago, the giants in Oze were in major trouble. They had been plagued by attacks from the Spindles and the Hag. Both groups took advantage of the giants' good nature and naivety to exploit and rob from them. The Spindles even arranged hunting tours—chartered trips to Ozeland—where paying customers could track and kill a giant just for the thrill of it."

"Are you serious?" Gillian covered her face with her hands.

"Peter felt the same. He sailed to their homeland and lived among them for many years. He taught them how to be wary of outsiders and how to fight when the occasion demanded it. His efforts worked; the slaughter of the giants was reduced to a trickle. Their quality of life also improved as he taught them how to produce food more effectively and how to concoct medicines to ward off common diseases. You can imagine how popular he became with the giants. But he also became a legend with other races who appreciated the giants."

Duncan broke from his story for a moment. A disturbance had erupted in the square below. A group of Cirque guards exited the building via the main doors. The activity was enough to cause a moment of excitement amongst the crowd.

"Anyway," Duncan continued, "three years ago, the Spindles launched a night-time raid on Ozeland; they were fed up with Peter. They captured him, sailed him back to Spindle. They threw the poor man into a Spindle dungeon. Most people do not survive more than a few weeks in those hell holes. Peter endured an entire year.

Then, out of the blue, the Cirque received a most unexpected offer from the Spindles. Lord Mora led the negotiation on behalf of the Cirque. Finally, an exchange took place: three imprisoned Spindle pirates were returned—along with a substantial payment of silver, I believe—in exchange for Peter. The Cirque also had to agree that Peter would never set foot on Ozeland again. Peter was not happy about the deal; he saw it as a clear victory for the Spindles, but we were very happy the great man ended up with us. Did you know he is close to one hundred years old?"

Gillian's draw dropped. "No! He doesn't look anywhere near it!"

Peter grinned. "I always enjoy seeing people's reaction to being told that. He'd been away for so long that none of the current Cirque Lords had ever met him before. He is truly a living legend!"

There was another disturbance in the square. Six more guards marched out. Duncan and Gillian watched them pass through the crowd and head north along the coastline.

"What does he do now?" asked Gillian.

"He teaches. He has around twenty followers here—there would be more, but Espanada is not an easy place to reach."

"You grew up here?"

"No, I'm a refugee from Amos Line, a region now occupied by Leprade."

Gillian nodded. She remembered the name from Nikolas's talk back in Three Widows.

"His followers are from all over the place. Perhaps if you don't find your way home; you would consider joining us?" Duncan smiled.

"Thank you, but I *will* be returning home, and even if for some reason I don't, I'm not really much of a follower."

Duncan laughed. "I'll mark you as undecided. Meanwhile, we should get you back to your room. You must be beyond tired by now."

Gillian yawned right on cue. "Yes, thanks, Duncan. It's been fun and informative, but you're right, I'm turning into a zombie."

Duncan looked at her blankly.

"A zombie, the walking dead. You see them in the movies. They..."

He continued staring at her, and she shook her head.

"Oh, never mind." She sighed. "I guess it's too hard to explain."

Duncan nodded. "I just have to pass a message on to the chef for Peter." Duncan got to his feet. "Sit tight. I'll be right back." He walked quickly into the kitchen via some swinging doors.

An eruption of noise sounded from the square. *More soldiers leaving?* Gillian walked over to the window to watch them depart. But the noise was different this time, and the crowd was no longer facing the Cirque. They had turned around, facing the sea. There were a lot of excited voices, and the noise reached a crescendo. Many of the watchers had walked down to or even beyond the shallow waters that marked the tideline.

Then she saw him. Tiny! He staggered up the beach, water dripping from his hair and his clothes. He looked all around him as he made his way across the sand. At the top, he turned towards a wooden jetty that stretched out into the sea.

Gillian did not wait a moment longer. She sprinted to the door and turned down the corridor to a grand staircase. She leaped down the staircase, taking four or five steps at a time. She vaguely registered hearing Duncan calling after her, but nothing was going to stop her. The main doors were right by the foot of the staircase. A single guard stood in front of them, a long sword in his hands. He looked totally shocked as she came flying towards him.

"Miss? What's happening?"

"Open the door! Open the door at once," she yelled a loudly as she could.

The guard gripped his sword tighter and raised it slightly, shaking his head. "I'm sorry, miss, I have orders…" he said, stumbling over the words.

Gillian reached into her pocket and retrieved the bracefire. She held it aloft in front of her. "In the name of Brunella and by the power of this bracefire, open the door *now*!"

"Okay, okay," said the guard, turning on his heel and pulling down a lever. The huge doors swung open, and as they did so, Gillian ran out into the now empty square. Within a few seconds she had caught up with the stragglers who were running towards Tiny. She zig-zagged around them, but as she made progress, the numbers increased, and she faced a wall of moving people, some of whom recognized her.

"The lost girl, the one who returned the bracefire!" someone shouted.

Soon, others joined in. Many stopped and turned around, inadvertently blocking her way.

"Let me through!' she yelled, brandishing the bracefire in front of her.

A path opened ahead as people scrambled to get out of her way. She was moving so fast; she ran straight into Tiny's leg. He didn't seem to notice the impact. His face was a picture of pain.

"Tiny," she shouted several times.

But there was no reaction. He stood still as a statue with large tears rolling down his face. Then she remembered; she stopped shouting and looked up at him, opening her mind. Instinctively, she also pointed the bracefire up at him.

A familiar fizzing feeling in her head indicated she was about to make contact with Tiny's mind. Then she connected. It was as though an express train hit her. For a few brief moments, she shared the emotions that had taken over Tiny's mind. A tidal wave of despair pulverized her feelings. Everything went dark. Her senses became totally overloaded. She shared his profound sense of loss, and the pain was excruciating. Mercifully, she blacked out, her legs collapsing under her. As she fell to the ground the last thing she heard was Tiny's ear-shattering, primeval yell of grief.

## Chapter 17

Jag was caught in a spider's web; dozens of threads were glued to his arms and legs. Each time he tried to struggle or break free, the sticky mucus spread. He wriggled this way and that, starting to panic, until he couldn't move at all. His head was held firm, and he was looking at a dark-grey wall. A diffused shaft of light flashed across the wall as a large door swung open. The hideous shadow of a human stick creature made its way into view. Its joints clicked, and its head jerked around as it searched for its prey. Then it saw him. Jag screamed as the creature rushed at him, mouth open, rancid fangs bared...

"Morning, Miss Muscle"

Jag slowly opened his eyes...the only part of his body he could move. He was lying on his back, completely immobilized by reams of bonding tape someone had wrapped tightly around him. The room was not brightly lit. He looked to his right as far as he could. There on the next slab lay Pinhorn. He was confined in a similar manner; except he was also locked in leg irons.

"Where are we? "asked Jag groggily. "Where are my friends?" He could use a glass of Anika right now.

"You're in hell. Somewhere called Brunella...or is it Ely?" said Pinhorn.

"Great!" muttered Jag. "We must be in Ely, which is the capital of Brunella. But what is this room?" he asked.

"Oh, you don't want to know!" exclaimed Pinhorn.

Jag could just about make out the bull on the bully's arm.

"Did you lead me here?" continued Pinhorn.

"What?"

"Did you set me up?"

Jag was speechless for a few seconds. "You think I brought you here?"

"I can't figure it out. Nothing has made sense since I followed you into that bloody tunnel."

Jag was stumped. "It wasn't us. We're trapped, too. Do you want to exchange knowledge? It could help us all."

After another pause, Pinhorn shook his head. "I don't trust you."

Jag drew a sharp breath. "You think I trust *you*? You were trying to beat the crap out of us a few minutes before this whole thing started."

"Are your friends here, too?" asked Pinhorn, ignoring Jag's response.

"Gillian and Freddie are here, but they left on a boat."

"Good friends, are they? Going off on a boat trip and leaving you at the mercy of these masochists."

A series of clanking noises interrupted their conversation. A door creaked open. Jag looked as far to the left as his confinement would allow. A short, balding man wearing a white lab coat walked into Jag's line of vision, clipboard in hand. Behind him walked a tall, emaciated figure with long, receding black hair. He was humming a little ditty to himself.

"What a surprise! Two little flies. Fit for the spider to dine on."

Jag shivered, reminded of the horrible dream he'd had.

"Welcome... Jag, isn't it?"

The tall man bore more than a passing resemblance to the creature that had featured in Jag's nightmare. Coincidence?

He poked Jag's stomach with his index finger. "The star prize, how about that, Bottle? It's a shame Master Leprade isn't here to enjoy the moment."

The little man nodded in agreement.

"You are wasting your time, Catchpole. He won't know how to open it," said Pinhorn.

"You're Catchpole?" Jag asked.

"So, you have heard of me? How flattering. It's always rewarding to hear that one has a certain notoriety, don't you think, Bottle? Please start preparing the prisoner."

The little man produced a small knife and started cutting away a section of the bonding tape that covered Jag's arm.

Catchpole looked on. "And for breakfast today, may I recommend bio-treacle!"

Over Catchpole's shoulder, Jag caught sight of Bottle preparing a syringe with a long needle.

"What are you doing?" Jag asked, panic setting in. He was struggling to recall the Catchpole story Nikolas had told them.

Jag jerked against his bonds at the sharp jab of the hypodermic in his arm, the liquid burning as it spurted into his bloodstream.

"Pinhorn, your comment was noted. However, it was rather rudely delivered. You would do well to note that now we have Jag, we probably don't need you anymore. Give Pinhorn a hundred please, Bottle."

"No!" yelled Pinhorn. "I take it back!"

From his position, Jag couldn't see Bottle delivering the electric shock, but he heard the crackling salvo of electricity at it struck Pinhorn. Even after Bottle had finished torturing Pinhorn, the boy's pitiful cries of pain sent chills of terror up Jag's arms.

Bottle cut away the remainder of Jag's tape. He had no restraints now, but the drug Bottle had administered made Jag feel very heavy. He could barely move his limbs and was completely at the mercy of his captors. Catchpole and Bottle carried him over to a sturdy pole with hooks attached at different heights. They lifted him, pulled his shirt over one of the higher hooks and left him dangling, his feet several inches above the floor. His shirt was stretched to the breaking point, the fabric cutting into him.

Catchpole looked up at Jag's face and smiled, obviously pleased with the pain he was suffering. "Now then. I'm not an unreasonable man; I do not want to punish you with more pain than is strictly necessary. However, it's important to calibrate one's electronic tools, don't you think? Hmmm? No opinion on the matter? I'm sure Bottle agrees, don't you, little man? Why don't you give him a couple of fifties just to make sure everything is in good order?"

Bottle raised his electric pistol and fired two rounds of charge into Jag's thigh. The pain was so great Jag was convinced he'd been struck with real bullets. The shock spread throughout his body. Each pulse felt like red-hot liquid passing through his veins.

"Enough!" Jag yelled. "What do you want from me?"

"Okay, very good," purred Leprade's henchman, clapping his sinewy hands together. "Now, we are ready to play. I expect you would like to know the rules? You know what? Pinhorn and I played this game yesterday. Pinhorn, would you be a good little plump boy and remind us of the rules?"

Pinhorn's voice was shaky, but he tried to shout. "Why don't you take your pathetic little electric toy thing and stuff it where the sun don't shine, you insect freak?"

Jag couldn't believe what he was hearing. Pinhorn was either far braver or far more stupid than Jag thought—perhaps both. On Catchpole's orders, Bottle fired a two hundred into Pinhorn's thigh. There was nothing phony about Pinhorn's cries of pain. Why was he doing this to himself?

Catchpole clapped his hands again. "Oh, I forgot to mention, I will be receiving a new Information Extracting Device this morning, courtesy of some friends in Amos Line. I hear it attacks the body and the mind simultaneously, and it has scored close to one hundred percent even against the most stubborn of subjects. Outside of the trials, you two will be the first to try it out. I bet you are excited!"

Jag said nothing, and Pinhorn was still trying to recover from his latest dose of electricity.

"So, Jag, I ask a question, and you answer. If I like the answer, you get to answer another. If I don't, you get a correction, and here's the fun bit—I think you are going to like it—each time you get a correction, the power doubles... Now, let's begin!"

Jag spent the next hour in living hell. He had no answers to any of the questions Catchpole asked. He did learn to at least try to give an answer because Catchpole classified not knowing as a lie. The pain Jag experienced at each increase in voltage had risen off the scale. Every muscle in his body hurt, he was having spasms, and he couldn't think rationally.

"Okay, I'm bored," said Catchpole, pretending to yawn. "And what do we do when the game gets boring, my learned friend, Mr. Bottle?"

"We up the stakes, Master."

"Spot on, Bottle," said Catchpole, slapping the little man on his back. "Anybody would think we'd been through this before!" Catchpole sat down. "I set a challenge for you. If you succeed, your friend here will be set free. He will be given safe passage to Gonk, no questions asked."

"And if I fail?" whispered Jag, his vocal cords semi-paralyzed from the shocks.

"If you fail, we execute him—immediately."

Jag recoiled with alarm. No sound came from Pinhorn. For a full minute, Jag tried to get on top of his nerves and emotions. What should he do? Nikolas's words came back to him: *to be interrogated by Catchpole was a death sentence in all but name.* If he was going to kill them anyway, what did they have to lose?

"Am I allowed to know what the challenge is before I choose?" he asked.

Catchpole thought about it for a minute, then reached into a hidden pocket and retrieved a very old-looking wooden box. The wood was inlaid with perfect circles.

"The challenge?" asked Jag.

"Open the box," said Catchpole, for once without his fake smile.

"Okay, I accept, but you will have to let me down," said Jag.

## Chapter 18

Jag was in full-on panic mode. Catchpole had given him "one bell" to find a way to open a box or become a witness to Pinhorn's execution. Jag only had a few minutes left, and he still had no idea how to open the box. Beautifully rendered inlays covered the cereal-box size container, but there was nothing about it that suggested it could be opened. Instinctively, he wanted to try smashing it but knew people far stronger than him had tried and failed using that approach.

"Thirty moments," announced Catchpole.

Jag took a quick look up; the black-robed, rebel henchman stood just a few feet away, smiling malevolently, and next to him stood a very muscular-looking RagaRaga holding the handle of a fearsome broadsword. Its blade was as long as his leg.

"Whoa, stop! Hold it, I have the solution," pleaded Jag.

"Six, five, four, three, two, one…time's up," said Catchpole.

"Kill Pinhorn and you will never know how to open the box…but I know where to find the answer."

The RagaRaga walked over to where Pinhorn lay and hoisted the giant blade above his exposed throat. He looked to Catchpole for the nod.

Catchpole looked over at Bottle. "What do you think?"

The little man in the white lab coat shrugged.

"Tell me, Jag. Where is the answer?"

"In a book," replied Jag, shaking. "In my backpack, wherever that is."

"Oh, I took a look at that last night. Mind-numbingly boring if you ask me. Stories from the distant past. There's nothing in there…" He looked over at the soldier and raised his hand.

Jag closed his eyes; he didn't want to see Pinhorn's face.

"You have to know what to look for," said Jag in a desperate last attempt to delay the inevitable.

"And you are an expert, I suppose?"

"Yes," said Jag, "I am."

Catchpole laughed. "What the heck. Let's give the book theory a go!"

He signalled to the trooper to lower the sword. "But don't go anywhere; I have a feeling we will need your services shortly."

The trooper stepped back against the wall and nodded.

"One further condition, Jag," Catchpole said. "If you do not find the solution in its pages, you will be the first guinea pig for my new toy!"

Bottle had already fetched Jag's backpack and passed it to him. Surprisingly, everything was still in it, although the contents were a mess. He carefully removed Nikolas's tome.

"It will take a while; I have to read through a chapter," said Jag.

"Then you shall read it aloud," said Catchpole, "and you'd better have an answer by the end. Because if you are playing me for a fool…" He looked to his assistant. "Bottle go see if the new toy is here yet. It should have arrived by now."

Bottle opened the door. For a moment, Jag looked up from the book. He glanced towards the exit. Could he make a dash for it? But no…he still hadn't shaken off the effects of the treacle drug. He wouldn't get far, and anyway, could he leave Pinhorn? A tempting idea but…

The door swung open again, and Bottle re-entered the room, pushing a large box on small metal wheels. Catchpole literally hopped with excitement.

"Perfect," he said, clapping once again. "My new toy! Isn't this exciting? Get on with it, Jag."

Jag looked down at the book. He thumbed through the pages until he reached the chapter he had read aloud to Ulma and The Vicar. Could the box in the story be the same as the one now sitting on Catchpole's chair? Either way, the book hadn't revealed the password, or had it? Jag was just buying time, and this was his last credit. This was probably the last thing he would ever read. He wished he could see his mother one more time…and Freddie—and Jag kind of missed Ulma. He felt an ache in his chest and stomach that had nothing to do with the torture.

*****

"Well?" said Catchpole.

"You didn't hear it then?" said Jag quickly, but the desperation in his voice belied his effort to appear confident they were onto something.

Catchpole signalled the guard to prepare for the execution and said, "They opened a box! So, what? Even if it is the same box, which is very unlikely, they didn't give the password!"

"Well, that's because it's a puzzle." Jag's heart thumped against his ribcage.

"Enough!" yelled Catchpole, his usually pale face turning bright red. "Now, you will both pay, you freaks from another world. Proceed, guard!"

There was a deafeningly loud bang from inside the crate. The lid blew clean off the base, hit the ceiling, and landed with a clatter, right next to where Pinhorn was lying.

Two shadowy figures leaped out. Dressed in black fatigues with loose black hoods concealing their identities, they tossed two smoke cannisters into the middle of the room. Within seconds, visibility became very poor. The two men removed their hoods; Jag couldn't believe his eyes.

"Good morning, Mr. Jonathan Ur-Jag. Williams and Trick Prisoner Extraction Service, at your disposal."

The guard started running at them, but Trick fired two rounds, and the man went down heavily in front of Jag.

"You worms...!" shrieked Catchpole.

"On the floor, insect man!" shouted Williams. "Face down, hands together."

Catchpole complied. Williams jumped onto his back and cuffed Catchpole's arms and legs.

"You vermin!" screamed Catchpole.

"Where's the other one?" Trick asked calmly.

Jag looked around the room. Where was Bottle? An open door indicated the little man had slipped out, which meant...

Alarm bells started ringing. Jag hobbled over to Pinhorn as quickly as his drug-addled legs would allow him. The two Mensans and Jag lifted Pinhorn. The thick layers of tape made him totally rigid, like an Egyptian mummy. They dropped him into the crate, the impact causing Pinhorn to yell out in pain. The rumble of a large number of troops running towards them down the passageway echoed from a distance.

"You are all going to be ripped apart," shouted Catchpole, thrashing around like a newly landed fish.

"In the crate," Trick shouted at Jag.

Jag hesitated.

"Now!" Trick added.

Jag dragged himself over the lip of the wooden box and landed on Pinhorn.

"There's a gun down there somewhere; use it on anyone who looks remotely hostile."

"But I..." protested Jag as the crate started moving. He fumbled around for the weapon. Finally, he felt a cold metallic barrel. Unfortunately, it was partially under Pinhorn and took some effort to extract. Jag lifted his head to shout at Trick. "Wait, the box! We can't leave without it."

The crate began to accelerate. They had to bring that box. By way of an answer, two objects landed on his head in quick succession—first the box and then his backpack. Jag had never been so happy to receive two bangs to the head.

"Okay," said Williams. "Now, stand up and shoot something!"

Jag adjusted his stance to keep the gun steady—a nearly impossible task with the trolley hurtling down the long passageway. Jag took a quick look behind—a dozen or more RagaRaga chased after them. Jag turned his head, and his heart sank. About the same number of RagaRaga blocked their path to the exit.

"Ahead! Let them have it, Jag!" ordered Trick breathlessly.

Jag fumbled with the strange gun. He'd never held one before, let alone fired one. He pointed it at the troops blocking their way and squeezed the trigger. The loud bang hurt his ears, and the recoil on his shoulder sent a spasm of pain down his arm. One of the troopers fell. Jag experienced a grim feeling of satisfaction.

"I shot one!" he yelled.

"Shoot another," replied Trick.

Jag ducked as they crashed into the line of RagaRaga. The impact threw him backward, and he landed hard again on Pinhorn. He clambered to his feet and peeked out; they had broken through the cordon and were now rolling across a large courtyard towards what Jag was certain had to be the town gate. Something was going on there, too. Guards were running about by the exit, firing at a fast-moving figure on the wall. The person was returning fire. As they drew closer, Jag recognized the Welsh accent.

"Godless plebs! Soulless infidels!"

The Vicar dropped out of sight, and moments later, the portcullis started rising. Williams and Trick directed the trolley directly at it. They threw flash and smoke grenades ahead of them, causing panic amongst the guards. Jag picked his targets carefully and shot several RagaRaga. Each time he hit his target; guilt surged through him.

The trolley banged and clattered as it passed through the gateway. Crossbow bolts and pellets deflected off the crate. A flash of pain raced up Jag's arm, but it barely registered, such was his emotional state. The Vicar emerged from the smoke to join the two Mensans as they continued to push the crate as quickly as they could.

"Okay, she's waiting over on the left. Steady!" The Vicar said.

They steered off the rutted lane they had followed out the gateway and accelerated into a dark copse of trees. They were on a downhill slope, and the crate careened off young trees and bounced violently against roots and rocks in the uneven ground. The crate was moving so fast, the Mensans struggled to slow its momentum. Finally, they brought the trolley to a halt, just shy of where Ulma stood waiting with a pair of ponies harnessed to a large flatbed trailer.

"Onto the flatbed!" shouted Trick.

They tried but couldn't lift Pinhorn out of the crate. Instead, they pushed it over onto its side, and he rolled out, still stiff as a board. They hoisted him up and then jumped on themselves. Ulma flicked the reins, and they cantered off.

"Where are we going?" Jag shouted.

"Fabrice in Gonk," Ulma replied.

Jag looked behind, expecting to see pursuers. But there were none. He didn't know why, and he didn't care. For a while, at least, they were safe. He gratefully unzipped his backpack.

"Nice to see you again, lost boy." Ulma looked over her shoulder, flashing a broad smile.

"You, too," he replied making eye contact with her and then looking away shyly. He opened his journal and selected a blank page. He picked up his pencil. Where to begin?

## Chapter 19

The sensation of someone applying a cold compress to her forehead pulled Gillian out of a deep slumber. She blinked up at the blurred images of people surrounding her. Were they talking to her?

"Hello?" she said.

That caused a reaction, but she couldn't make out what they were saying. Her frustration grew.

"Gillian, how are you feeling?"

"Who's speaking?" Her voice was croaky.

"Hey, Gillian, it's me, Ink."

"Hi, Ink, I think I may have caught up with my sleep."

There was laughter from around the bed.

"No kidding," said Ink. "I'm so happy to hear your voice again. You've been out cold for the best part of a day and a half."

As she recovered, Gillian learned there had been several people keeping watch over her—Ink, Freddie, Dell, Mora, Morgan, and Peter. Even Addford popped his head into the medical room from time to time, "just to see how the young lady is doing." It was Ink who brought her up to date with what had happened since she had been unconscious. Duncan had reached her shortly after she collapsed. He had carried her back into the Cirque. They'd summoned Mora, but he hadn't been able to heal what was beginning to look like a terminal injury. Duncan had fetched Peter, and he had prescribed the herbs that brought her back to health.

"That's twice he's saved my life in two days," said Gillian. "No wonder everyone loves him so much."

"To be fair, he didn't fix you by himself. One of the Fade assisted him. Just don't ask me which one!" said Ink.

Ink and Gillian laughed.

"But I am told that he or she will be one of those officiating at the Grand Cirque, so you have a one in three chance of thanking the right one!" Ink added.

"That is if she is up to attending today," Lord Mora said as he entered the room.

Addford and Peter followed on Mora's heels.

Mora stopped near the bed. "Gillian, it is wonderful to see you sitting up. How are you feeling?"

"Well, another glass of Anika water and I'll be the happiest girl in the world!" said Gillian, holding out her empty glass.

"No, my dear," said Peter sternly. "We've already given you more of that highly overrated poison than we should have. Ink, I'm holding you responsible if she somehow comes by any more."

"Understood," said Ink, taking the empty glass and putting it on the bedside table.

An awful, deep-pitched howl penetrated the room. Gillian cringed. The others covered their ears, though they didn't seem surprised by the terrible sound.

"What was that?" yelled Gillian.

"Tiny," said Ink.

"What? Where is he? We have to fetch him."

"He's where you last saw him," continued Ink. "He's mourning his brother."

"We have to help him."

"There is nothing you can do," said Mora. "Even Peter can't communicate with Tiny while he is in this state."

Peter explained the process. "He's been howling once every second bell or so. It will become less frequent as time passes, until eventually, he'll stop and move on."

"But that's awful," said Gillian.

"You would know," said Peter gently. "You experienced his feelings first-hand. I suspect the bracefire amplified the emotion. You were very lucky to survive the exposure."

Tears welled up in Gillian's eyes as the memories of that afternoon started returning. "What happened to Duncan?"

Peter placed his hand on her forehead. "He's with his fellow students. Sorry to say, he is holding himself responsible for what happened; he's very upset."

"It wasn't his fault," said Gillian. "Nothing would have stopped me getting to Tiny. Nothing."

"Young lady," Peter said, "I'm inclined to believe you."

"Okay, everyone," said Mora. "I need to speak to the patient and Freddie alone for a few minutes, as does Addford, I understand?"

"Indeed, Master," replied Addford.

"Freddie!" Gillian had almost forgotten about him. He had been sitting at the end of her bed. She'd never known him to be so quiet. He looked awful.

Ink gave him a hug. "Your number one nurse! Poor Freddie; he has hardly left your bedside."

"Well, I'd have a lot of explaining to do if I came home without you," Freddie quipped. But his usual vitality and energy were missing.

Gillian looked at him, but he avoided her gaze. He could be a real jerk at times, but underneath all that bluster he had a kind heart. Jonathan was very lucky to have Freddie as a friend.

Since Freddie had been asked to stay for the meetings, he remained as the others filed out.

"Sorry to rush this on you Gillian," said Mora, "but do you think you will be up to attending the Great Cirque?"

Gillian looked at the elder. Something about his expression gave away how important this was to him.

"Yes, I should be okay."

Mora sighed with relief.

"It's scheduled to start in two bells," he said. He didn't give her a chance to react to the impending deadline. "More good news: Rush has arrived and will represent the Western Wilds. We are fortunate to have her. She's one of the few Dory still in our part of the Turn and a brilliant soldier, too. I fear we will have need of her skills before too long. Yes, Freddie?"

"Why isn't Nikolas coming to represent Mensa?"

Mora looked slowly up and then down and then back at Freddie. "There's some history to this. Nikolas is my cousin, and I love and respect him. He was also a Lord and a very influential member of the inner-circle, but we had a falling out on a policy issue. I'm not going into details now, but the argument was serious enough that we could no longer work together at its conclusion. The inner-circle voted with me, and Salokin had no choice but to resign and return to Mensa. The Circle agreed he should continue as the junior representative in Three Widows. None of us wanted to see his talent wasted."

"Salokin?" Freddie asked.

"Oh. I'm sorry. I used his senior name. It's a tradition that anyone promoted from junior to senior rep change their name—usually employing the letters of their former name. Hence Salokin is Nikolas spelled backward." Mora laughed. "I don't think he was ever very keen on his new name. He changed it back immediately after he resigned." Mora paused for a minute and then asked, "Tell me, if you feel comfortable doing so, did Nikolas ask either or both of you to keep an eye out for a traitor in our midst?"

Gillian looked at Freddie. He shrugged. Gillian was at a loss. What should she say? Who to trust?

"Thank you... Your hesitation is all the answer I need. My cousin has long been obsessed with the theory that someone in a high office has been leaking critical data to our enemies. I don't buy it. I know all the high-ranking officials here, and I'm sorry if this comes across as a little arrogant, but I pride myself on my ability to read people. I am one hundred percent certain none of them would sell us out. But by all means, feel free to investigate the matter for yourselves. I'll cooperate willingly and will be happy to answer any questions you may have."

"Thanks," said Gillian. "We're sorry. We have been placed in an awkward position here."

"It's fine. Don't apologize. I fully understand how you must be feeling. I have to run; I need to prepare for the Circle. Please keep your meeting with Addford short because you need to get ready, too."

Lord Mora turned and left without another word. For a second, Gillian and Freddie were alone. But before they could discuss this latest development, Addford re-entered the room.

"Okay...very quickly," he said, checking the door before trotting over to Gillian's bed, "any leads regarding the imposter?"

"None," said Freddie. "In fact, I think our investigation just took a backward step."

He told Addford what had just happened with Mora.

"Okay, that's unfortunate, but I implore you to keep working on it. Push that conversation out of your mind," he said.

"That's easy for you to say!" said Gillian, raising her voice. "We are in an impossible position."

Addford put his finger to his lips. "Please, quiet. I have something for you. I can't give it to you now, but I will find a way of getting it to you tonight."

"What?" Gillian and Freddie said simultaneously.

"Documents—possibly letters from the insider. Okay, I have to go, and you have to get ready." He started for the door.

"Wait, Addford! If we do identify this person, who do we tell?" asked Gillian.

Addford turned around. "Me and only me. I will take it from there. I am in the outer circle chamber all day tomorrow and the following day. Bye for now." He turned and hurried out the door.

Gillian and Freddie exchanged a stunned look.

"Are you keeping up with this?" Freddie asked.

Before Gillian had a chance to reply the door swung open again, and Ink hurried into the room.

"Right, off you go, nurse Freddie. The young lady here has to be prepared for her big meeting."

"But I, err..." stammered Freddie.

"Off you go. You have to get ready, too. Perhaps Addford will give you a hand with your wardrobe," said Ink.

Gillian joined in with Ink's laughter.

"It's okay, Freddie. We'll talk later," said Gillian.

Freddie headed for the door.

"Oh, and Freddie," she called after him.

He turned around to look at her.

"Thanks" she said.
Freddie smiled, nodded, and then left the room.

*****

Gillian stood by the door to the inner-circle. She was about to enter the most hallowed room in the whole Turn. She felt nervous, but the was still dizzy from the trauma of her life-threatening experience and felt as though she was floating rather than walking. Her hair was stylishly bundled up on her head and she wore a simple pale-blue dress. Her only accessory was the hoop necklace Nikolas had given her. By prior arrangement, she was to be the last of the nine to enter the chamber. All the residents of the Cirque who were not permitted to enter the chamber were doing the next best thing by waiting in the outer chamber. From there they could watch the big guns come and go. Many of them would also expect to go straight into a briefing with their rep once the meeting ended and plans were disseminated. There had been an audible murmur when she passed through the second-tier room.

"You see? You look absolutely stunning," whispered Ink in her ear.

Marcus and Dell were sitting in the front row. Marcus was staring at her, but Gillian pretended not to notice him. She smiled at Dell, who grinned and gave her a thumbs up.

"Nicely done." said Ink.

Morgan stood by the door. His job was to open the door and let her in.

"Password please?" said the young officer.

"There's a password?" said Gillian. She didn't remember any mention of this in her preparations.

"Hug me." he replied, smiling and holding his arms out wide.

"Is that the password or a command?" said Gillian laughing and leaning forward to accept his embrace.

"Very good, you may enter." He grabbed the door handle and swung it open. "Good luck."

Anyone hoping to catch a glimpse of the inner-circle would be disappointed as there was a thick black curtain a few feet inside.

The door closed, the curtain opened, and Gillian found herself standing in front of the five other members of the inner-circle. They were all standing, positioned in front of their allocated seats. Lord Mora was closest to her, and he took her hand and saw her to her chair. She sat, and everyone else followed suit. The chair was not too comfortable, but maybe that was a good thing. She was still taking a number of herbal remedies, and despite the glamorous makeover Ink had given her, Gillian still hurt all over. She didn't want to pass out here, of all places. She looked at the faces around the table. Immediately to her right was Lord Mora and to her left Addford, who gave her an awkward smile. To his left was Saracen, who looked far from happy as he nodded and then shook his head repeatedly while he muttered to himself. Next to him was... *Oh my goodness!* She hardly recognized Freddie. He wore the military uniform of the Great Circle Guard, and his hair looked like it had met a comb for the first time ever. He grinned sheepishly at her and gave her a mock salute.

"Freddie, you look..." She couldn't think of a way to end the sentence.

"Oh, this little number?" he said, straightening the jacket. "It's just some old thing I threw on."

A striking-looking lady with long brown hair and high cheekbones occupied the last place at the table. She was studying Gillian carefully. For a moment, Gillian couldn't remember who the sixth representative was. Then Mora came to her rescue.

"Gillian, I believe you know everyone here except Rush, who is representing the Dory of the Western Wilds."

Of course! "Pleased to meet you, Rush," she said.

"Gillian, the honour is mine," the Dory soldier said in a dark voice, flashing a tantalizing smile. Her black hair cascaded down her back, and her long eyelashes fluttered.

Mora continued. "Also present in the chamber are three ranking members of the Fade movement. They are here to provide administrative support and to listen in on behalf of their order. The Cirque welcomes them and thanks them for the assistance they have given us...especially over the last few days."

The three Fade sat back away from the table in the shadowy area by the walls. As usual, they wore their hoods pulled well down over their faces.

Mora studied a note in front of him. "For the record, their names are Niam Te Yun, Fa Li Moon, and Ing Wo Pas. We welcome you."

Lord Mora stood. "There is but one item on the agenda, but it is possibly the most important agenda item to be discussed by this forum since the days when Brunella chaired the Cirque."

"In recent months we have seen a marked increase in the activities of our enemies to the south under the traitor Leprade, and from the islands to the north of us, Spindle and Hag. Individually, they are dangerous enemies; working in unison, they are capable of bringing about the total destruction of the Cirque and all it represents..."

Gillian took a good look at the old table around which they sat. She wasn't sure what type of wood it was, but she noticed the segment of table in front of each representative was uniquely designed to illustrate the characteristics of the region they represented. For Amos Line, hand-carved images of musicians and dancers, and a beach scene featuring bathers and children playing, and happy couples walking hand in hand through open fields covered the surface of the table. In the middle of the table was a centrepiece with four holes fashioned into it. She couldn't wait for a break in proceedings so she could take a closer look. But something she had just heard had caught her attention. What was it? She felt Mora's stare, and Gillian realized she had stopped listening. She snapped back to attention just at the exact moment Tiny issued one of his mournful cries. Even in the soundproof inner-sanctum of the Cirque, there was no refuge from Tiny's misery. She covered her ears, but her tears started again as they'd done each time she heard him.

Mora paused for a second and then handed the meeting over to Rush for the military briefing.

"Thank you, Master." Rush got to her feet. "Lord Mora, permanent and acting representatives of the six regions, and the good Fade now present, I have spent the last six weeks traveling the four corners of the Turn, meeting with friends and allies—the few we have left—and observing and analysing all I came upon. I will not spend time detailing and dissecting everything I heard. I request the Circle to accept the conclusions I now give you as being precise and accurate." Rush rested her hands on the table and spread her tapered fingers wide across the surface.

"In summary, a full-scale invasion of the Western Wilds and the Mensan valley is imminent. Our foes have formed an unholy alliance, which gives them an advantage in resources we cannot match. Leprade himself will oversee the combined forces of Spindle, Hag, and the Lepradians, and that is very bad news, indeed. He is as intelligent as he is evil, and as long as he is in command, their alliance is likely to stay strong, disciplined, and well organized."

"How certain are you of these conjectures, war lady?" growled Saracen.

Rush sat down. "I'm afraid it is far stronger than conjecture, Saracen. I would place its probability at one hundred percent. Well, okay, ninety-nine percent."

"Oh, good, there's hope then," said Freddie and earned himself a round of ironic laughter from the table.

"Seriously, though, I'm an outsider here and have no experience of war..." Freddie paused and looked at Mora.

The Lord nodded.

Freddie continued. "You have to at least analyse the one percent. Because if by the remotest of chances, it is the correct interpretation, you are better off knowing in advance."

"Very good, Freddie. Where did you develop that line of thinking?" asked Rush.

"Cricket, actually," said Freddie. "You see, back home, we have these things called test matches, which are kind of like a war but with less fatalities. Anyway, the game can last up to five days, and if one of the batsmen is particularly good, he can dig himself in and bat for maybe two days, chalking up a couple of hundred runs in the process. Obviously, the fielding side have to try to winkle him out…"

Gillian covered her face with her hands, and the remaining members of the Circle were all looking at Freddie with various degrees of confusion showing in their expressions.

"Maybe another day," said Freddie.

Poor Freddie thought Gillian. Just as he was starting to look the part!

"Thanks, Freddie," said Mora. "I'm not sure about this cricket thing, but your initial point was spot on. We have to find an answer—or die trying."

Saracen let out an unpleasant snarling noise.

"What do our forces look like?" asked a clearly distressed Addford. "Can we not request help from the Gonks? They have a large number of battle-hardened troops. Can they not spare a few?"

"Owlspin has done all he can to help us. The Gonks have their hands full keeping the RagaRaga at bay. Despite this, he has generously sent two units north under Captain Conroy," said Rush. "They should reach Mensa today. We have also heard the islands of Trellis and Crow are sending a unit each. But even with all this help we are still numerically far behind Leprade."

Gillian held up her hand.

"Gillian?" Mora acknowledged her request to speak.

"What about the bracefires? They have some sort of power, right?"

Gillian kept her gaze on Mora, but from the corner of her eye she noticed Rush appeared to be looking intently at her every movement.

Mora looked up. "Thank you, Gillian. The bracefires are the one percent."

## Chapter 20

Mora asked all the reps to remain in their seats for the duration of the exercise. "Everyone is wearing their Cirque hoop? Good. We will now have the bracefires slotted into their places. If the will of Brunella allows it, they will generate power that alliance troopers can tap into."

He gestured to the tallest of the three Fade. "Ing Wo Pas, please retrieve the box."

Ing Wo Pas walked to a section of the wall near the curtain through which Gillian had entered. For the first time, she noticed the Fade each had a small, coloured ribbon sewn into their hoods—Ing Wo Pas's ribbon was orange, and the other two were green and pale blue. Ing ran his palm across the wall and revealed two sets of parallel lines, which Gillian correctly guessed was the outline of a secret compartment. The door popped open.

Mora looked around the room. "Okay, before we start this, some of you may feel heat through your hoops. Don't remove the hoop. It won't get to the point where it is intolerable. Some of you may even feel a build-up of power inside you. Do not under any circumstances attempt to use the power. In this confined space you could unleash enough energy to kill everyone in the room, and that would seriously spoil my day. Please bring the box over."

"Please remove the lid," Mora said.

Ing very gently lifted the lid off the box and put it carefully to one side.

"There are five original bracefires in this box. Each has a unique slot on the table that it will slide into. Once it is in position it may or may not start generating power. No one should touch them other than a Fade or Saracen. Once these five have been positioned we will add the sibling bracefires held by Gillian and Freddie."

Saracen let out a howl of derisive laughter. "CP is not coming?" he asked Mora.

"No, only good people are allowed here. Can you help us?"

Saracen said nothing, but he stooped down until his eyes were level with the table and held up one finger.

"Okay, let's do this," said Mora, gesturing towards the Fade.

The Fade with the light-blue ribbon reached into the box and picked up a shining silver object.

"Beautiful," said Gillian. It was a ballet dancer.

The Fade walked three steps around the table and slotted the piece into a depression in the wood that Gillian hadn't spotted before. The ballet dancer stood in place, pirouetting and looking very much at home.

The second item drawn from the box was a silver palm tree. Rush's eyes immediately lit up.

"For those of you who do not know, this tree is a sacred symbol to the Dory people. The original tree still stands tall and strong. To a nomad, it represents two of the most important needs—water and shade. It is called the Lonely Tree, because it grows in a coastal area where there are no other trees."

The Fade slotted its base into another small indentation, this one in front of Rush. The Fade then repeated the ritual for each of the remaining pieces—the hammer, the goblet, and the book. The members observed the process in silence, the absolute quiet only adding to the growing tension. But Gillian neither saw nor heard any reaction.

"Now, we add the Mensan siblings," said Mora with the slightest quiver in his voice.

He gestured to the blue-ribbon Fade, who walked over to Freddie and held out his hand. Freddie reached into his pocket and pulled out the harvester and placed it into the Fade's palm. The Fade slotted the little silver statue into its allotted space, and...nothing happened. Gillian clenched her hands together. She had expected each placement of each bracefire in turn to cause some kind of reaction. But the pieces stood in place, completely motionless. They were down to their last chance. Blue Ribbon Fade approached Gillian to take the little silver sower. As he drew close, a combination of the candlelight behind her and movement in his oversized hood gave her the briefest of glimpses of his face. Enough of a glimpse for her to recognize him.

"I don't believe it!" she called out, jumping to her feet. She grabbed his hood with both hands and yanked it back off his head.

"Gillian, stop! What are you doing?" cried Mora.

"Steady, Gillian!" Freddie said. "Whoa! What the...?"

Without his hood concealing his face Fa Li no longer looked like a mysterious Fade monk. With his crop of short blond hair and his shy smile he became Farley, the Pendleton year eight student once again.

"Oh, boy," said Gillian. "We are stupid! It was so obvious—Farley/Fa Li." She ruffled his hair.

Freddie jumped from his seat and hurried around the table. "Okay, young Mr. Farley or Fade Fa Li—depending on which day of the week it is. You have some serious explaining to do!"

No one else in the room seemed surprised by the outing of Fa Li, but Mora appeared to be extremely frustrated by the delay.

"Gillian, Freddie, I can see you have just had a bit of a rude awakening, but we have to complete the bracefire ritual. Every second we waste now may cost several of our valiant troops their lives," said Mora.

Freddie raised his hand. "Lord Mora, you don't understand, this is pretty radical. Fa Li brought us here. He was living in our world, and he led us here like the Pied Piper of Hamelin."

Gillian put her hand on Freddie's shoulder. "Freddie, Lord Mora has a point. We need to finish this up one way or the other. But I agree with you; someone owes us an explanation once we're done."

Gillian passed the sower to Fa Li. With his hood still down Fa Li turned and slotted it into the position adjacent to the harvester.

The room was totally silent. There had been an atmosphere of anticipation, but now it was rapidly turning anticlimactic. They waited and waited some more. Eventually, Saracen slowly stood up from where he had been kneeling on the floor. He reached across the table and touched the Sower with the tip of his right index finger, then he reached towards Gillian with his other hand, gesturing for her to take hold of it. She did so and was surprised how cold his skin felt. He released his hand from hers for a moment and took her left hand and manipulated her fingers until she was mirroring the index finger touch of his right hand. She understood and pressed the finger against the harvester and then finally completed the bridge by taking hold of his left hand again.

For several seconds there was no reaction. Then she felt a slight tingling sensation in her finger. The energy worked its way up her arm, across her shoulders, and up her neck until she could feel it sparking in the centre of her head. The tingle turned to a buzz and the buzz into a deep, resonating vibration. The pulse got stronger by the second. She wanted to let go but realized she couldn't. She couldn't move.

A woman's voice cried out, "Ick stanched, hez iamse!"

"Please stop her saying that!"

But the woman repeated the words. "Ick stanched, hez iamse." And then, "Ick stanched hez lamse Brunella!"

*That's me talking!* Gillian's eyes flew open wide at the realization, and the pulse in her head erupted. From it, heat and power surged through every cell in her body. She saw and felt the blue electricity form a shimmering cloud around her, and once again, she felt its power—now her power. Saracen stood in front of her, face to face, searching her eyes. Then he removed his finger from the sower, and Gillian felt as though she'd been hit by a massive electric shock. She tumbled to the ground.

For a few seconds, she blacked out. When she came around, Freddie and Rush were helping her back into her chair. She was winded from the shock, and it took several minutes before she caught her breath. Freddie stood next to her, and Rush hovered just behind him. Saracen had returned to his chair. Mora leaned over him, and they were deep in conversation.

"How are you feeling?" asked Freddie.

"Not bad, considering... But I wouldn't recommend that experience to anyone else."

"Have you seen what you started?" Freddie nodded towards the table.

Gillian sat up in the chair. A small blue cloud enshrouded each of the bracefires, and a straight line of blue energy beamed between each of the artefacts. They emitted a quiet buzzing like that of a transformer.

"I think your work here is done!" said Freddie, looking happier than he had for some time. "You were standing in a cloud of blue gas. I was both terrified and amazed at the same time."

"I just hope that was the last time I have to do it," said Gillian. "You know, for a few seconds I had not only huge strength but also great knowledge. It's all gone now, but for a moment I knew so much…"

"What are you saying?" Freddie asked.

She whispered her answer. "Something has been bothering me about Lord Mora. When I was empowered, I knew why. But the answer is gone now."

"Well, what use is that then?" said Freddie.

"Shhh. Pass me over his note—quickly!" whispered Gillian.

"You can't do that!" Freddie's face grew red.

"Quickly, I'm just borrowing it," she said.

Freddie looked over at Mora one more time. He was still talking with Saracen. Freddie grabbed the parchment and passed it over. She started to read through his notes. They were just as he had read them.

"What are you looking for?" asked Freddie.

"I don't know… The way he writes?"

Mora's voice a couple of inches from her ear gave her a jolt.

"Mine, I believe?" he said, yanking the parchment out of her hand.

"Oh, my gosh, yes, sorry!" she said weakly.

Freddie rolled his eyes and looked away. Mora folded the paper and tucked it into his hip pocket.

"I'm not sure what you are looking for." He smiled. "But trust is something we value, and you just took advantage of it."

Gillian apologized. She also felt hard done by. Someone back at the farm had described this man as having a dark side. She had just taken a dose of it, and it wasn't to her liking.

"Okay, here's where we are," said Mora. He appeared to have put the incident behind him already. "First, all the bracefires have triggered. Saracen has confirmed we are getting as much power from them as we can hope for given the number that are missing. He insists we need the centre piece if we want to be certain of victory. That isn't going to happen. The legend is that the centre piece is composed of four gold candles, also known as the hope candles, but there is no record of them in any history book, and if you ask Saracen about them, he just laughs."

Gillian looked across at the centre of the table and noted the four large, round holes. They could be candleholders…

"Friends from Pendleton, you are free for the rest of the day unless something unexpected comes up. We will find you if need be. The other reps and our senior armed forces leaders will be discussing war strategy."

"What? It's all been decided?" said Gillian. "There's going to be a war?"

"We have no choice, Gillian. We are about to be attacked," said Mora testily.

"There are always options. Has anyone tried negotiating?"

This time, Mora's anger showed on his face and in his voice. "Gillian, how many wars have you fought? You would be well advised to limit your comments to topics you have some knowledge of."

Gillian jumped to her feet and stared at Mora. She was ready to take him on. How dare he? But she caught a glance from Freddie. He gave her a quick shake of his head. She stormed out of the room. She entered the outer chamber, and those waiting outside greeted her with loud applause and cheering. She tried her best to stem her tears and steer her way through the melee but achieved neither goal. She found Morgan blocking her path, closely followed by Marcus.

"Are those tears of joy?" said a smiling Morgan. "We are hearing good things. Tell us about it please?" Couldn't they see she was upset?

"Guys, I just want to be alone right now…" Freddie. Right now, she needed Freddie – the one guy she could trust and would do anything for her. She peered over Morgan's head and there he was. "Freddie, please," she called.

But he was walking away with Ink, and apparently, he hadn't heard her.

A woman in uniform squeezed through the crowd. "Marcus, Morgan, you are both required in the Brunella Chamber immediately."

The two men hurried off after the messenger. Other people moved to take their places, clamouring to get a piece of her, and now she knew no one.

"Please, everyone, step back, please…" she begged.

A deep, booming voice cut across the crowd. "You heard the lady! Everyone step back; she has duties to attend to. Gillian?"

There, standing in front of her, was Duncan, offering her his hand. Beside him was her detail, Violet.

"Service?" the little robot asked.

"Violet, if you wouldn't mind clearing a pathway?" said Duncan.

"Service!" yelled Violet and set about her task with gusto, bowling over anyone and everyone who found themselves in their way.

In no time at all, they'd exited the chamber.

"Thank you, Duncan, I was really in a mess in the outer circle," said

Gillian.

"Damsels in distress are my specialty!" Duncan looked back at her and laughed. "Where are you heading?"

"Oh, I don't know – somewhere quiet would be nice"

"I was just on my way to meet up with Peter and friends on a roof garden. Why don't you come too? You won't be subjected to the celebrity thing with them. They will just be meditating and sharing ideas. Does that qualify as quiet?"

He led her to one of the many spiral staircases that linked the multiple levels of the Great Cirque building. He had a very nice smile, and if he lacked the more classical good looks of Marcus or Morgan, he more than made up for it with his outgoing personality.

"Also, I owe you an apology. I didn't intend to get you in trouble the other afternoon," said Gillian.

"Yeah, you are one fast runner," replied Duncan, flashing her another smile. "This is it. Ready to meet the gang?" He led her out onto an open roof terrace.

*****

Jag and his friends had received a warm welcome in Fabrice. When they arrived, the guards took Ulma, Trick, and Williams to a large dining hall where a hot meal was being prepared for them. One of the guards took The Vicar to the healing rooms where Smedley was recovering. Jag accompanied a group of guards who stretchered Pinhorn to a small set of Fade rooms located in the Fabrice Cirque.

Once Pinhorn had been transferred from the stretcher to a bed, Jag took a closer look at his old nemesis. Pinhorn's skin was a deathly white, and he was struggling with his breathing. His eyes were half open, but he didn't respond to Jag's attempts to communicate with him.

Two monks, wearing oversized hoods that completely hid their faces, went to work on the patient.

"Are they Fade?" he asked the guard nearest him.

The guard looked surprised at the question but nodded. He watched the Fade for a while as they silently went about their task. There was nothing else he could do. He decided to go and meet the others and hopefully find something to eat.

As Jag made his way back to the dining hall, another guard intercepted him.

"Your friend is leaving. Do you want to say goodbye?" the guard asked.

Jag sighed. The Vicar must have decided the time had come to go. He had warned Jag earlier that this might happen.

"I get too emotional, see? Not good for my cold-blooded assassin image..." he'd said.

Jag nodded and followed the guard up a set of stairs to a viewing turret, high up on the Fabrice defensive wall. The Vicar exited the Gonk capital's northern gate and took a sharp left, taking him directly below Jag's position.

"Hey!" he yelled down at him. The Vicar looked up and gave Jag a sweeping wave. Smedley, who was strapped to The Vicar's back, looked happy enough, despite having a wooden peg in place of one of his front legs. He was going to miss the larger than life personality and his clever dog. As he watched the tall man with the three-pointed hat and his injured dog disappear into a dark wooded area, he wondered if they would ever cross paths again.

*****

This time he came within a few feet of the Dining Hall door before, yet again, having his progress checked.

"Lord Owlspin requests the pleasure of your company in his office." The tall guard tapped him on his shoulder and re-directed him. Jag would have to wait for his supper.

Owlspin's quarters were located adjacent to the Gonk Cirque building. Owlspin smiled broadly as Jag entered his office.

"I understand you've had quite an adventure, Jag," he said, brushing his long, curly hair back from his youthful face.

"I suppose I have really," replied Jag. He hadn't thought of it as an adventure.

"Well, I'd like to hear the story if you don't mind?"

Jag told his story with Owlspin listening to every word and asking many questions. When they were finished Jag took his chance to ask a question.

"Nikolas said you would be 'revealing' a task for me?"

Owlspin laughed. "Well, yes, I did, but it seems you've beaten me to it."

Jag raised his eyebrows. What did that mean?

"The box you took from Catchpole. We had reason to believe you might be able to help us retrieve it. May I see it?"

Jag retrieved the box from his bag and handed it to Owlspin. The young man studied it almost reverently, turning it slowly in his hands and running his fingertips over the engraved patterns. He paid particular attention to the circles. His face lit up as he returned it to Jag.

"It is very probable that this is the original cipher made by a figure of huge historical importance to the Turn."

"Robert?" said Jag.

"Yes!" said Owlspin. "You know of this legend?"

"I've read a little bit about him."

"That's great. So, you know that Robert and Timothy constructed a cipher, which, it is said, gives directions to a location where certain items of high value to the Turn are hidden?"

"I haven't read the whole story."

"The cipher has been missing for many, many years. How it came into Leprade's possession is unknown, but the rest of the Turn weren't able to rest knowing he had such a potentially dangerous item in his hands. Just one problem for Leprade—and a saving grace for us—he wasn't able to open it."

"I know that much. Catchpole was trying to make me open it."

Owlspin stood up and put his hand on Jag's shoulder.

"I am so sorry this happened to you. Leprade, Catchpole, and their subordinates are as evil as they are toxic. We became aware of you when a high Fade linked your name with the cipher. Of course, we were very keen to meet you. Though we had no idea what the connection was, we certainly didn't expect you to waltz into Brunella and pinch it from under Catchpole's nose!"

Jag shrugged and Owlspin smiled.

"This evening there is a possible window for us to contact Espanada. I'm sure you want to know how your friends are."

"Yes, very much." Jag held out the box towards Owlspin.

"No, please hold on to it—at least until the meeting. Off you go and take some supper; you must be very hungry. I'll have someone fetch you when the link is made."

Jag walked towards the door.

"Just one more thing," said Owlspin, looking at him through half closed eyes. "We haven't met before, have we?"

Jag nearly tripped up. "Have you ever been to Earth?"

"No."

"Then I would say there's definitely no chance we've met then."

As he left the room, Jag dug into his pack for his journal. What a strange thing to ask. He would definitely be including that last question in his notes.

*****

Duncan had persuaded Gillian to meet Peter and his followers. As they along the roof top, a booming cry served as a reminder of poor Tiny's misery. Once again, she wiped away tears as the giants' friend's followers greeted her. They had been sitting in a large semi-circle, listening to Peter, but broke off the lesson so they could say hello.

Duncan was right. The group of young people were very easy going and didn't crowd or harass her. She insisted they carry on with their agenda, and she would listen in. They covered a wide variety of topics, but the main themes were of tolerance and love. They involved her and listened attentively to her opinions. One thought rose uppermost in her mind: what a contrast to what she had left behind downstairs!

She spent a few minutes alone with Peter. He asked her what the leaders had decided, and she brought him up to date.

"It's so sad," he said. "This was avoidable. The smallest modicum of effort to talk to each other was all that was needed. Now, there will be needless bloodshed."

A tear fell from his eye, and Gillian instinctively wiped it away for him.

He laughed. "Not quite as sad as an old fool like me, tearing up over it, though!"

They both laughed.

One by one, the group members left to attend to their responsibilities. Finally, Gillian was alone with Duncan. They lay on their backs, observing the early evening stars—there wasn't a constellation out there she recognized. *Where am I?* she wondered just as she had done on the boat crossing.

"You know you could do far worse than join us," said Duncan.

"I have to go home. I miss my family, and I need to finish school."

"Maybe later then?"

"You are funny, Duncan!" Gillian laughed. "Tell me, how did you get Violet to respond to your commands. I thought details were supposed to be faithful to their owners?"

"Duncan pulled a screwdriver out of his pocket and showed it to Gillian. "It's amazing what a little mechanical knowledge and one of these can achieve!"

Once again, they were laughing.

"Speak of the devil" said Duncan.

Violet made her way to them over the roof garden.

"What's up, Violet?" said Gillian.

"Service?" she said.

"I'm confused, Violet. Did I call for you by mistake? Or do you have a message for me?"

"Service!" said a delighted Violet. "Gillian must come with me. There is a call for her."

"There's a *call* for me?" Gillian choked. "Out of the blue, there's a working telephone in this strange world?"

"Gillian must be fast. There is a limited call."

"And who is calling?" asked Gillian, stifling a yawn.

"His name is Jag. Shall I tell him you are busy?"

# Chapter 21

Jag shivered as he nursed his mug of hot tea. He was in the small chamber known as the Pipe Room, located in a basement some thirty feet or more beneath the Fabrice Cirque building. The Gonk had secured a connection to Espanada via one of the pipes. Owlspin had asked the engineer in Espanada to track down a select group to attend the meeting. They were waiting for the invitees to arrive. Gillian and Freddie were at the top of the list.

Apart from Jag, there were six others in the Gonk pipe room. Lord Owlspin, plus two of his commanders—Pudlington, a short, squat man with a handlebar mustache, and Fin, a tall, dashing man who had a whiff of perfume about him. Sitting in front of them were Ulma, Trick, and a Fade named Satchi who was the pipe expert. Jag could feel the pulse in his temple thudding louder and louder as each second passed. What if they hadn't made it to Espanada? What if they were dead? At least ten minutes had passed and…nothing.

Jag stood up and started walking 'round the chamber aimlessly. That wasn't helping. He distracted himself by returning to his chair and reviewing his latest journal entries, but he couldn't focus. He put the journal away and sat with his head on his knees, waiting.

*****

"Hello? Hello? Jag, they're telling me you're on the other end of this thing?" Freddie's voice was clear and unmistakable. "Tell me they're right!"

Jag stood up and lifted both arms in celebration. "Hi, Freddie. Yes, I'm here, and so is Ulma."

There was a deafening hoot from the other end. "Jagmeister! Is that really you? Say something again please." Freddie was sobbing.

"Yes, it's me. Have you been having an interesting time?"

Freddie was trying to catch his breath.

"Gillian should be here in a moment. In fact—hey, Gillian, guess who's on line three?" Freddie said.

"Not Jonathan?"

"Hello, Gillian," replied Jag.

The sound of Gillian sobbing came through the pipe. "Jonathan, we are so sorry we left you behind. I don't know why we let it happen."

"It's okay. Other people decided we should go different ways. We couldn't have changed it."

"We have so much to ask you and so much to tell you," said Gillian.

"Hopefully, we will find time for that later," said Owlspin. "I am sorry, but unfortunately, we have pressing matters which must take priority. Tell me, is Mora with you yet?"

"Yes, I am, Lord Owlspin," came Mora's response. "Without delay let me bring you up to date."

"Before you do, please confirm who else is with you, Lord Mora," Owlspin said.

A few moments passed before Mora replied sternly, "Those present can all be trusted. I have been out on patrol with them all."

"For the record, please, Lord Mora," said Owlspin calmly.

"As follows," said Mora grumpily, "me, Saracen, Rush, Gillian, Freddie, and a Fade, Fa Li Moon." He continued with his report.

He spent time talking about the various intelligence reports they had received and invited Rush to repeat her report. Then he moved on to the bracefire test, briefly acknowledging the part Gillian and Freddie had played in delivering them to the inner- circle and Gillian's role in firing the bracefire links.

"Unfortunately, Saracen has confirmed it won't be enough. We need more bracefires," said Mora.

"Or the four candles?" asked Owlspin.

"Tell me you have them?" said Mora.

"No, but we do have something that was very precious to Catchpole. We believe it is the lost cipher."

"That's incredible news! I thought it was in Leprade's possession."

"It was. Young Jag here spent a little time with the Lepradians. Catchpole has been trying to open it for years and tried unsuccessfully to persuade Jag to open it. Anyway, aided and abetted by his special forces crew of Ulma, Trick, and Williams, Jag relieved Catchpole of his prize." Owlspin smiled broadly at the reaction that came back down the pipe.

"Trick? Williams? How did they get involved?" said Freddie, laughing. "And Jag, we need to talk!"

"And you will," Owlspin promised. "I'm sorry, but there are two things we have to discuss. You will have gathered by now how serious this situation has become. Rebel forces have been mobilizing, an invasion of the mainland is, we understand, likely to happen late tomorrow. Lord Mora, please confirm your strategy."

"We are going to surprise Leprade like he's never been surprised before!"

"Tomorrow evening, his forces will land en masse on the Western Wastes. He will not be expecting much resistance. He certainly won't be expecting every troop we can muster, but that is what will be waiting for him in the dunes of the Western Wastes. Even as I speak, we're preparing boats to ship our troops east. Nikolas is organizing the forces available to us on the mainland. We are also promised highly motivated troops by our southern island friends, Trellis and Crow, and possibly Kites."

Gillian spoke up. "Sounds very positive but won't this leave Espanada exposed and vulnerable?"

"In a war, there are always risks, Gillian." Mora said, "We believe this one is well worth taking."

"What about the risk of a leak?" Freddie voiced the question.

There was anger in the lord's voice as he replied. "Young man, do you think we would allow any chance of this reaching enemy ears? We have taken every precaution. There will be no leak!"

If Freddie tried a follow up question, Jag didn't hear it. Had his friends made any progress with identifying the traitor?

"Jag, can we look at the box now?" said Owlspin.

Jag retrieved the ornate wooden container from his pack and placed it on a table in front of him.

"For those in Espanada, let me describe and explain." Owlspin delivered a concise description of the piece and gave a very brief outline of its known history.

Owlspin invited suggestions on how to open the box. Plenty of ideas were forthcoming at both ends, but the box survived being hit, bashed, ordered, and sung at. It remained solidly closed. The last few minutes of the window were chaotic as multiple conversations broke out simultaneously. Even Owlspin couldn't restore order. Jag was able to get Gillian's attention.

"Quickly describe the centre platform to me."

She did as he requested, and then Jag squeezed in one final request.

"The holes for the candles—what size are their diameters?"

"I don't know—about an inch? Jonathan, what—?"

A sudden clunk signalled the closing of the line.

Owlspin looked very frustrated. "I was sure Mora would crack it. Just needed more time. This pretty little box may contain within it the means of saving the Turn, and we are incapable of putting a small dent in it." A look of resignation was etched on his face as he looked round the chamber. "Catchpole and Leprade had this for years and got nowhere. Maybe it is just solid wood. Do you think the box can even be opened?"

Jag picked up the box and held it in his lap. "Yes, I'm certain of it," he replied.

"How can you be so sure?"

Jag held the box up in front of his eyes. "Because I've already opened it."

*****

The seven occupants of the Pipe chamber huddled around a table, looking at the contents of the wooden box. Jag had resisted the temptation to examine the contents when he'd first opened the box, so he was as excited as the others to see what it contained. He also decided not to share the secret of how to open it. He had learned that in the Turn, knowledge was power, and he and his friends would need all the leverage they could get if they were ever going to find their way home.

"But why didn't you open it while our friends were linked to us?" asked Owlspin, pulling back his long hair.

"Because now we know for sure that no one there can leak whatever we might discover," said Jag as he held up the first item from the box—a very, very old, hand-drawn map of the Turn. The fabric was so aged that it began to crumble a bit at the touch of his fingers. He laid it out carefully on the table and sketched a copy of it in his journal. On the horizontal and vertical lines, someone had written several letters, though they were not in order. There were no place names, just sketched depictions of hamlets and villages and other natural features, such as mountains, hills, forests, and rivers.

The second item was a crude eyepatch constructed of dry leather and frayed string. Again, there was no doubting that this was an ancient item.

"Pirates?" said Ulma and Trick at the same time.

"Could be." Owlspin nodded.

The third and final item was a piece of leather parchment, on which Jag could just about make out faded writing. He read the short message aloud:

"If you are needing strength and health
"seek out my likeness.
"I'm the mother of your wealth.

"Good stranger, the above will help you if you are worthy.
"I was initially named incorrectly.
"Speak me now and you will hear my name
"Follow me now and where I am will be plain.
"Strength through unity—may the Cirque protect you.
"R.I."

"Signed by R.I. By all the Cirque Lords! Is this message from Brunella herself?" said Fin.

"It certainly looks like it," said Owlspin, a broad smile on his face.

"I don't understand the message," said Ulma. "Can you make sense of it?"

"I think so," Owlspin said slowly. "R.I. were Brunella's initials before she changed her name to hide from her father."

"Yes," said Pudlington. "Initially my name was wrong. Radeem Isobel was her birth name. Radeem Isobel became Brunella, and thus, her initials were redundant or wrong."

"Her initials were correct, though," said Trick. "She didn't change her name because it was wrong. She changed it to keep herself hidden from her father. Are you certain we have the right person?"

A few seconds passed as the group considered the arguments.

"Let's come back to that because there is more to consider," Owlspin said. "'Seek out my likeness, I'm the mother of your wealth'?"

"I agree that has to be her," conceded Trick. "Who else fits that description?"

Jag looked 'round the table—no one challenged the theory.

"The eye patch?" added Owlspin. "Is everyone familiar with how Brunella ended her days?"

Everyone nodded except Jag. He raised his hand.

"Jag, she met a rather tragic end. She was on board a ship headed west beyond the southern islands. Exactly why, history doesn't tell us, but the ship sank, and all on board perished. Brunella's body washed up onto the shores of Crow. The island had once been notorious as a haven for piracy. But under her leadership, the pirates had been driven out, and law and order had been restored. The locals worshiped her, and when they found her remains, they buried her at the base of the cliff that looked out to the huge ocean to the west. Over the years that followed, the islanders set about creating a long-term memorial for her. They worked on the cliff, chiselling, cutting, and hammering, until they had fashioned a large granite representation of our greatest leader, standing tall, pointing out to sea. It stands there to this day."

Jag considered these details. There was a large gap in his knowledge of Radeem/Brunella. Starting when she ran away from home as a young girl and finishing at her tragic drowning, by which time she was already acknowledged as the greatest leader the Turn had ever known. He had to find time to read Nikolas's book. He nodded an acknowledgement to Owlspin but said nothing.

"Is the eye patch a reference to the Crow pirates?" asked an excited Trick.

Several of the others murmured their agreement.

Owlspin looked around the table. "So, the thing we are looking for is on the west coast of Crow, somewhere near the grave of Brunella. And we have one day to travel there, locate it, retrieve it, work out its function, and then bring it to the conflict where it might or might not tip the scales in the alliance's favour?"

Jag looked around the chamber. It was as if Owlspin had sucked all the air out of the room.

"I will retrieve it."

Everyone turned and looked at Jag.

Pudligton shook his head. "With respect, Jag, this would be a very challenging mission for someone who was born and bred here. For you, it will be virtually impossible. The southern seas are notorious for their unpredictability and—"

"The southern seas are irrelevant," said Jag.

"I'm afraid he's right, Jag," said Owlspin. "You cannot avoid them if you are heading for Crow."

"I won't be going anywhere near them because what we're looking for isn't there." Jag looked down at the table, avoiding all the eyes that fixed on him. "Trick already pointed out that the person the riddle refers to is not Brunella, but you chose to ignore him. Brunella changed her name to stop her father from finding her. Not because her name was wrong. She wasn't the author of the riddle if it refers to her final resting place because she would have been dead and unlikely to have anticipated her demise."

Owlspin buried his head in his arms.

Jag tapped the table and said, "It could, of course, have been written by a surviving relative, but that raises a bunch of other questions."

"This is killing me, Jag," said Trick. "If not Brunella, then who is 'the mother of our wealth?'"

Jag ran a mental checklist of those present and decided he could safely reveal the answer.

"The mother of your wealth was a pig named Rye."

## Chapter 22

Gillian lay face down on her bed, her head buried in her pillow. Marcus had advised her of her role for the upcoming battle, and she wasn't happy with it.

"They need you here, Gillian," said Ink as she checked the alignment of the sites on her crossbow. "If anything should go wrong with the bracefires, you are the only person who can re-start them."

"Why is Freddie going; he's not a soldier. He's too young to be involved in a war," said Gillian.

"We all are, Gill, but we have no choice. Freddie has already shown great ability as a fighter; we need him."

A loud howl of misery interrupted the conversation.

"Jeez, how long is he going to keep that up for?" shouted Gillian, covering her ears.

"Gillian!"

"I know… I don't mean it—poor Tiny." Gillian rolled off her bed, walked over to Ink, and gave her a hug. "I'm losing it. How long before you have to leave?"

"I'm already late. It takes a while to load the boats. We need to be on our way before daybreak. I have ten moments to get to the assembly point; can I borrow Violet to help carry my gear down?"

"Of course," replied Gillian. "Is Freddie not even going to come and say goodbye to me?"

Ink shrugged. "You know Freddie. He probably put his trousers on back to front, and he can't find anyone to fix them."

"Please send Violet back; I'll probably need the company," said Gillian as she helped Ink zipper her bag.

"Addford will be here," said Ink, stifling a laugh.

Gillian gave her a look.

"I'm sorry… Actually, won't Duncan be here?"

Gillian had forgotten about him. Of course, he would. She tried not to react, but Ink gave her that knowing look, and Gillian blushed.

Ink put her hands on her hips. "Okay! Just remember, you are staying here because you have a job to do. Duncan is not part of the job description."

After Ink had left, Gillian drew up a chair by her window. She had a partial view of the docking area. It was a hive of activity with lines of troops plus equipment and supplies being rapidly loaded. There was a knock on the door, and before she had a chance to ask who it was, Violet let herself in, crossed the room, and lay down on Gillian's bed.

"Violet, that's my bed!" protested Gillian.

Another knock sounded on the door, and Donald entered without being invited.

"Hey, you two, we're going to have to work on your manners," said a laughing Gillian.

"Message from the Freddie, for the Gillian," said Donald, talking to a cupboard.

"Do I look like a cupboard? I'm over here, Donald; what's the message from Freddie?"

The detail spun around and located Gillian. "The message from the Freddie is: 'Goodbye.'"

"Well, that was worth waiting for," said Gillian. "No service, you might as well hang out here until morning, too."

Donald trundled over to Gillian's bed, hopped in, and made himself comfortable next to Violet.

"Good thing I wasn't planning on sleeping tonight." Gillian sighed. She went back to her window. A strange boat floated just outside the harbour. It was small in length but sat high in the water. A giant funnel connected to the deck was blowing out large clouds of water vapor; within just a few minutes, the bay looked as though it was shrouded in sea fog. The boats set off, each in turn pushing off from the quay, turning ninety degrees, and then carefully edging their way out into the manufactured fog bank. From where she sat, the fog looked like a highly effective cloak. She thought about all the people she knew who were on the boats, and her tears started streaming. If even one of them didn't make it back, it would be tough to take, but the word was that they were likely to take a severe beating. She didn't want to think about what that would mean.

She looked over at the two details. They lay there snoring, pretending to be asleep, the effect ruined by their wide-open eyes. Then she noticed a stack of white paper under Violet's arm.

"Violet, what are you holding under your arm?"

"Top Secret."

"Okay, but who are you supposed to deliver them to?"

"Deliver to Gillian, but they are Top Secret."

"Can I have them?"

There was a long pause while Violet wrestled with the contradicting directions she had received.

"Please, Gillian, take them. Please note they are Top Secret."

"Right, I think you've made that clear."

She pulled the papers from under the robot's arm. Violet blinked a few times but said nothing. Gillian looked at the first page. It was a cover note:

Gillian, please review and see me. A

The second page appeared to be some kind of intelligence report:

Alliance sending three fully armed Cirque patrol vessels from 5o n to 20n—day after your receipt of this report. Maximize artillery ordinance return.

The third page was another:

More activity revealed overseas: Alliance expecting raiding party at 3W 2 days from your receipt of this report.

The fourth page read similarly:

Cr Island. dispatching unit to Gk 2 days after your receipt of this report.

Only alliance movement reported.

She flipped through the rest—they were all the same in style and content. None were signed, and none included a person's name. But they all appeared to contain confidential data the alliance would not want leaked. There was a pattern in them. Why couldn't Jonathan be here? He would figure it out in seconds. She put the stack of papers on her bed and opened the window. The cool morning air felt good. The fog had lifted, and there wasn't a boat in sight. How long before they reached the shores of the Western Wastes? How long before they clashed head on with the rebels? How long before her friends would fall at the hands of this ruthless enemy? She retrieved the papers from her bed and took them back to her window seat.

"Service?" Violet asked randomly.

"Oh, Violet. Nothing right now, thanks, unless you are an expert in document analysis."

"Analysis Service. Yes."

Gillian looked over at the mini-robot. Why not? There was nothing to lose. She handed the papers over to the detail.

"Here you go then, my friend. Can you see any recurring patterns in these documents?"

Violet held the pile in one hand and then read each page in about half a second and passed them back to Gillian.

"Well?" asked Gillian.

"Yes pattern."

"And?"

"M, A, O, R, M, A, R, O, A, M, R."

Gillian could see it now: the initial letters from one line of each report were a sign- off:

Maximize artillery ordinance return—MAOR

More activity revealed overseas—MARO
Only alliance movement reported—OAMR

Shuffle the letters a bit, and each one said MORA. He was signing off messages using the same cryptic device that newly appointed Lords employed to modify their name.

The man now commanding the entire alliance force was a traitor, and she had no idea what to do about it.

## Chapter 23

Jag gripped the chaise's safety rail as hard as he could. Sitting next to him was Ulma and she looked relaxed despite the wind and dust that was buffeting their ride.

Jag reflected on their rushed departure. Once he had explained to Owlspin and the others gathered in the Pipe Chamber why they had to send a party north rather than west, the Gonks moved very quickly to send them on their way. Owlspin had asked Jag if he would take on this critical mission. Jag had assumed he would be asked and said 'yes' - provided he had Ulma with him.

Pinhorn was still sick. Trick and Williams were to remain in Fabrice and bring him to Three Widows once he was fit enough to travel.

The two-seated chaise was harnessed to Jag's former roommate, David the donkey. Nikolas had sent him down to Gonk for their use. Jag was struggling to work out how Nikolas could have anticipated this event.

Fabrice was disappearing behind them, and as they bumped, bounced, and skidded along the crude road that was taking them inexorably in the direction of the Maria Mountains, Ulma asked questions.

"Tell me again how you worked this out," she shouted over the din of rushing air and the constant rattle of the chaise.

"It was a riddle," Jag shouted back at her. "'I was initially named incorrectly.' It had nothing to do with Brunella; in fact, she wasn't even born when the riddle was composed.

"The piglet Brough gave to Robert was incorrectly named. She should have been branded with R1, as in, Robert's first pig, but she was mistakenly marked RI—'Speak me now and you will hear my name…' RI sounds like Rye. They must have liked the joke because Robert and his adopted family called her Rye. Rye was 'the mother of wealth' because from her came generation after generation of hogs that were to earn a fortune for the family. Hold tight!"

The left wheel of the chaise struck a boulder, which sent the whole unit airborne for a few seconds before it dropped and skidded out of control. Jag covered his eyes until it eventually straightened out. How did the wheel not shatter?

"'Look me up on the map' is telling us to use the initials as a grid reference. R and I.

"And 'where I am will not be plain' tells us to forget the flatlands—we need to look in the mountains."

"R and I?" asked Ulma.

"Exactly—they mark a location in the mountains."

"Lost boy, will you teach me how to read some day?"

"Okay, if we can work it into our schedules."

"What about the pirate patch?" Ulma stood up, looking north towards the mountains.

"Nothing to do with pirates. Wait until we get there, and you'll see."

# Chapter 24

Gillian was sprinting along the passageway that led to the outer and inner circles. The corridors and stairways were deserted. The only others present were the two details who were following her, which was strange because she hadn't asked them to accompany her. Donald, in particular, had no reason for being there. But they gave her a measure of comfort, and she did nothing to stop them. She had to find Addford. She burst into the outer chamber. A mournful howl from outside reminded her of Tiny's situation. How she could use his strength right now. She jogged to the desk and chair where Addford usually worked, but there was no sign of him. Tears built up in her eyes. What else could she do? She walked up the slope to the perimeter of the outer circle and followed in a clockwise direction.

"Hey, you're up a little early!" came a familiar voice from behind her.

"Duncan!" she looked around, and there he was, a broad grin on his face.

His expression turned to one of concern. "Oh, no, are you crying? What's the matter?"

"I need to find Addford urgently. Have you seen him?"

"No, and we've been here all night. If he were here, we would have seen him. We are meditating on peace; this is a very sad situation. May I ask why you need to find Addford so urgently?"

"Well..." She looked at the stack of papers she was carrying.

"You wanted to do some quiet reading together?"

They both laughed.

"Tell you what. Come and see Peter. He will have some ideas; he always does!"

Gillian hesitated, then she thought about the kind, old man. "You know, I could use some of his comfort right now," she said.

A quarter of a turn 'round the cirque and there was Peter and his followers. They were sitting in a semi-circle, as was their custom, with Peter in the middle. He looked very frail. Doubtless, concern about the approaching conflict was taking its toll on the man.

"Well, here is a welcome guest," said the old man. "Come, sit with us for a moment or two as we contemplate this awful situation."

"Thanks, but I feel I must find Addford as soon as possible."

"Please, just for a moment or two. It will help clear your mind." Peter patted a cushion on the floor next to him.

Gillian relented; a few minutes couldn't hurt. She kneeled on the cushion. She was next to Duncan, and he gave her an encouraging smile.

Peter looked at Gillian kindly and said, "Yes, Addford. A nice chap, really. His demeanour tends to let him down a bit—gives people the wrong impression. All in all, a nice fellow, though. It's a shame we had to kill him."

Gillian thought she'd misheard. "What was that?"

"Yes, he was becoming a bleeding pain in the arse." As he spoke, Peter dropped the pitch of his voice and became much louder. In one swift movement, he rose to his feet. His stoop was gone; he stood tall, he looked thirty years younger, and he appeared thoroughly evil. He spun around in a circle once on his right heel, and as he did so, he produced a short dirk from the sleeve of his robe.

Gillian screamed. All the followers stood.

"Duncan?" she said.

He was standing over her, looking at her with a sneer. "You blew it, sister. I tried to bring you into the fold, but you weren't having it."

"What's happening?" Gillian yelled. "Who are you people?"

She tried to get to her feet, but Duncan kicked her ankle hard, and she twisted around and fell.

"My name is Kincade," announced the man who just moment before had claimed to be Peter the Benevolent. "I'm a Spindle, and I think that brings to an end one of my better performances."

Gillian had not heard the name before.

"Yes, an excellent performance," said Duncan.

All the followers started to clap as Kincade turned around to acknowledge them like an effete actor.

"She even fell for this crap!" he said, yanking the documents out of her hand with a crude laugh and tossing them into the air.

"You wrote these?" Gillian asked in disbelief.

"Yes, they are a bit weak, but they did the trick."

"So, where is Peter?" she asked him.

"Oh, the old git has been dead for years. I think we threw him off a cliff. Do you recall, Duncan?"

"He's the one we buried alive, Master," said Duncan, laughing.

"But Tiny and Freckles—couldn't they tell you were an imposter?"

"Funny you should ask. Tiny left Ozeland before Peter first visited, and anyway, he hasn't made it into the building yet. There aren't too many outside of Ozeland who have met Peter. Freckles did meet him, and I was a bit concerned about that, but he saved me a bit of a headache by drowning himself. Should have learned to swim years ago—giant ignoramus!"

Gillian literally saw red. No one was going to speak ill of Freckles to her. She could feel heat building in her necklace loop and realized the active bracefires were channelling strength to her. She jumped to her feet so quickly she sent Duncan spinning and then falling flat on his face. Fist clenched, she delivered a haymaker punch, and it connected with Kincade's chin, causing him to yelp and stagger backward.

"Get her!" he cried. "Cut her, cut her!"

Several followers brandished swords in front of her. Even with all the extra strength streaming into her, this was too much for Gillian to take on alone.

"Help us clear the bracefires, and we won't kill you," said Kincade, picking himself off the floor and holding a dirk in his hand.

"Yeah, right," Gillian shouted at him. "I know I'm dead already, but I'm going to take a bunch of you with me."

She tried to make eye contact with some of those in front of her, but a movement behind them distracted her. A Fade stood by the open door to the inner-circle, beckoning her towards him. How? She saw him throw something—it looped over her head and landed amongst the followers. There was a blinding flash and a deafening bang.

The flash didn't affect her because it was behind her. This was her chance. She charged forward, aiming for a narrow gap between two of the smaller followers. Adrenalin and bracefire power turned her into a wrecking ball, and two of the attackers flew backward as she blasted her way through the line. She sprinted for the door the Fade held open, hurling chairs and tables from her path. The second she crossed the threshold, the Fade slammed the door shut and released two heavy deadbolts, which sealed the door closed.

"Thank you!" cried Gillian, and then she saw the blue sash. "Fa Li! Of course, it had to be you!"

Fa Li motioned for her to sit, which she did as she tried to catch her breath.

Fa Li ran to the other side of the Cirque and disappeared through the small door the Fade had used during the Grand Cirque. Gillian buried her head in her hands. The respite from Kincade and his followers was only temporary. The only way in and out of the chamber was through the door she had just used to enter the room. It looked strong. It would take them a while to break it down. But it was only a question of time, and when they did break through, they would be in no mood to take prisoners.

*****

Jag and Ulma were high up on the old trail that led to the steep southern face of the Maria Mountains. They had been severely frustrated in their search for the trail. Jag had thought the map would make finding it easy. It didn't. The scale of the mountain only became apparent when they were up close to it. They had released David at the start of the foothills as Owlspin had directed. They unharnessed the donkey, Ulma whispered into his ear, and David had trotted off in the direction of Three Widows.

"We just let our transport go. How do we travel from here?" Ulma asked.

"That's a good question. I'm following directions. Hopefully Owlspin arranged something."

They found a large crack in the rock and followed it around to where it split forming a small clearing. Something about this space made Jag giddy and gave him a sudden burst of energy.

"I think it's time to try out the eyepatch," said Jag, passing it over to Ulma.

"Me?" she asked. "What am I looking for?"

Jag held his hand above his eyes, shielding them from the sun. "A large, circular rock with a hole in it."

They walked farther and farther into the mountains. Several times, Jag had the feeling they were being watched, but it was just a feeling. He scanned the area around them but saw nothing. He finally found what he felt sure was the correct location. The path ahead twisted several times, but then it came to a dead end. Jag slapped his hands together in frustration, but there was nowhere to go but back the way they came. Ulma was looking hard, constantly scanning up and down, left and right, but she found nothing.

Jag was overwhelmed by a sudden bout of self-doubt. This was stupid; they were never going to find it. If it even existed anymore. Besides, it was such a huge area to cover. This could take them weeks. Even if they did find it, chances were there would be nothing inside.

They came to a corner where the ledge turned hard to the right, and now he was hallucinating—up ahead by the turn he saw a monk in a brown robe pointing upward. Jag stopped dead in his tracks.

"What's wrong?" asked Ulma.

"See that guy?" asked Jag, but the man had disappeared. Where could he have gone?

"You need sleep, Jonathan Ur-Jag."

He trotted to the spot on the ledge where the stranger had stood. He peered down and then up.

"He was pointing up there," he said, pointing up the slope above them.

Ulma stood beside him and followed the direction he was pointing "You know you are getting desperate when you start following directions given to you by—"

"What?" asked Jag.

"I see it!" Ulma pulled the eyepatch off. "I saw it! I saw it, and now it's gone!" She put the eye patch on again and started jumping up and down with excitement.

She tried to pass the patch to Jag, but he had already closed one eye and was staring upward.

"Ulma, it's real!" Jag stood frozen in shock. "Can we climb up there?"

"Easy," she said and within seconds had clambered half the distance to the rock.

She stopped, turned, and jumped back down to the ledge, where Jag was struggling with the first foothold. She took his hand and guided him through the short climb. It was a struggle, but they finally stood in front of the large, circular rock with the dark hole.

"I don't want to look," said Jag.

"Why not?" Ulma's voice resonated with excitement.

"In case it's empty," he said.

"You could not have done any more, Jonathan Ur-jag." She stood on tiptoe and kissed him on his cheek. It was surprisingly comforting. Without thinking, he reached over towards Ulma and then with his index finger, he touched her lower lip very gently.

Ulma smiled, "Come on lost boy we're not done yet."

Jag turned his attention back to the opening in the rock. He put his hand into the dark recess. Nothing. He stretched his arm farther. Nothing. He shifted his torso as close to the opening as he could and stretched his arm, his wrist, and then his fingers. He touched something that shifted beneath his fingertips, and he explored the object with his hand. He was almost certain it was a wooden box. He was able to get enough purchase on it to drag it back to the opening. Finally, he had hold of it and pulled it clear of its hiding place. Ulma shrieked when she saw the ornate box. It looked like a much larger version of the cipher box they had taken from Catchpole. Jag sat with his back to the mountain, his legs hanging off the narrow ledge. Ulma sat next to him, pressed close as he lifted the hinged lid. There were pages of manuscript stacked at the top. They were in remarkably good condition. Jag lifted them out and skimmed the first two pages. He felt Ulma's eyes on him, awaiting his verdict.

"These are blueprints for a hypothetical form of government. Robert wrote them. *The* Robert." He put the parchment to one side and picked up the one remaining item, a red velvet bag tied at the top by a drawstring. Jag's hands were shaking. He pulled open the drawstrings, reached in, and retrieved a shiny silver pig. Jag ran his fingers around the legs. They were straight and round, each about an inch in diameter. A small tag was tied to one of the legs. He examined the worn piece of parchment and the short, handwritten note on it:

RYE—mother of our wealth, forged by Timothy and given to my

father for the protection of those who follow.

Brunella

Jag tried to stem the huge swell of emotion building inside him, but he couldn't. He grasped the prize icon Robert's mountain mentor had created all those centuries before, and he wept. Ulma cradled his head and gently stroked his hair.
He sat up with a start. "What is that?" he said, drying his eyes.
A large bubble was floating towards them from across the valley.
"By Brunella!" shouted Ulma. "Fade sphere!"

*****

Gillian felt sick. The banging and thudding on the door seemed to have been going on forever. It sounded like they had a battering ram; the door buckled every time they hit it, the impact so hard the whole room jumped with each blow.
But the door remained in place—so far. All at once, the attack stopped. There was an eerie silence broken by the malevolent tones of Kincade.
"Gillian, open the door, and we will go easy on you. The outcome of this battle is already decided. Mora and his rancid, butter-for-brains commanders should be arriving for the party any time now. Unfortunately, they have the wrong address—the party is here, and very shortly, Spindle, Hag, and Leprade rebels will take over this town."
Gillian became aware of a high-pitched whirring sound coming from the other side of the door. Fa Li was still in the Fade room—she wasn't allowed in there, but she wished he were with her.
"We will simply have to start the party without them! You see, the thing about Peter is that everyone trusted him." The whirring noise was now very loud. "I never once had to ask for information; they volunteered it to me. No fewer than three people told me they had decoded information about a rebel invasion of Mensa! Idiots!"
The whirring noise changed pitch as a drill bit broke through to the inner-circle and then promptly withdrew.
"If anyone is foolish enough to discuss state secrets in Spindle, they are hung from the nearest tree. Guess what? Spindle doesn't have a problem with leaks."
A small tube poked into the chamber through the freshly drilled hole. It spat out a steaming grey-green liquid, which gave off a steady cloud of gas.
From outside the building came the sound of a dozen war horns.
"Ah, listen," said Kincade. "You have visitors. Is there any sound prettier than that of a Spindle war horn? Sadly, you will not get to meet

them; the green gas is an old but entertaining chemical. Half a mouthful of it is a death sentence…rather slow and painful, I understand."

Gillian ran around the table to the Fade chamber door. "Fa Li!" she shouted.

No response. She pushed the door open and looked in. Fa Li was in the centre of the room working on a large lever, pulling it, pushing it, fighting it. It was like a large video game controller.

"Fa Li Moon, we are being gassed! We have to get out!"

Fa Li pulled the lever back toward shim one more time and then let it go. It carried on moving, but he appeared satisfied. He turned to Gillian and using his index fingers and thumbs made a circular image.

"Circle?" said Gillian. "What about the circle?"

The green gas was swirling at her feet a few inches above her ankles and rising. Whatever he had been doing he seemed to have finished with it because he made his way back to the inner-circle, which was now filled with green gas. The bracefire electrical fields glowed in the green cloud.

Fa Li made a charade of someone using a remote control.

"What?" She didn't understand.

Then he mimed a robot walking. Tendrils of gas were swirling round her waist—they had seconds left. Gillian snapped her fingers.

"Of course." She pulled the little remote from her pocket and pressed the intercom button.

After a couple of static crackles, a voice came over the remote's speaker. "Service?"

"Violet, please ask Donald for help, then attack the people who have trapped us in this room. Disable them or chase them out."

"Service!" came the excited response.

"It's a longshot but worth a go," said Gillian.

Fa Li nodded.

An instant later, all manner of bangs and crashes and yelling started outside the inner-circle.

"Deep breath and follow me!" said Gillian.

But Fa Li pushed in front of her and sprinted for the exit door. He released the deadbolts and threw the door open. They both burst from the chamber, gasping for air. The scene in the outer chamber was chaotic. Several of the followers lay on the floor; three others were fighting Violet. Donald was bashing a chair.

"Donald, that's a chair; help Violet!"

Donald redirected his efforts, and Gillian and Fa Li ran for the exit. They ran up a staircase, along the length of a corridor, and out the front doors into the courtyard. They stopped dead in their tracks. Ahead of them, facing the Cirque building, stood four rows of rebel troops. They appeared to be waiting for a command. They stood silent and still, their metallic weapons gleaming in the morning sun.

*They are going to take the place apart,* thought Gillian, and not a single alliance soldier was left in town to resist. The eyes of the entire mass of invading rebels turned to her and Fa Li.

Then one of the rebel commanders stepped forward. "Behold, the famed Espanada Defence Regiment! All two of them!"

He pointed at Gillian and Fa Li, and the rebel troops started laughing. For a few moments they seemed to relax; some of them even started shaking hands with each other. They would never have an easier victory.

"Make that three…" came a voice from high above them.

The laughing stopped. Gillian looked up. An alliance soldier stood on a ledge jutting out of the tower, cross bow at the ready.

"Four!" came another voice from just in front of them as another soldier pulled himself out of a hiding hole.

"Five."

"Six."

"Seven."

Alliance troops were appearing all over the place—on the rooftop of the Cirque, from a long-hidden ditch behind them, from packing crates that had been left by the front door. Others had been hidden in trees and behind walls that surrounded the Cirque. Within a few seconds there were hundreds of alliance soldiers, taking defensive positions. Gillian slapped Fa Li on his back. Apparently, Mora had double-bluffed the rebels—the alliance troops hadn't gone anywhere.

The courtyard fell silent again as the two sides took stock of each other. Fa Li and Gillian crouched low. The alliance was still heavily outnumbered, and there were still more rebels waiting to come ashore. Someone tapped her on her shoulder.

"Excuse me, miss, but you and your Fade friend are required elsewhere," said Freddie.

It was all Gillian could do to stop herself yelling out in excitement. Then a shot rang out from above them, one of the rebel troops fell to the ground, and all hell broke loose. The Spindle horns sounded the attack signal, the rebel lines advanced, the alliance defence sent a barrage of bolts, grenades, and arrows at the invaders, who responded with similar ordinance.

"Let's go!" yelled Freddie. "Fa Li, please lead."

The three ran back towards the Cirque building.

"Where are we going?" asked Gillian.

"To meet an old friend," said Freddie as he ducked to avoid incoming arrows.

## Chapter 25

"Jonathan, wake up! Oh, Brunella!" Ulma was shaking his shoulder.

Jag had been sleeping since boarding this extraordinary craft. He woke with a start; his tiredness still overwhelming him.

They were descending rapidly. Almost directly beneath them was a tall tower standing proud above a Cirque Building. But outside the Cirque there was a war going on.

"Espanada?"

"Yes," said Ulma. "We had to fly over the sea to get here."

The Bubble came to a halt a few inches above the roof of the tower and popped. Jag landed and toppled over. He tried to regain his feet, but Freddie and Gillian dived on top of him, hugging him and ruffling his hair.

"Quickly!" he shouted. "Do you know a place called the inner-circle? I have to go there. He held the Rye icon out in front of him.

"Blimey, what's that?" shouted Freddie.

"It needs to go in its slot...fast!" said Jag.

"I will take," came an unfamiliar voice from behind them.

They looked round; Fa Li had spoken. He was standing, hood down, with his hand held out in front of him.

"Farley?" said Jag, scarcely believing his eyes.

"Yup," said Freddie, "and that's just for starters."

"I'll go with you," said Jag, placing the silver pig in the Fade's hand.

"You sure about this, Jag?" asked Freddie. "There's danger everywhere here."

"He survived Catchpole," said Ulma. "He can handle this."

Freddie beamed at his friend. "We'll come with you."

But Fa Li frantically shook his head.

"I will find you afterwards," said Jag.

"Ok, but be careful, we don't want to lose you again. Also, the inner-circle was full of poisonous gas just a while ago," added Gillian.

"I have to help my people," said Ulma and set off down the stairs.

"Ok. I guess we're with you!" shouted Freddie.

He and Gillian raced after her.

Fa Li followed them down the first two floors, and then he and Jag broke off in a different direction.

What Jag guessed was the outer circle was quiet. Two very short people guarded the door, which judging by its ornate décor must be the door to the inner-circle.

"Halt, who are you, and where is your allegiance?" said the taller of the two.

"My name is Jag. We are here to return Rye to the cirque table."

The female robot exchanged glances with the male one. It was obvious to Jag that they had no idea what he was talking about.

"You may pass," said the female.

The inner-circle was sizzling with electrical activity. The gas that Gillian had warned them about seemed to have cleared. The bracefires were glowing white hot and shooting salvos of mini-lightning strikes into the space above the table. The strikes zigzagged and formed random geometric shapes before they splintered, allowing charged particles to strike back to the table where they terminated on one of the other bracefires. It was quite a show. Fa Li reached into his pocket and retrieved Rye. He held the master bracefire above the slots in the centre of the table. But he couldn't get any closer. At first, Jag thought Fa Li was struggling because the heat rising from the other bracefires was too intense. But he was miming a pushing action.

"There is a power field stopping you placing it?" asked Jag.

Fa Li nodded.

"Damn it!" Jag called out in frustration. Had all this effort been for nothing? His friends were outside fighting, relying on him to tip the scales in their favour and he was coming up short.

*****

Gillian followed Freddie and Ulma out the front door onto the courtyard. Chaos reigned everywhere, but despite the bracefire boost given to the alliance troops, they were being forced backward. The sheer number of rebels was the problem. Ulma dived into a melee, a dagger in each hand. Gillian found a discarded blade and went in after her. She realized instantly that she was completely out of her depth—she felt the power of the bracefire at her neck, but it wasn't as potent as it had been before.

She should have gone with Jonathan and Fa Li. She doubled back—a shooting pain raced up her arm. Someone had caught her elbow. She turned her head and stared at the face of a Hag warrior inches away. He licked his lips disdainfully then twisted her arm, causing an extreme burning sensation that went down to her fingers. She tried to twist around in the same direction to ease the pressure, but the Hag had her. Her instincts took over; she swung her knee up into the man's groin. The warrior collapsed in a heap. But two more Hag came running at her. They got within two feet when a ball bearing struck each of them in the forehead.

*Thanks, Freddie,* she mouthed silently.

That left three Hag by her feet. Ink lay a few yards away; she was in trouble, on her back, her face contorted in pain. Her right leg was cut and bruised. Any second now, a passing rebel would finish her off. Gillian ran to her friend and dragged Ink as fast as possible towards the Cirque building. She got her to the main door, but it was locked. She slumped down against the wall. Ink needed help, but Gillian didn't have healing skills—there was nothing else she could do. She pulled Ink close and held her hand.

The alliance was in trouble; the main corps were defending the space in front of the Cirque building for all they were worth, but the number of rebel fighters was overwhelming. The attacks kept coming, wave after wave. The alliance soldiers were on the back foot, and inch by inch, they were getting closer to the walls of the Cirque. They would soon be penned in and then— *Come on, Jonathan!*

*****

Jag and Fa Li burst through the entrance doors. The first person they saw was Gillian. She was sitting on the ground with Ink's head on her lap. Marcus was fighting off rebels with his broadsword, trying to protect the two girls.

"It didn't work!" Jag shouted as he kneeled beside her.

"Oh, Jonathan, I'm sorry."

Jag shook his head. There was another very loud, mournful cry from Tiny, temporarily blotting out the sound of battle. Jag looked up, startled.

"What was that?" he asked.

"Tiny. Freckles drowned, and Tiny can't get over it."

Jag took a moment to process the news. "He should be fighting! We need him!"

Two arrows whistled past their heads. The incessant sound of steel clashing against steel grew louder by the second. The rebel front line was closing in.

"I'm going to reason with him!" Jag jumped to his feet and ran straight at the line of rebels.

"Jonathan, no!" screamed Gillian. "Marcus, stop him!"

But Marcus had enough on his hands, protecting Gillian and Ink.

Jag heard her plea, but his instincts had taken over, and he continued to run headlong at the enemy.

"On your right, Jagmeister!" came the voice of his best friend as Freddie caught up.

"Freddie!" shouted Jag.

Fa Li was with them, too, gliding along on Jag's left. The young Fade stretched his arm out and passed Jag the silver pig. Jag took it and held it aloft as they approached the advancing wall of Hag warriors. Fa Li stopped to give aid to a fallen alliance soldier. Freddie had a sword in his hand and swung it twice as Jag and he hit the line. Two of the rebels went down, but the others fell back and adjusted their position. Others moved beyond them and re-formed, creating a line behind them. They were surrounded.

"Well, it's been a blast," said Freddie, spinning on the spot, waving his sword.

Jag stood completely still, holding Rye on his outstretched arm directly above his head.

"Thanks for coming with me, Freddie," he said quietly.

"I wouldn't have missed it for the Turn." Freddie flashed his sword at the two closest rebels.

Many of the Hag appeared distracted by the master bracefire, eyeing it suspiciously as they closed in. *This is hopeless,* Jag thought. *Mystical artefacts that don't do anything...what's the point?* But then he felt a warming sensation in his loop. Rye, too, was radiating heat. The loop and the bracefire were warm, then warmer, hot, very hot. But a cold metal gloved hand grabbed his ankle and in one movement pulled Jag to the ground. He lay prone on his back as a second Hag leapt onto him and straddling his stomach drove the point of his sword down toward at Jag's exposed chest. Freddie threw himself headlong between the blade and its target.

"No!" screamed Jag. His cry of emotion released the pent-up energy that had been building inside him.

He felt a surge of power around his neck. A blinding flash of electricity left his loop, passed inches in front of his face and into the pig. Multiple streaks of blue lightning shot out of Rye. The Hag who had been milli-seconds from skewering them took the brunt of the explosion. He was thrown fifty feet or more into the air with orange and red flames shooting out of his torso, his cutlass melting instantly. Another thirty or so of the closest Hag attackers were blasted left and right and up and down, killing them instantly. Jag's ears rang from the accompanying boom. The attacking circle was decimated. Freddie, who was untouched by the strikes, had rolled off Jag after the attacker was blown away and was screaming with delight.

"Jag! Brilliant. Let's go!"

Jag felt as though he'd used up every ounce of energy in his body. He had nothing left to give, but they had to get to Tiny. He wasn't that far, and they had a clear run to him. Apparently, the surviving rebel troops didn't want to share the experience of their fallen colleagues— they edged back as Jag waved the bracefire at them, but he was bluffing now. That one massive strike had drained all the power.

The bluff worked. The Hag backed off as they made their way to the giant. They finally reached Tiny and stumbled to a stop before him. The forlorn Ozelander stood motionless, gazing blindly out to sea.

"Jag don't try and communicate with him. It nearly killed Gillian," said Freddie.

Jag nodded but carried on. He didn't know if this was going to work, but it was worth the risk. He positioned himself in front of the Oze giant and thought only about Freckles, linking his death to the rebel soldiers and Ink and her wounds caused by the rebel soldiers. He rotated these two thoughts around his head again and again. Eventually, he felt a slight burning sensation and realized he was being read. Then the reading stopped.

Tiny opened his mouth wide and roared, the sound so loud that everyone in the area stopped whatever they were doing to cover their ears. His arms swung out either side of him. The furious yell had rocked Jag to the core. The giant turned and marched towards the invaders.

The sound of war horns washed over them. Freddie shouted and pointed out to sea.

Five large boats were approaching the beach. Their sails were white and embroidered with large blue '*O*'s. As they came closer, Jag could make out Nikolas standing at the front of the leading boat. Jag punched the air once, and Freddie gave him a big hug.

The unexpected arrival of the Mensans hard on the heels of the strange explosion sent panic through the rebel ranks. There was a lull in the combat as each rebel chose whether to continue attacking or to turn around and face the new threat from the sea. Their leaders were unsure what to do; clearly, they hadn't anticipated this scenario.

The alliance captains ran their boats at high speed straight onto the beaches. Led by Nikolas and Spike, they jumped clear of the decks and ran up the remainder of the incline to join the fray. The hand-to-hand combat intensified. Tiny was a giant possessed. He charged into the ranks of Hag troopers and kicked, punched, and stomped on anyone who came close to him. Nikolas walked quickly and nimbly around the battlefield, shouting encouragement and using a long cane as his weapon. He wasn't alone; a tall figure followed his every move, circling 'round him in a crouched position. Despite everything else that was going on, Freddie and Jag smiled; Nikolas's aged butler, Mit, looked every bit the part of a martial arts ninja bodyguard.

The combined alliance forces stopped the rebel's offensive in its track. Most of the enemy ran for the boats; a sizable number lay down their weapons and surrendered. A very small number carried on fighting but were dealt with quickly.

Marcus, his clothing ripped and bloodstained, walked slowly to where Gillian was sitting with Ink cradled in her arms. He squeezed Gillian's shoulder.

"Thank you," he said. Crouching down, he examined Ink. "She'll be fine. It's just her leg. Nothing Nikolas can't fix." He picked up Ink and carried her through the now open doorway.

Tiny made his way slowly up to the Grand Cirque building. As he approached, the Oze giant caught Gillian's eye, and he let her feel his thoughts for a second. She sensed deep sadness but also acceptance.

Little Flower, are you well?

Gillian ran to the giant and jumped up into his arms.

*****

Jag made his way slowly back to the Cirque, picking his way through corpses and debris from the battle.

Freddie put his arm round him, "Jag you are going to be a legend here! I'm so proud of you."

Jag acknowledged him with a nod, but he was feeling very down. So many people were dead and injured - and many as a direct result of his actions. And what of the others? Where were Ulma and her friends? Please let them all be okay.

From no-where a large hand picked him up at the waist and swung him over a broad shoulder.

Thank you, little soldier.

Jag felt tears welling up in eyes as Tiny gave him a brief glimpse of his inner emotions. There was still heavy sorrow there, but now there was the gentle glow of a warm light that was becoming stronger by the minute...

Then Tiny lifted him down and placed him with his back against the Cirque wall next to – Ulma.

"Nice work lost boy," she was giving him that sideways on smile that he had become so familiar with. He nodded and rested his head on his knees. His eyes were closing on him. He stole a quick look at her dark brown eyes and then let sleep take him.

"Wake up buddy." Jag opened his eyes with a start. "Freddie?"

"Look," said his friend. To Freddie's right was Gillian, who must have been asleep when he returned with Tiny and was still curled up now, with her head resting against the wall. Ulma and Tiny were not there.

"It's all over, bar the shouting." Freddie waved his hand in the direction of the now quiet battlefield. The only fighting that was still going on was out at sea, where alliance boats were chasing fleeing rebel ships. There was still a lot of smoke drifting around. Slowly, their friends returned from wherever the battle had taken them. Jag found himself completing a mental inventory of the people he knew. Ulma had been unscathed. Dell arrived from the seafront and Marcus from the Cirque;

where he had been tending to Ink. Both the brothers had numerous cuts and bruises, but no serious wounds. Fa Li had returned to the Cirque building to help tend the wounded. A striking looking Dory woman, who Freddie identified as Rush, had several wounds. Marcus immediately helped her into the Cirque building to request aid from the healers.

Finally, Mora and Nikolas spotted them and jogged over. Jag breathed a sigh of relief. They looked serious but satisfied.

"The day is ours," announced Nikolas, "thanks in no small part to you splendid people."

"We couldn't insert Rye!" said Jag.

"You didn't need to. You have the gift—you turned the tide of the battle. We are indebted to you," said Mora.

"That was but a fraction of the master bracefire's potential. But enough for our needs today. Its day will come," added Nikolas. "We have to locate and retrieve the remaining bracefires. It's a huge challenge for us but one we have no choice but to take on."

"Adrian tells us you also uncovered the spy Kincade. He had everyone fooled. You can say what you like about the Spindle, but as masters of deception they have no equal."

Gillian had woken as the two elders arrived. She rubbed her face with her hands. "I feel like I've lost a great friend—*friends* if you add Duncan. They were so convincing."

"Is that it then? Is the war over?" asked Freddie.

Nikolas laughed. "No, no. Unfortunately, this is just the beginning. No one has spotted Leprade; we think he escaped on one of the rebel ships. Kincade is probably with him. They are not likely to take this humiliation well. They will be back in no time and in greater numbers."

"Are you going to need us to continue the fight?" asked Freddie, clasping his hands together.

"No, you are welcome to stay if you choose, of course, but after all you have done for us, we owe you a safe passage home. Adrian and his Fade have identified a likely transition window two days from now." Nikolas pressed the palms of his hands together. "In two days, you will be going home."

# Chapter 26

The day after the Battle of Espanada, Lord Mora called a meeting of the Cirque along with troop commanders, the Mensan visitors and the 'lost'. There was no Fade presence. It was held in a large conference room located in Mora's quarters, whilst clean-up operations commenced in the Circle's chambers.

Jag sat back and took in the large conference room. The table at which they sat was round. Jag counted twenty-eight sitting round it (those present included Nikolas, all Marcus's troop, except Ink who was on bedrest). On the walls hung long tapestries with images depicting historical events in the Turn. Most meant nothing to Jag, but there was one which he felt sure was an illustration of Robert and Timothy studying the night sky in the Maria Mountains. On another tapestry there were three attractive women dressed in battle regalia singing in front of a large crowd – were they Robert's three daughters? If so, why were they singing? And why the military outfits? He realized he had barely scratched the surface of the Turn's past. He wished he'd read more of the book Nikolas had lent him, but the elder had requested its return. Jag had handed it to him as they prepared for the meeting.

Mora passed Jag a written message that he had just received from one of his aids. It was a note from Owlspin concerning Pinhorn. Jag read it and looked at his two friends. "They say Pinhorn's condition is stabilizing but that he will not be fit to travel for several more days."

Mora stood." You can't let this delay you. We will find a way of returning him as soon as he is fit enough."

This caused a lot of consternation between Jag and his friends. Fred and Gillian had no sympathy for Pinhorn and were happy to leave him behind. Jag, on the other hand, felt Pinhorn had come around to their side when faced with a common enemy.

"We will have a lot of explaining to do if we make it home without him." Jag said.

Freddie laughed, "We are going to have a lot of explaining to do whether Pinhorn is with us or not."

Jag let it go – what choice did they have?

*****

Lord Mora opened the meeting with a solemn reading of the names of those who had lost their lives defending the Cirque the previous day. Jag didn't know any of those who had perished but Gillian broke down when two of the last names were called; Deputy Commander Morgan and Corporal Clayton.

There was uncertainty about the fate of Addford.

"Addford is officially listed as missing." Said Mora. No-one had seen him since the day before the battle.

Gillian held her hand up, "Kincade told me they had killed him."

"Kincade is a pathological liar. The most likely outcome is that he was captured and taken to Brunella or one of the rebel islands." Mora said.

"Let me update you on Kincade." Mora continued, "I have a lot to answer for here. I represented the Cirque on the deal that brought 'Peter' to Espanada."

"He was so convincing," Gillian said, "It's crazy, but I am mourning the man he pretended to be."

"He escaped, along with Duncan," Mora said, "He may try and come back as another character. I think it more likely he will lay low for a while. But I'm certain we haven't heard the last of him. Sadly.

"As you are all aware Leprade never left his boat and he too escaped our clutches.

Scouting reports confirm that Leprade was heading south, probably to Brunella. Catchpole wouldn't be looking forward to his return. If Leprade hadn't already figured out that the cipher had been stolen from under Catchpole's nose, he will find out soon enough.

"In the interests of learning from this conflict are there any questions about the strategy we employed to take on the enemy?"

Gillian held up her hand; "Can you clarify how you duped the rebels into attacking Espanada and how you pulled off the deception with the fleet?"

"Thank you Gillian. We used the leak to misinform Leprade that we were mobilizing all our forces to the defence of Mensa. We guessed Leprade would gleefully divert his invasion force to take over the undefended Espanada. We went to great lengths to maintain this charade. Our homemade fog gave us the cover we needed to secretly change course. Instead of heading east we sailed west to the back of the island, and the troops disembarked and walked back to the town."

"A bold move," said Nikolas.

Mora shook his head slowly. "If Leprade had not taken the bait, I would have gone down in history as an idiot. There's a fine line between boldness and stupidity."

"Fortune favours the bold," said Freddie.

"On this occasion, yes Freddie. But I wouldn't recommend taking that path too often, unless you enjoy sleepless nights."

Mora sat down and said quietly, "Now it is time to recognize the critical roll, played by our guests from 'beyond'. Gillian, Freddie and Jag; you have demonstrated such courage, loyalty, and tenacity in our hour of need that there is no adequate way in which we can thank you enough."

There was loud cheering and clapping from all those present. They stood up as one and then bowed in the direction of the three. Jag felt his cheeks rouge and he stared straight down at the table top, waiting for them to finish. He could see Freddie out of the corner of his eye, lifting his arms in acknowledgement. Jag couldn't see Gillian's reaction.

When they finally finished, Gillian raised her hand. "If you really want to thank us, please make sure we find our way home tomorrow," Gillian said.

Jag looked up and nodded vigorously. His eye caught Ulma. She was sitting directly across the table from him. Why was she crying?

"We would also like some answers," said Gillian, "You are nice people, but I don't understand why you haven't been more open with us. Just for starters: what is the 'truth' with Fa Li? Which is he, Fa Li or Farley? What was he doing in our world? Does he cross over regularly? How was he able to register for our school? Where was he living? Does he have parents? Did he steer us to the tunnel? If so, why? Why us? I'm just starting; there are so many things we want to know. Haven't we earned your trust?"

Mora signalled Nikolas to speak and the Three Widows elder stood.

"Gillian, Freddie, and Jag, you have more than earned our trust. As I told you before, certain things are hidden from you for your own protection. This world is very different to yours. There is a mystic presence here that I believe is unique to the Turn. It determines much (though not all) of what happens. It has the ability to see the future – although sometimes the picture it paints is blurred. We have learned from bitter experience that you ignore its foresight at your peril. The Fade are deeply involved in the study of this entity. Many of the Cirque members past and present have also dedicated time to studying the phenomenon. Yes, Jag?

"You sent me a note which I opened when I was separated from Gillian and Freddie, was that…"

"Yes, that was a good example of a 'prediction' we received."

Freddie jumped to his feet," By who? I'm sorry, but why all this mystical *mumbo jumbo*? I don't buy it. We just want to know who's pulling off all these tricks and why?"

Nikolas bowed his head and slowly sat down.

Jag opened his journal and scribbled a summary of what he had heard.

The room remained silent for a few moments. Eventually, Freddie shook his head and sat.

Mora stood up, "Come, let us not dwell on this. We have just won a victory when all the odds were against us. We should be celebrating. I will talk with my cousin this evening and see what else we can safely share with you prior to your departure."

At the end of the meeting Mora announced there would be a victory party that evening.

"We owe it to the fallen to celebrate their lives."

Neither Freddie nor Gillian felt in the mood. Nor did Jag. Instead the three went to the downstairs room that Jag and Freddie shared. They ate snacks and exchanged details of everything that had taken place after their separation. Freddie and Gillian looked mesmerized as Jag matter-of-factly described his journey with Ulma, his meeting and companionship with The Vicar and not least, his capture and torture at the hands of Catchpole. Freddie grabbed his shoulders. "Dude! Are you okay now? It was so wrong of us to leave you alone. The electric shocks ...Jeez". Gillian was struggling to speak. She sat with her head buried in her hands.

"It sort of worked out." Jag said.

Gillian hugged him, "You have been so brave. No wonder Ulma is so sweet on you...."

Jag couldn't think straight he was so embarrassed. Did Ulma really like him? He thought she might, but she hadn't really been rude or mean to him recently, which Freddie had told him was the measure of such things. It was all too confusing. Teenage crushes, totally confusing – what's the point?

*****

Jag stared hard at the granite wall. He couldn't imagine an opening magically appearing in all that rock, but that was what they had been told to expect. He recognized this spot as the place where Ulma had found him when he woke after exiting the tunnel. That felt like so long ago, but when he checked his journal, he confirmed they had arrived in the Turn just a little over a week ago. He glanced to his left and then to his right, at Freddie and Gillian, respectively. Freddie looked less than happy, and Gillian was kneeling. She was crying openly.

Mora and Nikolas selected a small team to accompany and protect Jag and his friends on their journey to the gateway. They chose Adrian and Fa Li, Marcus, Ulma, Nikolas, Tiny, and Ink. They had sailed overnight in the same ship that had carried Nikolas and the Mensan troops into the battle. South sea islanders who were sympathetic to the alliance cause crewed the ship. It was large and comfortable and untroubled by the rebel boats that were no-where to be seen.

There had been some emotional farewells as they boarded the ship in the Espanada harbour. They'd suppressed the news of their imminent departure, fearing how people would react to losing their newly found heroes.

The boat set anchor for a short while at the point where they estimated Freckles had drowned. No one said a word. Those with the telepathic gift comforted Tiny as, flanked by Gillian and Ink, he placed a wreath of Oze bromias on the water.

Ulma hadn't spoken since they left Espanada. Jag wanted to talk to her, but he didn't know what to say.

Adrian was standing behind Jag. To his left were Nikolas and Fa Li. Adrian had been monitoring a curious-looking, handheld device, which most gave him information about the window. Adrian tapped the elder on the shoulder and held out three fingers.

Nikolas nodded. "Just a few moments now," he said. "Goodbye, my friends. What you have done for us is beyond measure. The people of the Turn will remember you always." He hugged each of them.

The Fade followed suit, and then Marcus, who had been standing watch on a large rock, jumped down and embraced Jag and Freddie.

"Thank you," Marcus whispered in Jag's ear.

Marcus hesitated when he came to Gillian, but she caught hold of both his hands and kissed him on the cheek.

"Sorry I upset you," he said to her.

But she was beyond being able to talk. She looked him in the eyes and smiled, despite the tears streaming down her face. Ink and Tiny took their turns, and there were more tears all round. Tiny communicated to Jag that he would see him again soon. Jag didn't respond.

Ulma had sat down several yards away, her gaze fixed on the horizon. Gillian and Freddie made their way over to her and hugged her together. Freddie looked back at Jag.

"Come on, you two!" Freddie said. "This is your last chance!"

A familiar heat warmed Jag's cheeks. Half of him wanted to run up to her and hold her; the other half wanted the door to open so he could escape. He glanced back in her direction just as she looked his way. Her dark-brown eyes locked with his. Ulma jumped to her feet and sprinted over to him, throwing her arms around him. She pulled herself tight against him and kissed him on the lips. For a second, Jag felt like he'd been hit with another surge of electricity from Catchpole's torture device. But there was something about the kiss that made him giddy. Slowly, he wrapped his arms around her. For a fleeting moment, he started to consider what his life would be like if he stayed in the Turn.

"Fa Li, please give them the fixers," said Nikolas.

Fa Li nodded and produced a small pouch from his pocket as Nikolas explained their purpose.

"These pills are necessary for your safe return. They will protect you in the rough and tumble of the transition."

Fa Li reached into the pouch and took out three yellow pills. He stepped in front of Gillian and signalled her to hold out her hand. He placed one of the pills in her palm and nodded. Gillian swallowed the pill whole. Fa Li repeated the procedure with Freddie, who tossed his pill into his mouth and swallowed it with a grin.

Then it was Jag's turn. Fa Li placed the last pill on Jag's outstretched palm. But with a deft sleight of hand, the Fade picked up the pill again as he moved his hand away. For a moment, Jag was confused. What was Fa Li playing at? Then he saw Fa Li motion him to swallow the fixer, and instinctively, Jag pretended to put a pill into his mouth and swallowed.

"Thank you, Fa Li. Jag, Freddie, and Gillian, I feel very guilty about what I just instigated, but there was no other option. The fixer pills are going to make you forget about your time here. This is necessary for the protection of both the Turn and your world."

There was a moment of silence as they took in the implication of what Nikolas had told them.

"*What?*" said Gillian. "We are going to lose part of ourselves. Don't you trust us?"

"I do trust you, but if you take home your knowledge of this world, there are all sorts of risks involved both to the Turn and to you individually."

"I feel like you're robbing us," said Freddie. "We risked our lives for you, and this is how you repay us. Why didn't you warn us before we took those pills?"

"Precisely because of the reaction I am getting now; you wouldn't knowingly take them, and I don't blame you. Jag, I'm afraid you will also need to leave your journal behind for the same reason. I'm sorry; I can't negotiate on this."

Jag opened his mouth to object, but he couldn't form the words. Instead he pulled off his pack and held it against his chest with a vice-like grip.

"Do you have any idea how important that journal is to him?" shouted Ulma.

"Before Nikolas could answer there was a loud splintering sound from the granite cliff.

"It's time," said Nikolas. "You will only have a few moments once the gateway is open. Jag, the journal please."

Jag's mind was racing. They were going to take the journal one way or the other. Best to do it on his terms. He pulled the journal from his backpack and passed it to Ulma.

Nikolas nodded. "Ulma will make a good custodian," he said.

Jag's guide and friend began to sob. "Don't you dare forget about me, Jonathan Ur-Jag."

There was another loud bang and then a body-churning vibration accompanied by the sound of scraping rock. The crack in the rock expanded rapidly, forming a hole just large enough for them to squeeze through.

Gillian and Freddie exchanged looks.

"We have no choice," said Freddie angrily and pushed himself through the gap.

Gillian cast a furious look at Nikolas and followed Freddie. Jag edged his way in and looked back to see Ulma bent double in distress, clutching his journal to her chest. Then he turned and stepped into the darkness.

"No!" shouted Marcus and dived across the entrance, trying to block it.

But he was too late. The nimble-footed Ulma had sprinted past them and through the rapidly disappearing gap. Moments later, the gateway closed with a resounding crunch.

End of Book 1

Jag returns in:

"Jag and the Three Widows"

For more information go to www.chrisdavy.net"

Notes and Acknowledgements:

Thanks to all those who helped me with the book. At the outset I naively thought I could do this project by myself. It turned out that I needed the assistance of a small army of people, ranging from publishing professionals through the heroic volunteers who gave up time and energy to help move the project along.

Special thanks to Sally Watson and Caroline Spindlow, both of whom went through the pain barrier, reading and re-reading multiple drafts of Jag. Their feedback and ideas ultimately helped shape the story. To all the beta readers who worked their way through and reported back on some pretty unrefined early drafts; Finlay Padwick, Zoe Watson, Archie Cox, Harriet Cox, Billie Watson, Isobel Harrison, Philip Wood, Hugh Watson, Ann Parish, Sam Carter and Katy Inglis.

Thanks also to Katie McCoach (katiemccoach.com); and the indefatigable Jill Noble-Shearer (jill.noele.noble@Gmail.com).

A big 'koszonom' to Levente Farkas (Flanddesign.com) for the cover art work and to Dan Parish (danparishltd.com) for re-producing Jag's map of the Turn. As well as Bryce Nicholson for his assistance with the website set up.

Thanks to Ildi and Audrey for their encouragement and assistance, and for putting up with me in general.

Finally, Gonzalo Urey, this is your fault mate – if you hadn't suggested this literary diversion, I'd still be happily focusing on my weekly fantasy report.

Work on the next Jag instalment is well underway. For status updates; questions; comments or if you just want to say 'hello,' please visit: www.chrisdavy.net.

Chris Davy was born in London, England and spent most of his formative years in the rural south-west of the country He attended private preparatory and secondary schools. But he didn't learn very much, preferring to stare out of the classroom window and day-dream.

In his mid-twenties he moved to Los Angeles, California, where he pursued a career in financial servicing. Today he is married with a daughter and lives in Altadena, California. His hobbies include; going to the pub, drinking warm beer and reminiscing about the old days. He still finds time to stare out of windows.

Printed in Great Britain
by Amazon